# AFFAIR WITH THE REBEL HEIRESS

BY

EMILY McKAY

AND

# THE MAGNATE'S PREGNANCY PROPOSAL

BY

SANDRA HYATT

MILLS & BOON

## "Well?" she prodded.

He gripped her shoulders, resisting the urge to shake her. "Stop. Interrupting. Me."

Her chin bumped up and she glared at him through stormy eyes.

Suddenly he couldn't remember what it was he'd been about to say. All he could think was that this was what he'd wanted for the past two months. He wanted to sleep with her. To strip her clothes off, lay her bare before him in a proper bed and spend hours worshipping her body.

"Well?" she demanded again. "Is that the best you can do?"

"No," he said. "This is."

Cupping her jaw in his hands, he shut her up the best way he knew how. He kissed her.

# AFFAIR WITH THE REBEL HEIRESS

BY

EMILY McKAY

Published in Great Britain 2011
Harlequin Mills & Boon Limited,
Eton House, 18-24 Paradise Road, Richmond, Surrey TW9 1SR

AFFAIR WITH THE REBEL HEIRESS © Emily McKaskle 2010

ISBN: 978 0 263 88093 9

51-0211

Harlequin Mills & Boon policy is to use papers that are natural, renewable and recyclable products and made from wood grown in sustainable forests. The logging and manufacturing processes conform to the legal environmental regulations of the country of origin.

Printed and bound in Spain
by Litografia Rosés S.A., Barcelona

For my mother, Judy Beierle, who has taught me
over and over to smile in the face of adversity,
to meet challenges with bravery and hope,
and to always, always find something to laugh about.

**Emily McKay** has been reading romance novels since
she was eleven years old. Her first romance came free in
a box of garbage bags. She has been reading and loving
romance novels ever since. She lives in Texas with her
husband, her newborn daughter and too many pets.
Her books have been finalists for RWA's Golden Heart
Award, the Write Touch Readers' Award and the Gayle
Wilson Award of Excellence. Her debut novel, *Baby, Be
Mine,* was a RITA® Award finalist for Best First Book
and Best Short Contemporary. To learn more, visit her
website at www.EmilyMcKay.com.

Dear Reader,

*Affair with the Rebel Heiress* is a very special book for me, not only because I love these characters and felt honoured to tell their story (I always feel that way), but also because it marks an anniversary for me: it's my tenth book!

I've been reading romances since I was eleven. I literally grew up reading Mills & Boon novels, Desire books and the old Bantam Loveswept titles. I spent so much money at the bookstore that my parents actually complained about it. (How crazy is that?)

Every time I turn in a book, or see the cover for the first time, or hold my book in my hands, I get this electric shock of excitement. I love being part of the Harlequin/Mills & Boon family, and I can't tell you how proud I am to have my tenth book with them out this month!

Now, about that book ... Some of you may remember Kitty Biedermann from *Baby Benefits*, which was out in 2008. She was Derek Messina's fiancée. She was the classic romance novel "other woman"— manipulative and self-centered. When I decided I wanted her to be the heroine of my next book, I knew I was facing a challenge. How could I transform her into a character people would love? I gave her plenty of spunk and sass along with a secret she'll go to great lengths to keep hidden. And of course, she had to have a great hero with whom to match wits. Enter Ford Langley, a charming business tycoon who's just not the type to back down from a challenge.

Did I pull it off? I think so. I hope you do, too!

*Emily McKay*

# One

Kitty Biedermann hated Texas.

That single thought had echoed through her mind from the time the flight attendant had said the words "unscheduled landing in Midland, Texas," until this moment, five hours later, when she found herself sitting in the bar adjacent the seedy motel in which she would be forced to spend the night.

The last time she'd been in Texas, she'd been dumped by her fiancé. Of course, he hadn't been just any old fiancé. He'd been the man she'd handpicked to save Biedermann Jewelry from financial ruin. So being dumped hadn't resulted in mere public humiliation or simple heartbreak. It meant the end of Biedermann Jewelry. So it was understandable that Kitty held a bit of grudge, not just against Derek Messina, but against the whole damn state.

Since being dumped by Derek, her situation had gone from bad to worse to desperate. She had needed Derek.

From the time she was a child, she'd been raised with one purpose—to land a husband with the smarts and business savvy to run Biedermann's. When Derek hadn't wanted her, she'd remained undaunted. But now, after six months of working her way through every single, eligible straight man she knew, she was beginning to feel…well, daunted.

With this latest trip to Palm Beach, she'd been scraping the bottom of the barrel. Geoffrey barely had two functioning synapses to rub together, but at least he could read, write and looked damn good in a suit. But even as meager as his qualifications had been, he hadn't wanted her.

Biedermann's meant everything to her. It was slipping through her fingers and there didn't seem to be anything she could do to catch it.

Now, with her elbows propped on the suspiciously sticky bar top and her chin propped in her palms, she stared at the murky green depths of her salt-rimmed margarita glass. She gave the glass a little shake, watching as the ice cubes within tumbled to the bottom of the glass. A lifetime of planning had fallen apart just as quickly. Was this rock bottom?

Her throat tightened against despair. Immediately she straightened, blinking in surprise. She was not given to fits of self-pity. Certainly not in public.

She shook her glass again, studying the contents. Exactly what was in this margarita? After a mere two drinks she should not be succumbing to such maudlin emotions.

Maybe this was what she got for giving the bartender a hard time. When she'd ordered a Pinot Grigio, he'd asked, "Is that like a wine cooler?" Apparently she shouldn't have doubted him when he said he'd make her a drink strong enough to knock her on her pampered, scrawny butt.

She was still contemplating the contents of her drink when she happened to glance toward the door and saw *him* striding in.

It was as if someone tossed a bucket of icy water on her. Every cell in her body snapped to life in pure visceral response. The stranger was tall and lean, somehow managing to look lanky but well-built all at the same time. He was dressed simply in well-worn jeans and a T-shirt that stretched taut across his shoulders, but hung loose over his abdomen. No beer belly on this guy. A cowboy hat sat cockeyed on his head, but he wore scuffed work boots instead of the cowboy boots she expected.

Her first thought—when she was capable of thought again—was, *Now* this *is a cowboy. This* was what women the world over romanticized. *This* was a man at his most basic. Most masculine.

Even from across the room, her body responded to him instantly, pumping endorphins down to the tips of her curling toes. Funny, because she'd always preferred her men sophisticated and suave. As well-groomed as they were well-educated.

She was, in fact, so distracted by this mystery cowboy who'd just sauntered in that she didn't see the other guy sidling up to her. The rough hand on her arm was her first clue someone had claimed the stool beside hers. Swiveling around, she realized that hand belonged to a guy who could not have been more different than the cowboy who'd snagged her attention. This man was short and, um…plump. He was bald except for a few wisps of hair grown long, combed over and plastered down with what she could only hope was some sort of styling product. His cheeks were rosy, his nose bulbous. He looked vaguely familiar, though she couldn't possibly have met him before.

"Well, hello there, little lady." He stroked a hand up her arm. "Whadda say we getcha some'tem cold to drink and we scoot on out to that there dance floor?"

"Pardon?" She—barely—suppressed a shiver of disgust at his touch. She tried to wiggle free from his grasp, but he had boxed her in between the bar and the woman on the stool beside her.

Why was he rubbing her arm like that? Did she know this man? After all, he *did* look familiar.

"You wanna take a turn around the room?"

"A turn at what?" she asked, genuinely not understanding him. She spoke four languages, for goodness' sake, but Texan was not one of them.

The man frowned. "Are you makin' fun a me?"

"No," she protested. Unfortunately, it was then that

she figured out where she knew him from. "Elmer Fudd!" she blurted out. "You look like Elmer Fudd!"

Normally, she would not have said anything, but she'd already gulped down two of those wicked margaritas. And all she'd eaten since lunch was a packet of airline peanuts. So her tongue was looser than normal.

Indignation settled over his pudgy features. He leaned toward her, scowling. "Whadja call me?"

"I…I didn't mean it as an insult."

"You *are* makin' fun a me." The man's face flushed red, only increasing his resemblance to the cartoon hunter.

"No! I…I…I…"

And there it was. She, who almost always knew exactly what to say and who could talk herself into and out of almost any situation, for better or for worse, was speechless. Horribly so.

She'd unintentionally insulted and offended a man who was probably armed right now. This was it. She was going to die. Alone. Miserable. In Texas. Murdered in a fit of rage. By a man who looked like Elmer Fudd.

Ford Langley could see trouble coming the second he stepped into The Dry Well, his favorite bar in Midland.

The Well was the kind of seedy dive that rednecks and oil rig workers had been coming to, through boom and bust, for sixty years or so. Since the Green Energy branch of FMJ, Ford's company, leased land for their wind turbines from a lot of the people in here, he figured they all knew who he was and how much he was worth. They just didn't care. Frankly, it was a relief places like this still existed in the world.

It was not, however, the kind of place women wore couture suits and designer shoes. Ford had three sisters with expensive taste. He knew a five-hundred-dollar pair of shoes when he saw them.

The woman sitting at the bar looked startlingly out of place. He'd never seen her there before. He came to The Well almost every time he visited Midland, and he definitely would have remembered this broad.

The word *broad* filtered through and stuck in his mind, because that's exactly what she looked like. The sexy broad who ambles into the PI's office in an old film noir movie. Lustrous flowing hair, long silk-clad legs, bright red lipstick, gut-wrenching sex appeal. With just enough wide-eyed innocence thrown in to make a man want to be the one to save her. Even though he knew instinctively that he would get kicked in the teeth for his trouble.

To make matters worse, she was talking to Dale Martin, who, Ford knew, had been going through a rough divorce. Dale had undoubtedly come in looking for what The Well provided best: booze, brawls and one-night stands. Given how completely out of his league the woman was, Ford could already guess which Dale was going to get.

When Ford heard Dale's distinctive drawl rising above the blare of the jukebox, Ford moved through the crowd, closing in on the brewing conflict, hoping he could cut trouble off at the pass.

He approached just in time to hear Dale accuse her of making fun of him. Hiding his cringe, Ford slung an arm around the woman's shoulders.

The stubborn woman tried to pull out of his grasp, but he held her firm. "I will—"

"Dale, buddy," he continued before she could ruin his efforts. "I see you met my date." He sent the woman a pointed look, hoping she'd take the hint and stop trying to squirm away. "Sugar, did you introduce yourself to my buddy, Dale?"

"It's Kitty," she snapped.

Dale was looking from him to her with a baffled expression. Which was fine, because Ford figured confused was better than furious.

"Right, sugar." Ford gave her shoulder an obvious squeeze. Winking at Dale, he added, "Kitty here's one of those feminist types."

She blinked, as if having trouble keeping up with the conversation. "Insisting that I be called by my given name and not some generic endearment does not make me—"

"She's a bit prickly, too." Based on her accent, he made a guess. "You know how Yankees are, Dale."

"I am not prickly," she protested.

But with Ford's last comment, a smile spread across Dale's face and at her protest, he burst out laughing, having forgotten or excused whatever she'd said to offend him. After all, she was a Yankee and obviously couldn't be expected to know better.

With Dale sufficiently distracted, Ford tugged the

delectable Kitty off her stool and nudged her toward The Well's crowded dance floor. "Come on. Why don't you show me what you can do in those fancy shoes of yours, sugar?"

At "sugar" he gave Dale another exaggerated wink. She, of course, squeaked an indignant protest, which only made Dale laugh harder.

When they were out of Dale's hearing range, she once again tried to pull away from him. "Thank you, I'm sure. But I could have handled him myself. So you can't seriously expect me to dance with you."

"'Course I do. Dale's watching."

Before she could voice any more protests, or worse, undermine all his hard work, he stepped onto the dance floor, spun her to face him and pulled her close. The second he felt her body pressed to his, he had to ask himself, had he really orchestrated all of that to avoid a fight or had he been angling for this all along?

She was taller than she'd looked sitting on the stool. With her heels on, her head came up past his chin, which was rare, since he dwarfed most women. As he'd suspected, her boxy suit hid a figure that was nicely rounded without being plump. She was delectably, voluptuously curved.

He felt the sharp bite of lust deep in his gut. Maybe he shouldn't have been surprised. He lived a fairly high-profile life back in San Francisco. As a result, he picked his lovers carefully for their discretion, sophistication and lack of expectations. He had enough responsibility without saddling himself with a spouse.

Unfortunately, it had been nearly six months since his previous girlfriend, Rochelle, had gone out for lunch one day with a friend who had kids and came home dreaming of designer diaper bags. He'd been happy to dodge that bullet and hadn't been in a hurry to find someone to replace her. Which probably explained his strong reaction to this woman. Kitty, she'd said her name was.

As he moved her into a shuffle of a Texas two-step, he felt her body relax against his. If his instincts were right, Kitty was smart, beautiful and used to taking care of herself. In short, she was exactly his sort of woman. She just may be the most interesting thing that had happened to him in a long time.

Kitty had never before found herself in this situation. Naturally she often danced with men she'd only just met. But she kept very careful tabs on the social scene in Manhattan. As a result, she usually knew the net worth, family history and sexual inclinations of every male in the room.

What some might consider mere gossip, she considered her professional obligation. She was in no position to date, marry or even notice a man who couldn't bring his own personal fortune to her family coffers. Unfortunately, ever since Suzy Snark had caught Kitty in her sights, the business of finding a rich husband had become increasingly difficult. Derek—damn him—had been the perfect choice. Until he'd gone and fallen in love.

But the truth was, she was tired of planning every move she made. This stranger with whom she was dancing, this cowboy, this man she'd never see again after tonight, made her pulse quicken.

From the moment she'd seen him sauntering through the door to the instant he'd pulled her body against his, she'd felt more alive than she had in months. Years, maybe. Somehow the scent of him, masculine and spicy, rose up from his chest and cut through the stench of stale smoke and cheap beer. His shoulders and arms were firm and muscular without being bulky. He had the physique of a man who worked for a living. Who lifted heavy things and shouldered massive burdens. The hand that cradled hers was slightly rough. This was a man who'd never had a manicure, never taken a Pilates class and probably didn't own a suit.

In short, he was a real man. Unlike the pampered men of her acquaintance. Most of whom, she was sorry to say, were likable, but were just a little bit…well, that is to say…well, they were sissies. And until this moment, she'd never realized that bothered her. She'd never known she wanted anything else.

Her face was only inches from his shirt and she had to fight against the sudden impulse to bury her nose in his chest. To rub her cheek against his sternum like a cat marking her territory.

It had been so long since she felt this kind of instant sexual attraction to someone. Geesh, had she ever felt this kind of attraction? She didn't think so.

Not that she planned on acting on it. A one-night stand was *so* not part of her five-year plan.

"I don't even know your name," she muttered aloud.

"Ford," he murmured.

He'd ducked his head before speaking so the word came out as warmth brushing past her ear. She suppressed a shiver.

"Like the car?" she asked.

He chuckled. "Yep. Like the car."

Geesh, indeed. Even his name was masculine. Why couldn't he have had a name that was just a bit more androgynous? Like Gene or Pat. Or BMW.

She didn't manage to stifle her chuckle.

"You're imagining me named after other car brands, aren't you?"

Her gaze shot to his. "How did you know?"

"It's pretty common. People usually think one of two things and you just seemed the type to wonder, 'What if he'd been named Chevy?'"

"Are you saying I'm predictable?" Even though the lighting was dim, she could see that his eyes were whiskey-brown. And just as intoxicating as the tequila in her drink.

"Not at all," he reassured her. "You could have been thinking Dodge."

"It was BMW, actually. I can't see you as something as clunky as a Dodge." Was she *flirting* with him? What was wrong with her?

"So you're a woman who appreciates precision engineering."

*Actually, I'm a woman who enjoys precision in everything.*

The words had been on the tip of her tongue. Thank God she swallowed them. Instead she asked, "What's the second?"

"Second what?"

"You said people usually think one of two things. If the first is other car names, then what's the second?"

His lips quirked in either amusement or chagrin. "They wonder if I was conceived in the back of a Ford."

"Ah." Perhaps that had been chagrin, then. And was that the faintest hint of pink creeping into his cheeks? As if he were just a tad embarrassed. "And were you?"

"That," he said firmly, "is a question I was never brave enough to ask my parents." They both chuckled then. A moment later he added, "But I have three sisters and their names are not Mattress, Kitchen Table and Sofa, so I think I'm safe."

She nearly asked what the names of his three sisters were, but she stopped herself. Somehow that seemed inappropriate. More personal, even, than the discussion of his conception. She didn't know Ford. Didn't want to know him longer than the length of this song. Personal details like the names of his sisters didn't matter. So instead, she gave in to her temptation to rest her cheek against the strong wall of his chest and to breathe in deeply.

After a moment he said, "I hope you don't judge Dale too harshly."

"Dale?"

"The guy hitting on you earlier."

"Ah. Him." She'd forgotten he even existed.

"He's been going through a rough divorce. His wife left him for a guy who's twenty-three years old."

"Ouch. That's got to be hard on the ego."

"Exactly. Which is why he's been a mite irritable lately. But what exactly did you say to him that made him so mad?"

She cringed, hesitating before answering him. "I said he looked like Elmer Fudd."

Ford seemed to be suppressing laughter. "I can't imagine why that offended him. Everybody loves Elmer Fudd."

"That's what I tried to tell him!"

They both chuckled. But then she looked up. For a moment, space seemed to telescope around them, blocking out everything else. The smoke, the crowd, even the blare of the music faded until all she could hear was the steady *thump-thump* of the bass echoing the thud of her heartbeat.

She felt her nerves prickle in anticipation. Desire, hot and heavy, unspooled through her body. Her very skin felt weighed down. Her thighs flushed with warmth.

Who knew that laughter could be such a turn-on?

Their feet stopped shuffling across the floor. That ridiculous grin seemed frozen on her face for an instant, but then it faded, melted away by the intensity of his gaze. There was a spot just over his ear where his otherwise straight hair curled. Before she could think, her fingers had moved to his temple to tease that wayward lock of hair.

He took her hand in his, stilling her fingers. He cleared his throat, and she expected him to say something, something funny maybe, something to lighten the tension between them, but he said nothing.

Who had ever imagined that she'd feel this needy lust for a stranger? Not just a stranger, but a cowboy. A Texan. When she'd sworn she'd never even set foot in this damn state again. She *so* hadn't seen this coming.

That's when it hit her. Here, tonight, was a night out of time. She would never be here again. She would never see him again.

In this strange place, with this man she didn't know, she had complete immunity. Freedom from her well-planned life. From her routines and her expectations of herself.

Tonight she could do whatever she wanted with no consequences. She could allow herself to do what she would normally *never* do. She could be stupid and reckless.

Without giving herself the chance to harbor second thoughts, she rose up on her toes and pressed her lips to his. His mouth moved over hers with a heated intensity. The sensual promise in his kiss made her shiver. She arched against him, letting her body answer the call of his. She slipped her hand into his and walked off the dance floor, tugging him along behind her.

As she wove her way through the crowd, the tempo of her blood picked up. After a lifetime of carefully planning, of controlling her actions and emotions, he could be her one rebellion. Tonight could be a vacation from her life.

And even if this was a mistake, he'd make sure she didn't regret it.

# Two

*Two months later*

"You've got to stop moping around," Jonathon Bagdon said, then added, "And get your feet off my desk."

Ford, who'd been sitting with his work boots propped up on the edge of Jonathon's desk while he scraped the tip of his pocketknife under his nails, looked up for the first time since his business partner walked in the room. "What?"

Jonathon swatted at Ford's boots with the leather-clad portfolio he'd been carrying. "Keep your feet off my desk. Christ, it's like you're ten."

Ford's feet, which had been crossed at the ankles,

slid off Jonathon's desk. He lowered them to the floor and ignored the insult.

"The desk is worth twenty thousand dollars. Try not to scuff it."

Finally Ford looked up at his friend, taking in the scowl. He glanced over at Matt, the third partner in their odd little triumvirate, who sat on the sofa, with one leg propped on the opposite knee and a laptop poised on the knee. "Who shoved a stick up his ass this morning?" Ford asked Matt.

Matt continued typing frenetically while he said, "Ignore him. He's just trying to bait you. He doesn't give a damn about the desk."

Ford looked from one to the other, suddenly feeling slightly off-kilter. Together the three of them formed FMJ, Inc. He'd known these men since they were kids. They'd first gone into business together when they were twelve and Jonathon had talked them into pooling their money to run the snack shack at the community rec center for the summer. One financially lucrative endeavor had led to another until here they were, twenty years later, the CEO, CFO and CTO of FMJ, a company which they'd founded while still in college and which had made them all disgustingly rich.

Jonathon, though always impeccably dressed and by far the most organized of the three, might impress some as overly persnickety. But those were only the people who didn't know him, the people who were bound to underestimate him. It was a mistake few people made more than once.

In reality, it was unlike Jonathon to care whether or not his desk was scuffed, regardless of how much it was worth.

Still, to mollify Jonathon, Ford abandoned the chair he'd been sitting in and returned to his own desk. Since they worked so closely together, they didn't have individual offices. Instead, they'd converted the entire top floor of FMJ's Palo Alto headquarters to a shared office. On one end sat Jonathon's twenty-thousand-dollar art deco monstrosity. The other end was lined with three worktables, every inch of them covered by computers and gadgets in various stages of dissection. In the middle sat Ford's desk, a sleek modern job the building's interior designer had picked out for him.

With a shrug, he asked, "Is Matt right? You just trying to get a rise out of me?"

Jonathon flashed him a cocky grin. "Well, you're talking now, aren't you?"

"I wasn't before?"

"No. You've been picking at your nails for an hour now. You haven't heard a word I've said."

"Not true," Ford protested. "You've been babbling about how you think it's time we diversify again. You've rambled on and on about half a dozen companies that are about to be delisted by the NYSE, but that you think could be retooled to be profitable again. You and Matt voted while I was in China visiting the new plant and you've already started to put together the offer. Have I left anything out?"

"And…" Jonathon prodded.

"And what?" Ford asked. When Jonathon gave an exasperated sigh and plopped back in his chair, Ford shot a questioning look at Matt, who was still typing away. "And what?"

Matt, who'd always had the uncanny ability to hold a conversation while solving some engineering problem, gave a few more clicks before shutting his laptop. "He's waiting for you to voice an opinion. You're the CEO. You get final vote."

FMJ specialized in taking over flailing businesses and turning them around, much like the snack shack they'd whipped into prosperity all those years ago. Jonathon used his wizardry to streamline the company's finances. Matt, with his engineering background, inevitably developed innovations that helped turn the company around. Ford's own role in their magic act was a little more vague.

Ford had a way with people. Inevitably, when FMJ took over a company, there was resentment from the ownership and employees. People resisted, even feared, change. And that's where Ford came in. He talked to them. Smoothed the way. Convinced them that FMJ was a company they could trust.

He flashed a smile at Matt. "I can do my part no matter what the company is. Why do I need to vote?"

While he spoke, he absently opened his desk drawer and tossed the pocketknife in. As if of their own accord, his fingers drifted to the delicate gold earring he kept stored in the right-hand corner.

The earring was shaped like a bird, some kind of sea

bird, if he wasn't mistaken. Its wings were outstretched as if it were diving for a fish, its motion and yearning captured in perfect miniscule detail.

Ford's fingertip barely grazed the length of its wingspan before he jerked his hand out and slammed the drawer shut.

It was her earring. Kitty Biedermann's. The woman from the bar in Texas.

He'd discovered it in the front of his rented pickup when he'd gone to turn the truck in. Now he wished he'd left it there. It wasn't like he was going to actually return the earring to its owner.

Yes, when he'd first found the earring, he'd had Wendy, FMJ's executive assistant, look Kitty up, just to see how hard it would be to hunt her down. But then Kitty Biedermann turned out to be a jewelry store heiress.

What was he going to do, fly to New York to return the earring? He was guessing she didn't want to see him again any more than he wanted to see her. But now he was stuck with this stupid bird earring.

As much to distract himself as anything, he rocked back in his chair and said, "Okay, let's buy a company. What do they do again?"

"What do you mean, what do they do?" Jonathon grumbled. "This is the company you researched."

Ford nudged his foot against the edge of the desk and set his chair to bobbing. "What are you taking about? I didn't research a company."

"Sure you did." Jonathon held out the portfolio.

When Ford didn't take it, Jonathon settled for tossing in on Ford's desk. "The same day I sent out that first list of companies to consider, you e-mailed Wendy and told her to dig up anything she could find on Biedermann Jewelry. Since you seemed interested in them, Matt and I voted and…"

Listening to his partner talk, Ford let his chair rock forward and his feet drop to the floor. With a growing sense of dread, he flipped open the portfolio. And there was the proposal. To buy Biedermann Jewelry.

His stomach clenched like he'd been sucker punched.

Had Wendy misunderstood his casual, *Hey, see what you can find out about Kitty Biedermann?* But of course Wendy had. She was obsessively thorough and eager to please.

With forced nonchalance he asked, "Have you put a lot of work into this deal yet?"

"A couple hundred man hours," Jonathon hedged. "Biedermann's is circling the drain. We need to move fast."

Matt normally wasn't the most intuitive guy. But he must have heard something in Ford's voice, because he asked, "What's up, Ford? You having doubts?"

"It's a pretty risky deal," he said simply. Maybe he could gently redirect their attention.

But Jonathon shook his head. "It isn't really. Biedermann's has always been a strong company. They've been undervalued ever since Isaac Biedermann died last year. But I can turn them around." Jonathon's lips quirked in one of his rare grins. "Kind of looking forward to the challenge, actually."

Ford had seen that look in Jonathon's eyes before. Jonathon was ready to gobble up Biedermann's. Any minute now he'd be picking his teeth with the bones of Biedermann's carcass.

Unless Ford stopped him.

Which he could do. All he'd have to do is explain about Kitty. And the earring.

But what was he really supposed to say? *Don't buy the company because I slept with her?* He usually preferred relationships to last a little longer than one night, but he wasn't above the occasional fling when the chance presented itself. He'd never had a problem walking away the next day. He just wasn't a long-term kind of guy. He wouldn't even remember her name if it hadn't been for that lost earring.

"So what do you say?" Jonathon asked. "We all in?"

"Sure." And he sounded convincingly casual about it, too. He pushed his chair back and stood. "Hey, I'm going to the gym. That damn chair makes my back hurt."

"Don't be gone long. We've got work to do."

"When do you leave for New York?" he asked.

"Not me, we," Jonathon corrected. "As soon as I can get the board to agree to a meeting."

"Great." It looked like he was going to be able to return that earring after all.

Kitty sat at the head of the conference table, concentrating all of her considerable acting skill on looking relaxed. Today was the first of what would probably be many meetings to negotiate the deal with FMJ. She would never feel good about this, but what choice did she have? Everything she'd tried on her own had blown up in her face. Marty, Biedermann's CFO, had assured her this was her only option. Her last, best hope to salvage anything from Biedermann's.

Still, the thought of selling the company twisted her gut into achy knots. Beidermann's had been in her family since her great-great-grandfather had moved to New York from Germany and opened the first store in 1868. For her, Biedermann's wasn't just a company, it was her history, her heritage. Her family.

But it was also her responsibility. And if she couldn't save it herself, then she'd hand it over to someone who could, even if doing so made her stomach feel like it was about to flip itself inside out.

She should be more comfortable sitting at this table than most people were in their own bedrooms. And yet she found herself strumming her fingers against the gleaming wood as she fought nausea.

Beside her, Marty rested his hand over hers. He seemed to be aiming for reassuring, but his touch sent a shiver of disgust through her.

He stroked the backs of her fingers. "Everything will be all right."

She stiffened, jerking her hand out from under his. "I beg your pardon?"

"You seemed nervous."

"Nonsense." Still, she buried her hand in her lap.

She didn't handle sympathy well under normal circumstances. Now it made her feel like she was going to shatter. He looked pointedly at the spot on the table she'd been drumming on, to which she replied, "I'm impatient. They're seven minutes late and I have a reservation for lunch at Bruno's."

Marty's lips twitched. "You don't have to pretend with me."

Something like panic clutched her heart. So, he thought he saw right through her. Well, others had thought that before. "Don't be ridiculous, Marty. I've been pretending to be interested in your conversations for years. I'm certainly not going to stop now."

For an instant, a stricken expression crossed his face and regret bit through her nerves. Dang it. Why did she say things like that? Why was it that whenever she was backed into a corner, she came out fighting?

She was still contemplating apologizing when the door opened and Casey stuck her head through. "Mr. Ford Langley and Mr. Jonathon Bagdon are here."

Awash in confusion, she nearly leaped to her feet. "Ford Langley? Is here?"

Then she felt Marty's steady hand on hers again. "Mr. Langley's the CEO of FMJ. He's come in person for the negotiations."

She stared blankly at Marty, her mind running circles around one thought. Ford Langley.

He was here? He was the CEO of FMJ? Impossible. Ford Langley was an ignorant cowboy. She'd left him in Texas and would never see him again.

She must have misheard. Or misunderstood her assistant just now. Or misremembered the name of the stranger she'd slept with. Or perhaps through some cruel trick of fate, the CEO of FMJ and the stranger shared the same odd name.

Each of these possibilities thundered through her mind as she struggled to regain her composure. Mistaking her confusion, Marty must have spoken for her and told Casey to show in the people from FMJ.

She barely had time to school her panic into a semblance of calm before the door to the conference room swung open and there he was. Fate had pulled a much crueler trick on her than merely giving two men the same name. No, fate had tricked her into selling her beloved company to the same man to whom she'd already given her body.

What had he expected?

Okay, he hadn't thought she'd jump up, run across the room and throw her arms around him. But he sure as hell hadn't expected the complete lack of response. The coolly dismissive blank stare. As if she didn't recognize him at all. As if he were beneath her notice.

Her gaze barely flickered over him as she looked from him to Jonathon. Then she glanced away, looking bored. Someone from Biedermann's had stood and was making introductions. Ford shook hands at the right moment, filing away the name and face of Kitty's CFO.

She looked good. Lovely, in fact. As smoothly polished as the one-dimensional woman in the Nagel painting poster he'd had on his wall as a teenager. Beautiful. Pale. Flat.

Gone was the vibrant woman he'd danced with in The Well two months ago. By the time the introductions were done, one thing had become clear. She was going to pretend they'd never met before. She was going to sit through this meeting all the while ignoring the fact that they'd once slept together. That he'd touched her bare skin, caressed her thighs, felt her body tremble with release.

Which was exactly what he should do, too. Hell, wasn't that what he had *planned* on doing?

Just as Jonathon was pulling out his chair, Ford said, "Before we get started, I wonder if I could have a word alone with Ms. Biedermann."

Jonathon sent him a raised-eyebrowed, do-you-know-what-you're-doing? kind of look. Kitty's CFO hovered by her side, like an overly protective Chihuahua.

Ford gave the man his most reassuring smile while nodding slightly at Jonathon. He knew Jonathon would back him up and get the other guy out of there. Jonathon wouldn't question his actions, even if Ford was doubting them himself.

Something was up with Kitty and he intended to find out what it was.

Kitty watched Marty leave the conference room, fighting the urge to scream. An image flashed through her mind of herself wild-eyed and disheveled, pulling at her hair and shouting "Deserter! Traitor!" like some mad Confederate general about to charge into battle and to his death, all alone after his men have seen reason and fled the field.

Clearly, she'd been watching too many old movies.

Obviously her time would have been better spent practicing her mental telepathy. Then she could have ordered Marty to stay. As it was, she couldn't protest without Ford realizing how much the prospect of being alone with him terrified her.

The moment the door shut, leaving them alone in the room, he crossed to her side. "Hello, Kitty."

She stood, nodding. Praying some response would spring to her lips. Something smart. Clever. Something that would cut him to the bone without seeming defensive.

Sadly nothing came to mind. So she left it at the nod.

"You look…" Then he hesitated, apparently unsure which adjective best described her.

"I believe 'well' is usually how one finishes that sentence." Oh, God. Why couldn't she just keep her mouth shut?

"That's not what I was going to say."

"Well, you seem to be having trouble finishing the sentence," she supplied. "Since I'm sure I look just fine and since I'd much rather get this over with than stand around exchanging pleasantries, I thought I'd move things along."

He raised his eyebrows as if taken aback by her tone. "You aren't curious why I'm here?"

That teasing tone stirred memories best left buried

in the recesses of her mind. Unfortunately, those pesky memories rose up to swallow her whole, like a tsunami.

As if it were yesterday instead of two months or more, she remembered what it had felt like to be held in his arms. Cradled close to his body as they swayed gently back and forth on the dance floor. The way he'd smelled, musky yet clean against the sensory backdrop of stale smoke and spilled beer. The way her body had thrummed to life beneath his touch. The way she'd quivered. The way she'd come.

She thrust aside the memories, praying he wouldn't notice that her breath had quickened. Thankful he couldn't hear the pounding of her heart or see the hardening of her nipples.

Hiding her discomfort behind a display of boredom, she toyed with the papers on the table where she'd been sitting. She couldn't stand to look at him, so she pretended to read through them as she said, "I know why you're here. You came here to take control of Biedermann's." Thank God her voice didn't crack as she spoke. It felt as if her heart did, but that at least she could hide. For the first time since he walked into the room, she met his gaze. "You can't honestly expect me to welcome you. You're stealing the company I was born to raise."

His expression hardened. "I'm not stealing anything. FMJ is providing your failing company with some much-needed cash. We're here to keep you in business."

"Oh, really. How generous of you." She buried all her trepidation beneath a veneer of sarcasm. As she always did. It was so much easier that way. "Since that's the case, why don't you just write out a nice hefty check and leave it on the table on your way out. I'll call you in a decade or so to let you know if it helped."

"A big, fat check might help if all you needed was an infusion of cash. But the truth is, Biedermann's needs a firm hand at the helm and you can't have one without the other. You know that's not how this works."

His words might have been easier to swallow if he'd sounded apologetic instead of annoyed. No, wait…there wasn't really any way that anything he said could be easier to swallow.

"No. Of course that's not how it works. You'll go over the company with a fine-toothed comb. You'll tear it apart, throw out the parts you don't like and hand the rest back in pieces. In the end, everything my family's worked for for five generations will be gone. All so you can turn a quick profit."

"Tell me something. Is that really what's bothering you?"

Of course it wasn't what was really bothering her. What was really bothering her was that he was here at all. Her safe, what-the-hell-I'm-stuck-in-Texas fling hadn't stayed where it was supposed to. In Texas. What was the point of having a fling with a stranger if the man ended up not being a stranger at all?

But she couldn't say that aloud. Especially given the way he was looking at her. With his expression so intense, so sexual, so completely unprofessional, it sent a wave of pure shock through her system.

"W-what do you mean?"

"Come on, Kitty. This anger you're clinging to isn't about Biedermann's at all. This is about what happened in Texas."

She quickly buried her shock beneath a veneer of disdain. "Texas. I'm surprised you'd have the guts to bring that up."

"You are?"

"Of course." She strolled to the other side of the conference table. "I'd think you would be the last person to want to hash that over. But since you brought it up, maybe you can answer a question for me. Was anything you told me true or was it all pretense?"

"What's that supposed to mean?"

"You know. That whole charade you put on to pick me up back in Texas. That aw-shucks, I'm just a simple cowboy trying to make a living act."

"I never said I was a cowboy."

"No. But you had to know that's what I thought."

"How exactly was I supposed to know that?" His facade of easy charm slipped for a moment and he plowed a hand through his hair in frustration. He sucked in a breath and pointed out in a slightly calmer tone, "You weren't exactly forthcoming about who you were, either."

"I did nothing wrong." True, she hadn't exactly presented him with her pedigree when they'd first met, but surely it didn't take a genius to see she didn't fit in at that bar. If there had been an obvious clue he didn't, either, she'd missed it entirely. She refused to let him paint himself the victim. "I don't have anything to apologize for. I'm not the one who pretended to be some down on his luck cowboy."

"No, you're just the one who gave me a fake phone number instead of admitting you didn't want to see me again."

"If you knew I didn't want to see you again," she asked, "then why did you go to the trouble of hunting me down?"

"I didn't hunt you down. What happened in Texas has nothing to do with FMJ's offer."

"Then how exactly did the offer come about anyway?" she asked. "If you didn't go back to work and say, 'Wow, that Kitty Biedermann must be really dumb to have fallen for my tired old lines. I bet we could just swoop in and buy that company right from under her.'"

His gaze narrowed to a glare. "You know that's not how it happened."

"Really? How would I know that? What do I really know about you other than the fact that you're willing to misrepresent yourself to get a woman into bed with you?"

"I never lied to you. Not once. And despite the fact that you're acting like a brat, I won't start now."

"Maybe you didn't lie outright, but you certainly misled me. Of course, maybe that's the only way you can get a woman into bed."

Ford just smiled. "You don't believe that. The sex

was great." He closed in on her, getting right in her face as if daring her to disagree.

God, she wanted to. That would serve him right.

But when she opened her mouth, she found the denial trapped inside her. Between the intensity of his eyes and the memories suddenly flooding her, she just couldn't muster up the lie.

Instead she said the only thing that popped into her mind. "You can't convince me that FMJ is prepared to buy Biedermann's solely so you can get laid."

He grinned wolfishly. "Boy, you think highly of yourself."

"You were the one who brought up sex," she pointed out.

"You didn't let me finish. I was going to close with the suggestion that we both try to forget it happened."

"Oh, I won't have any trouble with that," she lied easily, barely even cringing as she waited for the bolt of lightning to strike her down.

"Excellent." He bit off the word. "Then you agree from here on out, it's all business?"

"Absolutely." Her smiled felt so tight across her face she was surprised she could still breathe. But she kept it in place as she crossed back to the door.

Jonathon and Marty were waiting in the office outside the conference room. If they'd picked up on the tension, neither commented. Thank goodness. She simply wouldn't have had the strength to come up with any more lies today. Between the lies she'd told Ford and the lies she was telling herself, she was completely out.

"Everything okay?" Jonathon asked, more to Ford than to her.

However, she didn't give the treacherous bastard a chance to answer. Instead, she dug deep and pulled out one more lie. "Mr. Langley was just assuring me Biedermann's is going to be in great hands with you." She held out her hand to gesture him back into the conference room. "Why don't you come in and we'll talk money."

Kitty's head was pounding by the time she finally made it back to her office alone. The simple truth was nothing could have prepared her for this.

She thought she'd been ready, but she hadn't, really. Not to sit in a conference room and listen politely while strangers discussed her beloved Biedermann's—while they calmly talked about compensation packages. While they talked about key positions in the company they'd need to replace.

Oh, they'd started by reassuring her that she would stay on as president of the subsidiary, but she knew she wouldn't have control. Not really. She'd be a figurehead, at best. A pretty adornment to make things look good. It'd be pathetic if it wasn't so sad. But the really pathetic thing was she would let herself be used that way.

She loved Biedermann's. She'd do whatever it took to save it. Even if she had to sell her soul to the devil. Or in this case, Ford Langley.

# Three

If she thought her day couldn't get any worse, she was wrong. She ran into Ford in the elevator bay.

"Fantastic," she muttered as she punched the elevator button. "Thousands of people work in this building and I get to ride down with you."

"I waited for you."

"How kind." She didn't bother to meet his gaze or to inject any real graciousness in her voice. She certainly hoped he wasn't so dense that he couldn't hear her sarcasm.

"I wanted to apologize." He seemed to be speaking through gritted teeth.

Well, she certainly wasn't going to make this any easier for him. "For your behavior earlier?" she asked as the elevator doors began to open. She prayed there'd be someone else in the car with them, but her prayers went unanswered. Which was the norm of late. "Don't worry. I didn't expect better behavior from you. After all, I know what Californians are like."

It was a twist of something he'd said to her at that bar in Texas, when he'd teased her about being a Yankee. His gaze flickered to hers and for a second they seemed to both be remembering that night.

Damn it, why had she brought that up? She didn't want to remind him about that. She certainly didn't want him to think she remembered that night with anything approaching word for word accuracy.

"What I meant," he said, following her into the elevator, "was that the meeting seemed hard for you. I can't imagine it's easy to sell a company that's been in your family for generations."

She shot him a scathing look. "Please don't tax your mental capacity trying to imagine it."

The doors closed, sealing them inside. For a moment he thought she'd say nothing more, just ride with him in silence. Maybe this was it. Maybe she really was as cool a number as she'd seemed in the boardroom. Maybe selling her family company meant nothing more to her than—

Then abruptly she let loose a bitter laugh.

*Okay, maybe not.*

"You want to know the really funny thing?" she asked as she punched the 1 button. "This is exactly what I was raised to do."

"Run Biedermann's?" he asked.

"Oh, God, no. Don't get me wrong. My father adored me. Treated me like an absolute princess. But he never thought I was capable of running Biedermann's. I was supposed to transform myself into the perfect wife. I was supposed to catch myself a rich husband to run Biedermann's for me."

She slanted him a look as if to assess his reaction. Her tongue darted out to slip along her lower lip and his body tightened in response. He was not supposed to want her. This was about business. Not sex. Now, if only his body would get that memo.

Apparently she'd gotten it though, because she continued on as if the energy between them wasn't charged with the memory of soul-scalding sex.

She shook her head wryly. "His attitude was archaic, but there you have it."

"So you decided to prove him wrong," he surmised.

"No, I didn't even do that. I really tried to marry the perfect man to take over Biedermann's. I had him all picked out. Even got him to propose." When the elevator doors didn't shut fast enough for her liking she started punching the close button repeatedly. "He just decided to marry someone else instead. I won't bore you with the details of my love life. Not when they're available online in several different gossip columns."

The elevator started to drop and again she laughed.

"See, that's the funny part, right? Flash-forward a year. I've made a complete mess running Biedermann's, just like my father predicted. You swoop in to rescue the company. FMJ is going to take care of everything. But—" she hastily added, as if he were about to argue with her. "I'll still get to play at being president of the company. You'll be watching over my shoulder, so there's no chance I'll make things worse. I'll just get to sit there, looking good, while a big strong man fixes things for me. It's the job I was raised to do."

"Kitty—" he began, but the doors opened and she cut him off as they did.

"My father would be so proud."

She said it with the cavalier indifference of someone who was truly in pain. But damn, she was good at hiding it.

If he hadn't met her under other circumstances, if he'd never seen her with her guard down, he'd probably even be fooled. But as it was, he saw right through her.

If she'd been weeping and moping, maybe he could have ignored her despair. Or handed her off into the care of someone who knew her better. But these bitter self-recriminations…well, he remembered how he'd felt after his father died. The grief, the anger, the guilt, all rolled into one. He wouldn't wish that on anyone.

He fell into step beside her, and said, "Look, you're going through a hard time. You shouldn't be alone tonight. It's Friday night. Why not let me take you out for—"

"It's not necessary. I have plans."

"Plans?" he asked. "After a day like today?"

She waved a hand, still putting on a brave face. "It's

something I couldn't get out of. A commitment from weeks ago."

He quirked an eyebrow, waiting for her to supply more information.

Finally she added, "It's a fundraiser for The Children's Medical Foundation. At The Pierre. Very posh. You wouldn't be comfortable there," she finished dismissively.

She was either trying to insult him or she'd made up the engagement to put him off. He didn't believe for a minute that she planned on going to this charity event, even if she had bought the tickets months ago. She was just trying to get rid of him. But he couldn't stand the thought of her all alone, wallowing in her misery.

"Great." Why not pretend to buy her story? "I'll come with you."

She shot him a look icy enough to freeze his eyebrows off.

Okay, so he couldn't exactly imagine Kitty wallowing in anything. Here in New York she was as cool and collected as they came.

But he'd seen her outside her element. He'd seen her vulnerable. He knew that a passionate, emotional woman lurked beneath the surface of her icy cool perfection. If he peeled back the layers to reveal that woman, he'd probably find someone who could use a shoulder to cry on.

Kitty stopped in the lobby, ignoring the other people filtering out onto the street. "You don't need to do that."

"I don't have plans."

"Your partner—"

"Has a teleconference with some people in China."

"Who called a meeting for a Saturday morning?" she pressed.

"You know what they say." He flashed a smile. "If you don't come in on Saturday, don't bother coming in on Sunday, either."

"I'm fine," she insisted.

But she wasn't. He could see the strain in the lines around her eyes and in the tightness of her mouth. Of course, there was a chance his attempt to be kind was only making matters worse, but his gut told him to keep pushing. He was almost past her defenses, but charm alone wouldn't get her to open up. He needed to change tactics.

"Oh, I get it," he said. "You don't want to be with me."

"Exactly."

"You're probably afraid of how you feel about me." A lock of her hair had fallen free of its twist. He reached out and gave it a quick tug before tucking it behind her ear. He let his fingers linger there, at the sensitive place along the back of her ear.

She rolled her eyes. "That's not going to work."

"What?" he asked innocently.

"You're trying to bait me," she accused.

"Hey, I understand. You don't want to be alone with me. Can't say I blame you." He dropped his eyes to her lips. He let himself remember what it had been like to kiss her. To feel her breath hot on his skin. When he met her gaze again, he knew she remembered it, too.

"It's probably wise. We should spend as little time together as possible."

Her breath seemed to catch in her throat and her tongue darted out to lick her bottom lip. Then she seemed to shake off the effects. Her eyes narrowed in obvious annoyance. "Fine." She turned and started to walk away. "If you're so desperate for something to do tonight that you'll pull that cheap trick, you can come along. But don't blame me if tickets to this fundraiser are outrageously expensive at the last minute."

He smiled as he fell into step beside her. The spark was back in her eyes. The bite was back in her words. She'd be fine.

"I'll pick you up at your place," he offered.

"That's not necessary."

"I don't mind."

"Well, I do," she countered. "You don't honestly think I'm going to tell you where I live, do you?"

"You don't honestly believe I don't already know, do you?"

She turned and shot him an assessing stare. "You know where I live? What did you do, hire a private investigator?"

"I didn't have to. Jonathon has a whole team that researches that kind of thing when we're looking to acquire a company."

"I don't know whether to be creeped out or impressed." She reached the street and raised her hand to hail a cab, but this time of night the streets were packed. "Creeped out wins, I think."

"This is just company policy."

"What, all's fair in love and war?" she asked with an edge to her voice.

"This isn't love or war. This is business."

He held her gaze as firmly as he said it.

She jerked her gaze away from his, turning her attention to the passing cabs on the street. "This may be only business to you. But for me, it's both love and war. I love Biedermann's. And I've spent the last six months fighting for its survival. This may not be personal for you, but it's deeply personal for me."

A look of surprise crossed her face. Like she hadn't meant to admit that. Or maybe she just wasn't used to talking about her emotions.

After a minute he said, "Maybe that's part of the problem."

"Part of what problem?" He was about to respond, but she stopped him before he could. "And don't you dare tell me that 'the problem' is that I care too much. That I'm too emotionally involved to make rational decisions. Because I don't believe that my emotional state has anything to do with the flagging economy or the fact that malls across America are doing lower volume sales across the board." Her voice rose as she spoke, betraying her frustration. "If I could miraculously turn off my emotions and stop caring about Biedermann's, it wouldn't make a bit of difference. So if it's all the same to you, I'm going to go right on caring passionately about—"

Her voice cracked and she started blinking rapidly. Like she was trying to hold back tears.

He reached out a hand to her. "Kitty, I'm sorry—"

But a cab finally pulled up before he could finish the sentence. "Don't be sorry," she ordered as she opened the door. "Just find a way to fix it. Because if you can't, then we're both screwed."

She didn't look back as she climbed into the cab. He watched her go in silence.

She was one tough cookie.

Every other woman he knew was more in touch with her emotions. Or—he corrected himself—maybe just more willing to use her emotions to get what she wanted. Any one of his sisters would have been boo-hooing up a storm halfway through the meeting. But Kitty had just sat there in silence. Listening to every word that was said, but commenting little herself.

If it hadn't been for her outburst in the elevator, he might never have known how upset she truly was. She was unlike any woman he'd ever known. She wasn't willing to use tears to get what she wanted. He had to admire that.

But in other ways, Kitty was exactly like the other women he knew. She herself had admitted that she'd been on the lookout for a rich husband.

But somehow the poor bastard had slipped away. Or the lucky bastard, as the case may be. Frankly, he didn't know whether to feel sorry for the guy or not. Kitty was a hell of a woman.

Sure, he'd used steak knives that were less sharp than her tongue, but for him, that was part of her charm. He had enough women in his life that he had to walk on eggshells around. Thank God he didn't want to get married. Otherwise he might be tempted to drop to his knees and propose right now. He nearly chuckled imagining the scathing response that would earn him.

Ford had developed a certain cynicism about the institution at a very young age. He'd been about nine or ten when he first discovered that his father had a long-term girlfriend living one town over. Eventually, that girlfriend had developed into a second family, complete with two curly-haired little girls, quite close in age to his own sister.

At first the way his father balanced both families disgusted Ford. By the time he reached adulthood himself, it was no longer his father's behavior that troubled him. By then he'd realized both his mother and the other woman knew about each other. They'd been content to let the situation slide. As long as there was enough money to go around.

Since his father's death, Patrice and Suz had become friends in some sick little way. As for the girls, they now treated each other like the sisters they were. He seemed to be the only one who found the situation odd.

Now, standing on the curb watching the spot where Kitty's taxi had disappeared into the night, Ford nearly laughed himself. If she thought her revelation about her family would scare him off, she had another think coming. His family had more drama than a Greek tragedy.

Ford tucked his hands into his pockets and started walking toward the nearest subway station. It wasn't far back to the hotel and it was a nice night. He might as well enjoy the weather.

Only then did he feel the earring still in his pocket. It was just as well he hadn't returned it to her today. She might have been tempted to cram it down his throat.

Kitty's apartment, a walk-up in the eclectic Murray Hill neighborhood, surprised him. He'd have pegged her for an Upper East Side girl, or at the very least he imagined her in some glossy new high-rise. Instead, she lived in a prewar building that had seen better years.

When she let him into her fourth-floor apartment she wasn't dressed yet. She left him waiting in her living room for nearly an hour. Probably just to tick him off.

Her apartment was smaller than he'd expected, sparsely furnished with a few antiques. With the exception of a couple of framed black-and-white family pictures, the walls were bare. Either her taste was minimalist or she hadn't lived here long.

Ford spent the time hanging out on the sofa, first answering his e-mail on his iPhone, then reviewing some specs Matt had sent him, and then finally playing Tetris on his phone.

He might have left, but the truth was, the tension was palpable. Too much remained unsaid between them.

Under any other circumstances, he would have let it slide, being something of an expert on unresolved emotional issues. But with Kitty, it was different. He'd never before been in a position where he'd have to work with a woman he'd slept with. The last thing he wanted was some emotional complication mucking up the coming negotiations. If she was going to have a problem working with him, he wanted to clear the air now.

Finally her bedroom door opened to reveal Kitty encased in a shimmering deep purple gown with a low-cut, heart-shaped neckline. Her dark hair fell in sleek waves about her shoulders. He nearly laughed at the expression of surprise that flickered across her face when she spied him.

He stood. "You look lovely."

She fell into step beside him, not bothering to suppress an exasperated sigh. "You're still here."

"Much to your disappointment, I'm sure." He put a hand at her back to guide her to the door, only to discover a generous expanse of naked skin.

"Not at all," she murmured, suddenly all charm. "I had trouble with my zipper. You can't imagine how worried I was you might get tired of waiting and leave."

"Trouble with your zipper? For over an hour?"

"It's a long zipper."

He leaned away to look pointedly at the back of her dress. A delicate triad of beaded straps criss-crossed at her shoulders. Her skin was left bare all the way to just below her waist. The sparkling fabric molded to her bottom before falling in a straight line to the floor.

Just over the crest of her bottom he could see the faint outline of the zipper hidden in the seam. It couldn't have been more than four inches long.

"So I see."

Kitty was no scrawny fashion model. She had a body that managed to be both slender and voluptuous. Her bottom was lusciously rounded. Just looking at it made his blood throb with lust.

She elbowed him in a way that was both playful and seductive. "Stop looking at my zipper," she murmured huskily as she locked her door.

He shrugged as they started down the stairs. "If you don't want people looking at your *zipper,* you shouldn't display it quite so prominently."

"That's sexist," she chided.

"No, it would be sexist if we were at work and I ordered you to display your zipper. Or I hired you or fired you based on the size of your zipper. But this is a social situation, so I don't think either of those apply. Besides, a woman doesn't wear a dress like that unless she wants to be looked at."

He hailed a cab when they reached the street.

Kitty frowned, her bottom lip jutting forward in a pout. "Oh. We're going in a cab. How…prosaic."

"I try to avoid hiring a driver when I come to the city. They spend too much time looking for parking and driving around. It's a waste of gas and resources." He held open the cab door for her, admiring the swath of leg revealed as she slid into the car.

"Hmm. Like I said. How prosaic."

He climbed in beside her. "Being aware of the environment isn't prosaic." A hint of his annoyance slipped into his tone. "FMJ has made most of its money in green industries. Our image as a green company is a priority. Not just for the company, but for all of us."

She yawned delicately, but with obvious boredom. Annoyed by her attitude, he nearly called her on it, but before he could, it hit him. "You're doing this on purpose, aren't you?"

She looked taken aback. "I…I don't know what you mean. Doing what?"

"This." He gestured toward her body-skimming dress. "The sexpot dress. The self-indulgent pout. The childish behavior. It's all a way of keeping me off balance."

She blinked, and he couldn't tell if he'd insulted her or if she was merely surprised he'd seen through her. "You're just trying to distract me. To avoid that conversation we need to have."

"However did you get that idea?"

"Probably because you've been pushing me away ever since I walked into the conference room today. You've made it obvious that you don't want to relinquish control of Biedermann's. You may have fooled everyone else into thinking that's the only thing going on. But I can see right through you. I know the truth."

Oh, God. What did he mean? He knew *the truth?* What truth? That she was a total fraud? That she had no idea what she was doing?

He leaned closer, a seductive grin on his face. "I know what you're really afraid of."

"Afraid of?" she squeaked.

He brushed his thumb across her lower lip, once again sparking the desire that heated her blood every time he touched her.

She should not be attracted to him. He was so not what she needed right now. Or ever, for that matter. Geesh, he wasn't even wearing a tux. Okay, so he looked fabulous in an Armani jacket thrown over a gray cashmere sweater and black pants. And, yes, the understated elegance of his outfit made him look outrageously masculine. Never mind that he carried it off. Never mind that the day's worth of stubble on his jaw made her fingertips tingle with the urge to touch him. Never mind that she could tell already all the other men at the fundraiser would look overdressed and foppish by comparison. She couldn't possibly be attracted to a man who didn't even know when to wear a tie.

"Yes," he continued. "You're afraid of the attraction between us."

As his words registered, she was flooded with an odd sense of relief. He was still talking about sex. About what had happened between them in Texas.

Maybe it shouldn't have made her feel better, but somehow it did. Physical intimacy she could handle. Men had been pursuing her since she hit puberty. She knew how to handle that. She knew how to entice without promising anything. To lure and manipulate a man while staying just out of his reach.

What she didn't know was how to handle a man who was interested in her. Not her body. Not her net worth, but her.

Thank God, Ford was proving no different than any other man she'd ever met. She'd learned long ago the secret to keeping men at arm's length.

The mere suggestion of sex was enough to distract the average man. The possibility that you might one day have sex with him made most men so befuddled they never bothered to look beneath the surface.

To that end, she let herself sway toward him slightly, as if she couldn't resist his draw. Then she ran her tongue over the spot on her lip that he'd touched. It was a gesture sure to entice him, but she found it disconcertingly intimate. She could almost taste him on her tongue.

Suddenly memories flooded her of their one night together. How could she have forgotten what it had been like to kiss him? To feel his hands on her body? To give herself over so completely to his touch?

She felt her breath catch in her chest, found herself leaning toward him, not in a calculated way, but as if he were a magnet and the heart pounding away in her chest were made of iron, pulling her inexorably toward him.

He cleared his throat, breaking the spell he seemed to have cast over her. Nodding toward the cab door on her side, he said, "We're here."

When had that happened? Damn him. She was supposed to be distracting him. Not the other way around.

Feeling befuddled, she looked from him to the

crowded street outside her window, to the cab driver rattling off the fare. Her mind was embarrassingly sluggish, but finally she got moving.

Staying one step ahead of Ford was going to be harder than she'd thought. This was going to take some serious work.

Then just when it seemed like things couldn't get any worse, a camera flashed a few feet away. Great. Just what she needed.

Paparazzi.

# Four

Ford stood near the bar, nursing a tumbler of weak Scotch, wishing he could have ordered himself a Sierra Nevada Pale Ale. He would have thought that at five hundred bucks a ticket, they could have stocked the bar with some decent beer. But of course, the best beer in the world wouldn't have distracted him from what was really bothering him. His date.

From the moment the first camera had flashed outside the hotel and she'd practically leaped from his side, she'd been avoiding him. At first, he'd assumed she just didn't want their picture taken together. That she was averting the potential scandal. But things hadn't improved since they'd made it into the event.

She'd immediately sent him off to get her a glass of

white wine and she'd been dodging him ever since. Not that he wasn't having a grand ol' time, between the event organizer who'd hit him up for a ten-thousand-dollar donation and the drunk society maven twice his age who'd been hitting on him. He hadn't had this much fun since his root canal.

Then he spotted Kitty across the room. On the dance floor. With another man. A guy who couldn't have been more than five-six and had very clingy hands.

Ford wasn't used to women blowing him off. After all, he'd only come out tonight because he'd wanted to make sure she was okay. After the near waterworks in the elevator, he'd been worried about her emotional state. Judging from the way she was laughing at Mr. Grabby's joke, she was doing just fine. But enough was enough.

He handed his drink to a passing waiter and wove his way through the crowd to the dance floor. He cut in, sweeping Kitty into his arms before she could protest. But he could tell she wanted to. As her hand settled into his, a scowl twisted her perfect features.

"I'm starting to think you're avoiding me."

"Whatever gave you that impression? After all, it's not like you wheedled your way into coming with me uninvited or anything."

He grinned at her, some of his annoyance fading at the bite of her sharp tongue. In Texas she'd been relaxed and open. Who would have guessed he'd find her bristly defenses just as appealing. "I'm a grown man. I don't wheedle."

"Hmm…" She paused as if considering her words. No doubt searching for the best way to skewer him. "How about coerce? Or maybe bully? Are those descriptions more to your liking? Are those masculine enough for you?"

He stared down at her, studying her expression. As they danced, his body brushed hers. He couldn't help remembering what it had felt like to dance with her in that bar in Texas. There, her body had melted into his; here, she held herself more stiffly. This was less a dance, more a battlefield.

"I don't like to think," he said seriously, "that I've bullied you into anything."

She arched an eyebrow. "Then perhaps you shouldn't be trying to buy my company out from under me."

"That's business."

"I thought you said it was *all* business?" she countered smoothly.

"That's not what I meant and you know it." She felt good in his arms again. Solid, yet soft. Curved in all the right places. Tempting and a little bit dangerous.

Suddenly he couldn't remember why he was supposed to leave her alone. Something about the business deal, right? It was a bad idea to mix business with pleasure. He knew that.

But Biedermann's was in serious trouble and FMJ looked like the only people stepping forward to help out. Besides, if everything went as planned, this would leave her even richer than she was now. Kitty was a businesswoman first and foremost.

But she was also a woman. A very desirable, powerful woman. He'd be an idiot to ignore the tension simmering between them. Not just because the sex would be fantastic, but because the more they tried to ignore it, the more likely it was to get in the way of business. He couldn't let his former relationship with Kitty muck up this business deal. He wouldn't let his buddies down like that.

Ford smiled. "What's going on with Biedermann's is all business. This thing between us isn't business at all."

"There is no thing between us."

Her voice was so emotionless, he almost believed she meant it. But his body had been inside hers. He'd watched her face as she climaxed. Women didn't forget that kind of thing. Sure, he could let her go on pretending they had no past, but that would just make things worse down the road if this blew up in both their faces.

"There was something between us back in Texas. I'm betting there still is."

She hesitated, her feet missing the rhythm for a moment. But then she picked up the beat again and fell into step. "You're wrong."

"And you're avoiding the obvious," he said. "You're acting like we didn't have hot, steamy sex in the back of my truck."

Her gaze narrowed into a glare. "And you're acting like a sixteen-year-old girl who put out on prom night and now wants to hear the quarterback still respects her."

He nearly chuckled at the image, but that seemed to only irritate her more.

She leaned closer to whisper vehemently, "You want to know the truth? Yes, the sex was hot and steamy. But it was just sex. Sex with a nameless, faceless stranger. It was never meant to be anything more than that. If you'd wanted a long-term relationship you should have put an ad up on one of those Internet dating sites."

"Trust me. I'm not a relationship kind of guy. I'm just not willing to be whipped. Least of all by you. Why would I? So far, you've been insulting, arrogant and generally a pain in the ass."

Surprise flickered across her face and he might have felt a twinge of guilt if every word he said wasn't true. Possibly even an understatement.

"Don't get me wrong," he continued. "It's kind of cute. In a spoiled brat kind of way."

"Cute? Spoiled brat?" She sputtered as if searching for a response. "How da—"

"How dare I? I dare because whether you like it or not, we have to work together. Whether *I* like it or not, for that matter. I thought talking about what happened in Texas might make things easier for you." Though the music continued to play, they'd slowed to the point they were no longer dancing. "Apparently I was mistaken. You don't want to talk about it? Fine. Just make sure you don't bring any of this baggage into the boardroom when we start negotiations."

She pulled her hand from his. Her gazed narrowed to a venomous glare. "Thank you for clearing that up for me. Here I was worried FMJ's offer might have been motivated by some chivalrous impulse on your part."

"Sorry, sugar." He softened his words with a grin. "I don't have a chivalrous bone in my body."

"I'm glad you've disabused me of that notion. Now I can go about being my normal…what was that phrase you used? Oh yes, pain in the ass…without feeling bad about it. That makes things much easier."

Shooting him one last haughty look, she spun on her heel and left the dance floor.

"I 'disabused her of the notion'?" he muttered to the empty spot where she'd been. "Who the hell talks like that?"

He stood there for a minute until he realized the couples around him were staring with interest. He flashed his best charming rogue smile and shrugged. "Women."

Several men tried to hide their smiles. A couple laughed outright. The women either rolled their eyes or just looked away. But he could see in their eyes that they were more amused than they wanted to be.

If the audience was keeping score, it looked like he'd won another round. It didn't feel that way, though. If only he'd believed her when she said she wasn't interested in sleeping with him. Hell, he'd even be satisfied with believing himself.

Kitty's heart pounded in her chest as she maneuvered through the maze of bodies on the dance floor. Nausea clung to her, sticky and thick. She wasn't sure how much longer she could maintain any semblance of calm around Ford. Her nerves were frayed to the point of exhaustion.

Selling Biedermann's was something she'd never

thought she'd consider. Just meeting with FMJ to discuss it had been abhorrent. But she'd done it. She'd dug deep to find strength she'd never known she had and she'd done the right thing for the company. And this was how fate had punished her.

Why, oh, why, did it have to be him? Why did he have to be the *F* of FMJ? Six billion people in the world and the one she never wanted to see again just happened to be the one who held her future in his hands. It was cruelty piled on top of humiliation. It was completely…nauseating.

She flattened her hand against the restroom door and shoved her way inside. The room was thankfully empty. A fact that she only had a second to appreciate before another wave of nausea washed over her. She bolted for the closest stall just as bile mixed with the rich appetizers she'd been so hungry for when she'd first arrived.

Talk about humiliation.

As if throwing up—in public—wasn't bad enough. As Kitty knelt on the bathroom floor with one hand propped on the toilet paper dispenser and the other wedged against the wall, she heard footsteps outside the stall.

"Oh, my, are you all right?" asked a wavering voice from behind her.

The voice sounded kind—benevolently maternal. Kitty wasn't taken in. Too many "kind" women were starving for gossip.

"I'm fine," Kitty managed. She raised her left leg, felt around in the air a bit for the door, then kicked it shut.

"Is there something I can get you, dear?"

Hmm…a cool washcloth? A glass of water? Retrograde amnesia? Any of the above would do.

Kitty shoved the hair out of her face and straightened, wiping at the corners of her mouth with the back of her hand.

"Perhaps I could notify your date that you're not feeling well?"

Nosy and persistent, then. Kitty stood, smoothing down her dress. In her haste, she stepped on her hem and pulled it out. But that couldn't be helped. Praying she looked better than she felt, she left the sanctuary of the stall. Kitty turned to see an elderly woman hovering by the sinks. Though she had to be nearing ninety, the woman was well-dressed and obviously took pains with her appearance.

Kitty remembered something her grandmother had often told her. There's no situation that can't be improved with a fresh coat of lipstick.

Sayings like that had made Kitty roll her eyes as a teenager. Inexplicably, Kitty chuckled. "I think I'll just freshen my makeup."

The older woman smiled. "Always a good idea, if you ask me."

Kitty faced the mirror. Her hair had lost its smooth sheen and now looked tousled beyond repair. Her face was ashen, her lips dry. Even her eyes seemed to have developed dark circles. She could only suppose they'd darkened to match her exhaustion.

And here she'd thought she looked pretty good just a few hours ago when she'd left the condo.

She sighed. By the sink there was a selection of hand lotions and perfumes, along with a bottle of mouthwash and a stack of tiny cups. She filled one of the cups with water to rinse out her mouth.

Spitting as delicately as she could, Kitty said, "This is quite embarrassing. I don't think I've ever thrown up in public before."

"Think nothing of it, dear. Every woman goes through it."

Kitty raised her eyebrows. "Every woman—" she started to ask in confusion.

"Well, not every woman. But when I was pregnant with Jake, my second, I couldn't keep anything down, either."

"Oh, I'm not… That is, I've just been under a lot of stress."

The woman gave her a pointed look. "Is that what they're calling it these days?"

"I'm not—" But Kitty's protest died in her mouth. "Pregnant."

Her vision tunneled, fading to black at the edges but staying piercingly bright in the center, where she could see her reflection in the mirror. Pale. Frightened. Terrified.

*What if she was?*

She couldn't be. But even as she thought it, reality came crashing back.

She was losing Biedermann's. Ford was back in her life. Running her company. So why wouldn't she be pregnant?

* * *

Ford stood in the grand ballroom of The Pierre, scanning the room one last time as the nasty truth sank in. Kitty had left him standing on the dance floor, dashed off for the bathroom and then—somehow—sneaked past him on her way out.

As unpleasant as the idea was, there was no other explanation. Kitty was nowhere to be found. Hell, he'd waited long enough for her to put in an appearance.

Maybe he had it coming. After all, this wasn't an actual date. He'd pushed his way in. Bullied her into agreeing, to use her word.

Still, he wasn't going to let her get away with this.

Forty-five minutes later, he was standing at her door, a lavish bouquet of orchids in his hands.

Her hair was loose about her shoulders, no longer sleek, but tousled as if she'd been running her fingers through it. Her face had been scrubbed clean of makeup, leaving her cheeks rosy. Her mouth was still impossibly pink, though.

She'd changed out of her dress and had a long silk robe cinched tight around her waist. The result was that she looked like one of those forties movie starlets. Somehow, even devoid of makeup and expensive clothing, she still exuded class. As if she'd been simmered in wealth since childhood and now it fairly seeped from her pores.

She eyed him suspiciously, her gaze dropping to the orchids and then back to his face. "What are those for?"

Since she didn't seem inclined to invite him in, he

elbowed past her into the apartment. "They were my excuse to get in the building. One of your neighbors was leaving. I told him I was here to apologize for a date gone bad so he'd let me in."

"And he believed you?"

"What can I say? I was persuasive."

After a moment of indecision, she closed and bolted the door. "Don't worry. It won't happen again. I'll hunt him down and kill the jerk."

"Don't do that. If you're mad at me, take it out on me." While she considered his words, he surveyed her apartment. A dingy kitchen led off from the living room and he headed there with the flowers. "Do you have a vase?"

"I thought the flowers were just a ruse."

"That's no reason not to enjoy them. Do you have any idea how hard it is to find flowers at midnight on a Friday night?"

He grabbed a vase out of one of the cabinets. It was an ornate job with elaborate curlicues. As he filled it with water, he waited for her response. She always seemed to have some snappy comeback.

It was her silence that alerted him something was wrong. He dropped the flowers into the vase and turned, thinking maybe she'd retreated to her bedroom or even left the apartment. Instead he found her sitting on the living room's sole sofa with her elbows propped on her knees and her face buried in her hands.

His nerve endings prickled with alarm.

He sent up a silent prayer. *Please don't let her be*

*crying.* Between his three sisters, Patrice and Suz, he'd faced down his share of weepy women.

The one thing his vast experience with crying women *had* taught him was that running like hell would only make things worse.

"Hey," he began awkwardly. "What's—"

Then Kitty stood, her eyes red, but dry.

No tears. Thank God.

She crossed to stand before him, her posture stiff with anger. "What's the matter?"

She got right in his face, stopping mere inches from him. "I'll tell you what's the matter."

She shoved a hand against his shoulder. Surprise bumped him back a step. "You are the matter."

She bopped him on the shoulder again. This time he was ready, but she was stomping forward, so he backed up a step anyway. "You come here and push your way into my company. Into my life. Into my apartment. You push and you push and you push."

With each *push* she shoved against his chest and with each shove he stepped back, trying to give her the room she needed. But she followed him step for step.

"Maybe it's time someone pushed back."

By now he was—literally—up against a wall. With his back pressed to the living room wall, he had nowhere else to go. She stopped mere centimeters away from him, her hands pressed to his chest, her eyes blazing with anger.

"I'm—" he began.

But she didn't let him finish. "Don't you dare say

you're sorry. Sorry won't cut it. *Sorry* doesn't even *begin* to cut it."

"I—"

"Well?" she prodded.

He gripped her shoulders, resisting the urge to shake her. "Stop. Interrupting. Me."

Her chin bumped up and she glared at him through stormy eyes. "Well?" she demanded again.

"I—" What?

Suddenly, he couldn't remember what it was he'd been about to say. All he could think was that this was what he'd wanted for the past two months. He wanted to see her again. To sleep with her. To strip her clothes off her, lay her bare before him in a proper bed and spend hours worshipping her body.

"'I—I—I—'" she copied, mocking his stammer. "Is that the best you can do?"

Man, she was annoying sometimes.

"No," he said. "This is."

Cupping her jaw in his hands, he shut her up the best way he knew how. He kissed her.

# Five

What exactly did she have to do to insult this man? She'd sneered at him. She'd acted like a tease. She'd ditched him in the middle of their date. She'd insulted him and made fun of him. And now he was kissing her?

What was wrong with him?

Worse still, what was wrong with her?

A hot and heavy make out session with Ford was the last thing she needed right now. She wanted peace and quiet to process the events of the night. She wanted to kick Ford out of her apartment. She wanted him out of her life. She wanted to go on kissing him forever.

After months of living on memories, he was actually kissing her. Months of pretending she'd forgotten him, of believing she'd never see him again, of shoving him out of her mind during the day, but then dreaming of him when she slept. After months of waking in the middle of the night, panting, heart racing, body moist and heavy with need. After months of that, he was here. In her apartment. Kissing her.

His tongue nudged into her mouth, tracing the sensitive skin behind her lip. She shuddered, opening herself fully to him. He tasted of smoky Scotch and heat, of neediness and lust. So familiar, even though she'd only been with him once. Her body sparked to life beneath his touch.

Suddenly it didn't matter that he'd sneaked back into her life uninvited. It didn't matter that he'd deceived her. That he pushed too hard. That she couldn't intimidate or control him. All that mattered was that he just keep kissing her.

Her body remembered his touch as if it were yesterday. No matter what lies she'd told him earlier, *she* remembered. She remembered every second of their time together. As if for those few hours they'd been together she'd been more alive than at any other time in her life. As if she'd been more herself than she was in real life. The way he'd kissed her then. The cool night air on her skin when he'd kissed her in the parking lot of that god-awful bar. The heat of his hands against her flesh. The cold metal of his truck door pressed against her back.

His fingers had fumbled as he pulled her shirt over her head. She'd lost an earring. Yet when he'd touched her breasts, he hadn't been clumsy. His touch was deft. Gentle. His fingertips rough as they'd pinched her nipples, sending fissures of pleasure through her body.

He'd shoved her skirt up to her waist and his jeans had been rough against the insides of her thighs. He'd shoved her panties aside, touched her *there.* A slow, rhythmic rasping of his thumb that had driven her quietly wild. By the time he'd plunged into her, she was already on the brink of climax. The feel of him pumping inside of her combined with the chafing of his fingers had sent her over the edge.

Now, kissing him in her living room, with memories flooding her, his touch was so achingly familiar. Her body trembled with need. Moisture seeped between her legs as desire pulsed through her. She was ready for him already.

His arm snaked around her back, holding her body to his as he walked her backward, one step, then two, still kissing her. His mouth nibbled hers as if he would devour her one tiny bite at a time. And she felt powerless to stop him.

The backs of her knees bumped against the arm of the sofa just as his hand cupped her breast through the bodice of her robe. The silk provided little protection against his roaming hands, not that she wanted any. She felt her nipple tighten, hardening to his touch. Heard a groan stir in his chest.

He pulled his mouth from hers. "This isn't how I wanted this to happen."

But he poured kisses along her neck as he said it.

Proof that he was as powerless against her as she was against him.

Her hands clutched the lapels of his jacket. Pulling back, she tried to glare at him. Which was hard to do through the fog of her desire.

"How *you* wanted it to happen? What about what I want?"

He grinned wickedly, his hand flicking open the folds of her robe. Brushing the outside of her panties, he said, "I think I know what you want."

Her panties were damp with her need for him. She knew it. Maybe it should embarrass her, this desperate lust for him, the way he only had to kiss her and she went wet for him, but it didn't. Not when she knew he felt the same way. She may be wet, but he was hard. Panting. Pulsing against her hand when she ran it down the front his pants.

"You do, don't you?" Her voice came out husky. "Know what I want, I mean."

"I do."

His gaze was disconcertingly serious as he muttered the words. For an unsettling second, she considered the possibility that maybe this was about more than just sex for him. For both of them. But she shoved the concern aside.

Sex was all they had. All she wanted.

Because she couldn't think about anything else. Anything beyond this minute. This very second. She couldn't think about the mistake she might be making. Or the mistake she'd already made.

She couldn't think about the pair of pregnancy tests she'd hastily thrown out when the doorbell rang. Couldn't think about the twin pink lines on those pregnancy tests. She couldn't think about the baby already growing in her belly.

Logic told him to slow down, but she didn't let him. One minute he was merely kissing her, the next she was tumbling over the arm of the sofa, pulling him on top of her. He barely caught himself in time to keep from squashing her. He braced one hand on the back of the sofa and the other right beside her head.

For all her height, she felt tiny beneath him. He didn't want the weight of his body to pummel her. "That was close," he muttered.

"Not nearly close enough," she purred, bucking against him. Her hips rocked against his. Not in a light and playful way, but frantically, as if she were seconds from losing all control. One of her legs crept up the outside of his thigh, hooking around to anchor her hips to his.

Then she bucked against him one last time, rolling him off the sofa altogether, following him down onto the floor. Thank God for plush carpet, though even that hadn't been able to keep the breath from being knocked out of him.

Or maybe it was just her that took his breath away. Kitty. Demanding. Arrogant. Unapologetic. And sexy as hell.

She walked her hands down his chest, slowly pushing

herself into a seated position astride his hips. Her robe gaped open, barely covering her breasts as it caught on her nipples. The sash was still tied at the waist, but the robe revealed enough for him to see she was naked except for her underwear. A little scrap of fabric that felt silky and damp beneath his touch. Just kissing him had made her wet. His erection leaped at the very idea, straining against the front placket of his pants.

Head thrown back, she shifted her hips forward, grinding herself against him. She groaned low in her throat, a sound both erotic and unbearably tempting. How could he resist her? Why would he even try?

He slipped his thumb under the hem of her panties and found the nub of her desire. He stroked her there and the moan turned into a chorus of yeses. The steady chant echoed through his blood, pounding against the last of his restraint.

When she reached for his zipper, it didn't even occur to him to stop her. With a few quick movements, she'd freed him. He lifted his hips as she pulled at his pants, not even bothering to take them all the way off.

She nudged the fabric of her underwear out of the way, then lowered herself onto him. With one smooth movement, he was inside of her. Hot, tight, and unbearably sweet. He squeezed his eyes tightly closed, trying to reign in his pure lust. Sucking a breath in through his teeth, he narrowed his focus. Pleasure rocked through his body, but he stayed just ahead of it. He didn't want to come too quickly. He wanted her right there with him.

He moved his thumb in slow, steady circles, matching the rhythm of her rocking hips. With his eyes still closed, he focused on the sound of her breath, the quick gasps and low moans. The yeses had dissolved to a series of meaningless guttural sounds.

He felt her muscles clenching around him. Then he made the mistake of opening his eyes. He looked up to see her poised above him, her back arched, her breasts thrusting forward as her hands clutched her heels. With her neck arched her hair fell down her back in wild disarray. He'd never seen anything more primitive, more primal, more gut-wrenchingly erotic.

And then she focused her groans into a single word that sent him spiraling beyond control.

"Ford!"

Sleeping with Ford just about topped the list of stupid things she could have done. Ford had said she'd had a hard day and he didn't know the half of it.

And as if sleeping with him wasn't bad enough, she'd *slept* with him. When he'd picked her up and carried her to her bedroom, she'd actually tugged him down onto the bed with her, draped her body over his and promptly fallen asleep. She'd snuggled with him, for cripes sake.

When she'd peeled herself off him in the morning to sneak away for a shower, she prayed he'd at least have the common courtesy to disappear. But no. Not Ford. He made coffee.

How the hell was she supposed to defend herself against a man who'd made her coffee?

"Oh," she said joylessly. "You're still here."

"We have to talk."

"So you keep saying." She crossed the narrow kitchen to the coffeepot and poured herself a cup. "Maybe you think we're ready for couples' therapy."

He cut to the chase. "We didn't use a condom last night."

Ah. So that was why he'd stuck around.

Hoping to antagonize him into storming out, she said, "I suppose you blame me for that."

"I didn't say that. I just wanted to let you know you don't have to worry about your health. I get tested annually for anything that—"

"I know," she interrupted him. "When I got back from Texas I had myself tested. Yes, we were pretty safe, but as we both know condoms aren't one hundred percent effective at anything."

She broke off sharply. *Please don't do something stupid. Like cry. Or tell him the truth.*

"So," she continued. "I knew that wasn't a concern."

*Just keep sipping your coffee. He'll leave soon and you can do all the stupid things you want.*

He pinned her with a heavy stare. "Do I need to worry you'll get pregnant?"

It took all her willpower not to spew coffee all over the kitchen. Instead she equivocated. "Do I look worried?"

"That's hardly the point. You never look worried."

Well, at least she still had someone fooled. With a

self-effacing shrug, she said, "When you're raised the way I was, you learn to keep your emotions to yourself."

"Well, you learned well, then." There was a hint of something dark in his voice. Bitterness maybe, but she didn't want to consider what he might mean by that. She couldn't let herself think too much about his emotions just now.

She ignored his comment. "You don't have to worry about last night."

"You're certain?"

"Let's just say that if I got pregnant from last night, it would be a medical miracle."

Thank God he didn't press her for a more precise answer. Still, she didn't breathe deeply until he'd left and she'd thrown the dead bolt behind him.

Maybe doing something stupid like this was inevitable.

She stood in her kitchen for a long time, sipping her coffee, making excuses for her behavior. What she wanted most was to simply crawl back into bed with her sketch pad and MP3 player. To spend the whole day pretending the rest of the world didn't exist. Of course, she didn't have that luxury.

Come Monday, Ford would start pressuring her to cement the deal with FMJ. Whatever else happened, she couldn't afford to sleep with him again. There was too much at stake, for Biedermann's and for her. After all, she was going to be…

Kitty broke off her train of thought to stare down at her nearly empty coffee mug. Could pregnant women even drink coffee? Shaking her head, she dumped the last splash of coffee in the sink and washed out the mug. She'd have Casey look that up on Monday.

She paused in the act of drying the mug. Yeah, that'd be subtle. No one would ever guess she was pregnant, between puking every few minutes and having her assistant research the effects of caffeine on pregnancy.

At some point, she'd have to tell Ford about the pregnancy, but she wasn't ready for that just yet. She needed more time to process it. To figure how she felt about the tiny life growing inside of her and what it meant for her life.

She had no idea how Ford might respond to the news he was about to be a father. But she knew that whatever his reaction was going to be, she'd need to have her own emotional defenses in place before she dealt with him.

How long could she justify not telling him? A couple of days maybe. But she had to tell him and she had to do it soon.

The very thought made bile rise in her throat. She dashed for the bathroom, only to have her nausea fade, leaving her feeling queasy. The minty zing of her toothpaste helped. When she put away the toothpaste, she saw the two pregnancy tests she'd taken the previous evening.

She'd stopped to pick them up at a drugstore on the way home from the fundraiser. Her heart had pounded the whole time, sure she'd see someone she recognized. Or that at the very least someone would comment on the absurdity of a woman in formal wear buying pregnancy tests late at night. She hadn't cared. She'd needed to know.

She had still been reeling from the shock when Ford had shown up on her doorstep. He'd caught her at her most vulnerable. Again.

But it wouldn't happen a third time. From now on, she'd be prepared to deal with him. But first, she had to deal with other issues. She pressed a hand to her belly.

Logically, she should still be freaking out about being pregnant. But for some strange reason, she wasn't. Maybe some weird pregnancy hormone had been working its magic on her subconscious for the past two months. Whatever the reason, she felt strangely at peace.

Why did being pregnant have to be such a bad thing? All her life she'd dreamed of being part of a bigger family. She'd longed for sisters and brothers. How many times had she made her grandmother read *Little Women* to her? Dozens.

The only thing she'd wanted more than siblings was a real mother. Her grandmother had done her best. She'd loved her and cared for her, sure. But she hadn't done the things other mothers had done—or rather the things Kitty had imagined other mothers did. She'd never climbed onto the jungle gym at the park. She'd never built forts out of old sheets draped over the furniture. She'd never crawled into Kitty's bed to cuddle her and chase away the monsters.

Those were things Kitty's childhood had lacked. But they were experiences she could give to her child.

She could lavish this child with love. She could become the kind of mother she'd always wanted for herself. She could create the family she'd craved for so long.

What about Ford? What kind of father would he be? She bet he'd be the kind of dad who coached Little League and charmed all the teachers into rounding up his kids' grades. He'd spend too much on birthday presents, and…

Whoa. Where had all that come from? Wondering what kind of father Ford would make was the last thing she should be worrying about. It was a completely absurd exercise. Like wondering whether or not the tooth fairy was ticklish. Ford was Mr. Not-Willing-to-Be-Whipped.

There was no way he'd be interested in coaching Little League. This morning, he'd given her the perfect opportunity to tell him about the baby, but she'd balked. She hadn't exactly lied, but she hadn't told him the truth, either. And she suspected it had less to do with her mental defenses than it did with the possibility that she already knew how he'd react.

Ford wasn't looking for long term. Not with her. Not with a child. When he found out the truth, he would cut and run.

At least, dear God, she hoped he would. She could only pray he wouldn't do something noble like offer to *marry* her.

She'd been a burden all her life. For once in her life, she wanted to pull her own weight.

Yes, being pregnant now was inconvenient, what with everything that was going on at Biedermann's.

But it didn't have to be a bad thing. Not at all. The more she thought about it, the more convinced she became. She could be a good mother. She could do this. This was one dream that would not be snatched away from her.

True, she'd probably never be able to run Biedermann's the way she'd dreamed of. But being a failure as a CEO didn't mean she'd also be a failure as a mother. After all, her father had been a fantastic CEO, but a less than stellar parent. That was proof enough, if she needed it, that the two jobs didn't require the same skills. It came down to this: she'd have to be a good parent, because she was likely to be the only parent her child ever knew.

Whenever he and Jonathon traveled together, they got a hotel suite. The combined living space always made it easier to have teleconferences with Matt and to work late in the evenings. It was an arrangement that had worked well. And Jonathon certainly didn't care that Ford was returning to the hotel, having obviously been out all night. And had he slept with any other woman, Ford would have kept his mouth shut.

But Kitty was not any other woman. This morning she'd seemed fine. But the truth was, he had no idea what she was really feeling. He couldn't dismiss the possibility that he'd screwed things up. And if he had blown this deal because he couldn't stop thinking with a certain male part, then Jonathon deserved to know the truth.

"I made a mistake," he admitted as soon as he walked into the hotel suite.

Jonathan didn't even bother looking up from his laptop. A fruit plate and a bowl of oatmeal sat untouched beside his computer. "That's never a good announcement at 7:00 a.m. on a Saturday morning. But you're a big boy. I'm sure you can handle it."

"I slept with Kitty."

Jonathon's head snapped up. "Kitty Biedermann?"

"It was stupid, I know," he admitted.

A pot of coffee and a couple of cups sat untouched on the room service tray, so he poured himself a cup. He looked up to see Jonathon with a bemused half smile on his face.

"We just got here. That's fast, even for you." When Ford didn't answer, Jonathon's smile morphed into a contemplative squint. "That's not it, is it? You knew her already."

"I did. We met in Texas about two months ago." He took a sip of the coffee, relishing the heat as it burned its way down his throat. A stiff drink was what he really wanted for a conversation like this. Scalding hot coffee wasn't a bad second, though.

Jonathon studied him for a long moment, absently popping a grape in his mouth as he did. "You were the one who wanted to buy out Biedermann's."

Ford shook his head. "Biedermann's was on your list."

Jonathan stabbed a bite of cantaloupe. "Technically, that was the NYSE's list. I just referenced it when I was looking for another company to buy. There were seven or eight other companies on that list. You were the one who did all that research on Biedermann's."

Jonathon paused, chewing slowly as he watched Ford. "Unless you weren't researching the company at all. You were researching her, weren't you?"

"Look. I made a mistake. It wouldn't be the first." Ford took another drink of his coffee, wishing again it was something stronger. "I asked Wendy to find out what she could about Kitty Biedermann. She was overly enthusiastic. I didn't even know Biedermann's was on the list until you'd done most of the work."

"You should have said something then."

"I didn't think it would be a big deal. Neither of us was looking for a long-term relationship. I knew what happened in Texas was just a one-night stand and it would never happen again."

Jonathon quirked an eyebrow. "Which explains perfectly why you just slept with her a second time."

"It's not a big deal."

"So you keep saying. Are we going to have a problem with the acquisition?"

Ford thought back to Kitty's attitude. Last night she'd been passionate and demanding. This morning she'd been coolly reserved. "I don't think so," he said honestly. "She's devoted to Biedermann's. She'll do the right thing for the company. As for me, she's not emotionally involved. She's just not the boil-a-bunny type."

"How well do you know her?" Jonathon asked.

"Well enough to know that…" Then he noticed that Jonathon leaned over his laptop as he spoke, typing rapidly. Ford just rolled his eyes. "You're looking her up on Google, aren't you?" In answer,

Jonathon just shrugged. "After all the information about her that Wendy dug up, you think you're going to find something on the Internet that we didn't already know?"

Jonathon shrugged. "It never hurts."

Annoyed, Ford continued speaking. "I know her well enough to know she's not going to back out of a business deal for personal reasons."

Jonathon tapped his fingers across the mouse pad while he waited for the slow hotel wireless connection to load the results page. "I hope you're right. Kitty owns nearly sixty percent of the company. If we don't have her on board, the deal will never go through, regardless of whether or not we can convince anyone else."

"I know that." His tone was a little sharper than he'd intended.

Jonathon raised his hands in a gesture of defense. "Just reminding you." He clicked on a page, then sat back, waiting for it to load. "If she backs out now, we've wasted a decent chunk of change. And I don't like wasting time, either."

"She's not going to back out. Selling Biedermann's to us is going to make her a lot of money. That's all the incentive she needs. She's been rich all her life and we're going to make her richer. There's nothing else we need to know."

But by then Jonathon had leaned forward to read whatever Pandora's box Google had pulled up. He let out a low whistle.

"What?" Ford demanded.

"You might want to read what Suzy Snark has to say before you say anything else that'll get you in trouble."

Tension seized Ford's stomach. "Who?"

"Suzy Snark. She's a gossip blogger here in New York. Talks about Kitty every once in a while." He looked up at Ford. "You didn't really read that report from Wendy, did you? Suzy Snark was mentioned multiple times."

The tension that had started in his gut seeped through the rest of his body, leaving him frozen on the spot. He should just cross the room and take the damn laptop from Jonathan, but no matter what orders his brain issued, his feet weren't following them.

Finally he said, "Stop being so damn cryptic and just tell me what the damn thing says."

"Trust me, you're going to want to read this yourself."

He took the laptop from Jonathan and sat back down on the sofa, only vaguely aware of Jonathan walking away to give him privacy. As he read, his tension coalesced into cold, hard anger.

A few minutes later, Jonathan returned, holding out a shot of Scotch from the hotel's courtesy bar. Ford carefully set the laptop on the coffee table before accepting the drink. He took several long drinks, then realized his knuckles were turning white from gripping the glass too tightly.

Finally he stood and headed for the door with grim determination, almost too angry to speak.

"Where are you going?" Jonathan asked.

"To find Kitty."

# Six

By the time Monday morning rolled around, Kitty felt marginally more prepared to face Ford. After he left her apartment Saturday morning, she'd decided she simply couldn't face him again so soon. So she'd abandoned the familiarity of her apartment for a hotel not far from Biedermann's offices. She'd spent the weekend with her phone turned off, huddled under the blanket watching an *I Love Lucy* marathon and ordering room service. She'd bawled when Little Ricky was born and then found herself unable to stop crying. Poor Lucy always tried to do the right thing, but always made a mess of things. Sometimes her own life felt like an episode of *I Love Lucy,* but without the laugh track or the comforting presence of Ethel Mertz.

Maybe this mess would seem more bearable if her own pratfalls could be cushioned by the unconditional love of her own Ricky Ricardo. Maybe if Ford...

No, she stopped herself. She couldn't think like that. He wasn't hers. He never had been and he certainly wouldn't be now that she was keeping this secret from him.

Maybe, she justified to herself, one lie of omission deserved another. In Texas, he hadn't told her that he was a business tycoon whose company was worth billions. So Saturday morning, she didn't tell him the whole truth, either.

But of course, she hadn't outright lied. After all, he truly didn't need to worry that she'd gotten pregnant then. By the time they'd had sex, she was already two months pregnant.

All of her rationalizations almost made her feel better. Until Monday morning rolled around and she found Marty pacing in her office. With his tie loosened and his hair tousled, he looked as bedraggled as she felt.

She dropped her handbag on the chair by the door and shrugged out of her coat before tossing it carelessly on top. "Honestly, Marty, have you even been home? You look as if you slept here."

Marty knew her as well as anyone did. Keeping the truth from him would be quite the challenge. Today was a day to channel her inner bitch if there ever was one.

He ignored her comment. "Where have you been all weekend? I've been trying to reach you since Saturday. We all have."

Kitty's stomach tightened. This didn't sound good. "I went away for the weekend." Another lie. Sort of.

What could she possibly have done wrong now? She hadn't even been here. Running his fingers through his hair again, Marty asked, "Have you been online this morning?"

She faked a yawn to cover any panic that might have crossed her face. "You know I can't stand staring at a computer screen before coffee. Speaking of which, could you be a dear and get—"

"No, Kitty. Not this morning." He rounded her desk and popped open her laptop. "Come have a look."

By the time she reached it, the Suzy Snark blog was loading onto the screen. At the top of the page was a picture of her and Ford climbing out of the cab in front of The Pierre Hotel. Whatever nasty comment Kitty had been about to make was swallowed by her dread.

She stared blankly at the screen, her eyes unable to focus on the jumble of words on the screen. After a second, she realized Marty was looking at her expectantly.

"Well," he said.

She dropped petulantly into her office chair. "Why should I care what some gossipmonger has to say?"

"You should care because it affects your business."

"I sincerely doubt it."

"Are you even going to read it?"

You bet your booty she was. But not now, with Marty looming over her, watching the painful process. "Maybe later. After coffee."

Marty twisted the laptop to face him and began reading aloud. "Christmas has come early for those of us who love juicy gossip—"

"Honestly, Marty," she interrupted. "Is this really necessary?"

"Yes." His tone was unexpectedly firm. "You need to read this before anyone from FMJ shows up."

She mimicked his tone. "Fine. Then be a dear and get me that mocha latte and I'll be done reading it by the time you get back."

As soon as he was gone, she leaned forward and began the laborious process of reading.

Christmas has come early for those of us who love juicy gossip. Readers of this column are probably wondering why Kitty Biedermann's love life has been so dull lately. Ever since her breakup with Derek Messina, she's been nursing her broken heart in private. But no longer!

This time she's set her sights on entrepreneur Ford Langley of FMJ. The two were seen together at the posh Children's Medical Foundation fundraiser just last night. It's not surprising the enterprising Kitty would try to land such a hunky catch. The shocker is that they may be entering into professional negotiations as well as personal ones. There are rumors that Biedermann's is about to get gobbled up by FMJ.

And that's not even the biggest news. An inside source says Kitty may be expecting more than just a hefty bonus from FMJ. The only question is, once Langley finds out about Kitty's little bundle of joy, will he still be interested in saving Biedermann's Jewelry? Or will the heiress have to raise her baby and run her company all on her own?

Kitty felt bile rise in her throat as she sat back in her chair. Oh, dear lord.

Before she even began to ponder the issue, Marty reappeared. The mocha latte he set down in front of her did nothing to settle her stomach. His stony expression did little to quell her fears.

"I got a decaf. Just in case she's right." He must have read her answer in her expression, because he propped his hip on the edge of her desk and muttered a curse. "How did she find out?"

"I don't know," she admitted.

"Guess."

But she couldn't guess. She'd known herself for less than seventy-two hours. How had Suzy-stinkin'-Snark found out about it?

"I bought a pregnancy test," she said aloud. "Someone must have seen me do it."

Marty sighed. "And if it was someone who reads the blog and recognized you, they would have contacted Suzy right away."

Marty's obvious annoyance rankled. "Why are you acting all put out over this? This is my private life she's exploiting."

"And it affects our business. Why were you out with Ford anyway? Did you think making a conquest of him would make this buyout any easier on you? Do you really think FMJ is going to want to do business with you when you act like this?"

She could only stammer in response. For years she'd put up with Marty's passive-aggressive kowtowing, and now—the one time she could have really used him in her corner—he was turning on her?

Kitty was saved from having to formulate a defense when Ford appeared at the door.

"Oh, goody," she muttered. "Because I wasn't feeling beleaguered enough."

Ford swept into the room with all the subtly of a tsunami, and he brought flotsam and jetsam in his wake. Jonathon and Casey followed him.

"I assume you've both seen it."

Kitty opened her mouth to answer, but before she could, he turned to her assistant. "We're going to have to make a preemptive strike. We'll schedule a press conference. But not for this afternoon. We want to appear proactive, but we don't want to lend credence to the blog by appearing to be reacting to it. So announce the press conference, but schedule it for a few days out. Wednesday maybe. Jonathon, why don't you and Marty get started on that? Casey, you can—"

Fear propelled her to her feet. "A press conference?" She tried to scoff convincingly. "Over a piddling gossip blog? Isn't that overreacting?"

Ford turned the weight of his gaze on her. He crossed his arms over his chest. "Not at all. FMJ's acquisition of Biedermann's hasn't been officially announced yet. It doesn't look good that the news was leaked."

Right. The acquisition. The news of her pregnancy had overshadowed everything else. She'd forgotten that the blog even mentioned the buyout.

"But," she protested. "It was leaked to a *gossip* blog. One that no one is likely to read. And it's even less likely that anyone who does would care about business."

"This blog may have a wider readership than you think. We all read it within a few hours. We have to assume others have, too. If we work fast, we can minimize the damage."

"Why should we respond at all? We certainly don't want people thinking that whatever this woman posts online is true."

Marty's gaze had been ping-ponging back and forth between them. Ford narrowed his gaze at the other man, giving him a why-are-you-still-here look. Before Marty could respond to the unspoken question. Jonathon ushered both Casey and Marty out with such practiced ease, she couldn't help wondering if he and Ford had orchestrated the move.

"Wow," she murmured. "I'm impressed. Normally it's impossible to get Marty out of my office when he's got a bone to pick." She gestured between Ford and the door through which Jonathon had just vanished. "Did you guys plan out that two-pronged approach? Not that I mind. If we have to talk about that blog, I'd much rather do it without an audience."

"Damn right we have to talk about that blog. Was she right? Are you pregnant?"

* * *

"Does it matter?" Kitty countered smoothly.

Her lack of denial was all the confirmation he needed. Ford gritted his teeth against the questions he wanted to throw at her. As prickly as she was, it wouldn't take much to push her into a full-fledged argument.

"I'd prefer a quiet wedding, but I'll leave that up to you. We should—"

She spun to face him. "We're not getting married."

"Of course, we're getting married." A hard note crept into his voice. "I'm not going to desert my family."

For a long moment, she seemed to be considering him. Then she patted her belly with exaggerated care. "Well, lucky for you, this baby and I aren't your family."

Kitty stood there, one hand propped on her hip, chin up, all defiant bravado.

"You're saying it's not mine?"

"I'm not *saying* it isn't yours. It *isn't* yours."

"But you are pregnant?"

Her chin inched up a notch. "What I am is none of your business. Not your burden. Not your problem."

"You couldn't be more than a couple of months pregnant," he pointed out.

"What's your point?"

"The timing is perfect for me to be the father."

She quirked an eyebrow, her expression full of arrogance. "What, you think I came back from Texas so satisfied that I couldn't even imagine being with another man?"

"I suppose I would like to think that. But the truth is, you're not the type to sleep around."

"Oh, really?" she asked, her voice brimming with challenge. "And you're such an expert on me? How long have you known me, Ford, really? A week? It's less than that, isn't it? The truth is, you have no idea what I'm capable of."

If she was lying, she did a damn good job of it. There wasn't so much as a sputter of doubt in her eyes to give her away.

He waited for the surge of relief. Pregnant or not, she was letting him off the hook. All he had to do was take her at her word and walk away.

He studied her standing there, taking in the defiant bump of her chin, the blazing independence in her eyes. She was dressed in slim-legged pants and a fuzzy sweater that made her look touchable. But that was the only hint of softness about her, otherwise she was all hard angles and bristly defenses.

Kitty was pregnant. There was a baby growing inside her belly. A tiny life. Maybe his. Maybe not.

But his gut said it was his. Every possessive, primitive cell in his body screamed that her child must be his.

Of course, that didn't mean it *was*.

"You're right," he said finally. "I don't know you well, but I'm a good judge of character. I know you well enough to know you're capable of lying to get what you want. The only thing I don't know is what it is you want."

She squared her shoulders and met his gaze. "What I want is to save Biedermann's. If FMJ can do that, then we'll have a deal. If not, I'll find someone else who can."

* * *

"Are you sure you don't want Marty here?" Ford asked as he sat down at the conference table. "He is your CFO."

"I'm sure." They were working late, trying to get all the details of the acquisition hammered out before the press conference later in the week. Thanks to Suzy Snark, they needed to work much faster than they might have otherwise. Instead of sitting herself, she stood near the windows, staring out at the cityscape below. Marty made her so damn nervous. She'd asked Ford to set up this meeting between him, her and Jonathon precisely because she couldn't ask the kinds of questions she needed to with Marty in the room.

Of course, Jonathon made her nervous, too, with his steady gaze and his brilliant head for numbers. He was exactly the kind of person who made her feel twitchy with fear. But Jonathon couldn't be avoided. She no longer trusted herself to be alone with Ford.

Which was why she waited until Jonathon had settled into a chair at the conference table before speaking.

"If I'm going to hand my family's company over to your tender care—" Kitty stressed the words *tender care,* letting them hear her doubts that their management of Biedermann's was likely to be either tender or careful "—then I need assurances that you actually have a plan in place."

Jonathon cleared his throat. "If you've read the proposal we sent, you'll see your compensation package is—"

Ford interrupted him. "I don't believe it's her compensation package she's worried about."

She looked over her shoulder, surprised by his comment. He sat at the table, leaning back in his chair, one ankle propped up on the opposite knee. The posture was relaxed, but there was an intensity to his gaze that made her breath catch in her chest.

"Yes." She forced fresh air into her lungs. "Exactly."

Now, Ford sat forward, steepling his hands on the table before him. "Unless I'm mistaken, Kitty is the rare CEO who is less worried about what she's going to get out of this settlement than how the company is going to be treated." He pinned her with a stare that she felt all the way to her bones. "Am I right?"

In that instant, the intensity of his gaze laid her bare. All the artifice, all her defenses, the image she'd worked her whole life to build and maintain seemed to vanish like a whiff of smoke, leaving her with the disconcerting feeling that he could see straight through to her very soul.

"You are," she said simply.

"I don't understand." Jonathon frowned, looking down at his laptop as if he expected it to sprout flowers. "Why did you ask to meet with us alone if you weren't worried about your end of the deal?"

"I thought you'd be more honest in private." Which was also true and was as good an excuse as any. "I don't care how much money I walk away with. I don't care what kind of golden parachutes you offer to the board members. I care about whether or not the stores themselves survive. When this is all over with, is there going to be a Biedermann's in nearly every mall in America? Are there going to be any of them left?"

The question hung in the air between them. Since they seemed to be waiting for her to say something else, she continued.

"If FMJ gobbles us up, that may solve the immediate problem of our declining stock prices, but that's only part of the problem." She turned to Jonathon. "Our stock price wouldn't be going down if we had strong retail performance. I want to know how you plan to improve that."

She expected Jonathon to answer. After all, he was FMJ's financial genius. However, it was Ford who spoke.

"You're right. For too long, you've been relying on people shopping at your stores because they're already at the mall. However—"

Ford broke off as his cell phone buzzed to life. Reaching into his pocket, he grimaced as he pulled out the phone. "Sorry."

He turned off the volume on the phone, but left it sitting on the conference table by his elbow. "It's not enough…"

Even though he continued talking, her attention wandered for a second. She'd seen the name displayed on the phone when it rang. *Patrice*. What were the names of his sisters? Chelsea, Beatrice and…something else. Certainly not Patrice, though.

Not that it mattered in the least. He probably had the numbers of dozens of women stored in his phone. Hundreds maybe. It wasn't her business.

She forced her attention back to his words.

"We don't want shoppers to stop in at Biedermann's because they're at the mall. We want to attract them to the mall because there's a Biedermann's there. We need Biedermann's to provide them with services and products that they can't get anywhere else."

"We have strong brand recognition," she protested. "We offer more styles of engagement rings than any other store."

"But engagement rings are a one-time purchase. You need something that will bring customers back again and again."

The phone by his elbow began to vibrate silently. Again she glanced down. This time the name display read Suz.

"You can answer it if you need to," she said.

He frowned as the phone stopped vibrating and the call rolled over to voice mail. "I don't."

"Are you sure? Second call in just a few minutes."

Jonathon was scowling, clearly annoyed. He quirked an eyebrow in silent condemnation when the phone started vibrating again a few seconds later. Rosa this time.

Was that the third sister's name? She couldn't remember.

"Just answer it," Jonathon snapped.

Frowning, Ford stood as he grabbed the phone. "Hey, miha. What's up?" With a slight nod, he excused himself from the room.

For a long time, Kitty and Jonathon sat in silence, the tension taut between them. She suspected he didn't like her any more than she liked him. With his frosty demeanor and calculating gaze, every time she glanced at him she half expected to see little dollar signs where his pupils were.

However, after a few minutes of drumming her nails against the armchair, her patience wore out. Or perhaps her curiosity got the better of her.

"Does he always get so many personal calls at work?"

Jonathon scowled, but she couldn't tell if he was annoyed by the interruption or by her questions. "It's after hours. But his family can be quite demanding."

"Those were all family members?" Maybe she'd misremembered the names. Or perhaps misread them?

Jonathon's scowl deepened. Ah, so he hadn't meant to reveal that.

"I know he has three sisters, but—"

"If you're curious about his family, you should really talk to Ford about it."

And let him know she was scoping out his potential as a father? Not likely.

She met Jonathon's gaze and smiled slowly. "The problem, Mr. Bagdon, is that whenever Ford and I are alone, we end up doing one of two things. Neither of them is conducive to talking about his family."

Mr. Cold-As-Ice Jonathon didn't stammer or blush. Instead, he held her gaze, his lips twisting in an expression that she might have imagined was amusement in a man less dour.

"Interesting," he murmured.

"What?"

"You expected me to be either embarrassed or distracted by your honesty."

"But you're neither?" she asked. What was it with these guys from FMJ that none of them reacted the way normal men did?

"Certainly not enough to be tricked into telling you the information you're fishing for."

Well, if her motives were going to be so transparent, then she might as well be honest. "Very well, then. Let's be frank. I am curious about Ford, but I don't want to ask him about his family."

"Because…" Jonathon prodded.

She smiled. "If there's one thing you and I can both agree upon, it's that the relationship between Ford and I is complicated enough as it is. Yes, I could talk to him about it, but I wasn't merely being provocative with my earlier comment. Every time Ford and I are alone we're either fighting or having sex. I don't see any reason to add emotional confidences into an already volatile mix merely to satisfy my curiosity."

Jonathon studied her for a moment, his expression as nonplussed as it always was. Finally he nodded. "Very well. What do you want to know?"

What didn't she want to know might have been a better question. Ford seemed such a dichotomy. She thought of the easygoing charmer she'd met back in that bar in Texas. He'd seemed such a simple man. Not stupid by any means, but uncomplicated. It was that quality that had drawn her to him in the first place. With his laid-back charisma and magnetic smile, he'd coaxed his way past her defenses as easily as he'd mollified Dale.

That alone should have made her suspicious. A man that could assess and defuse a tense situation like that was no mere cowboy. Far more telling was the way he'd charmed her. She never let down her defenses. Never let anyone close. She should have known that any man who could tempt her into a quickie in the parking lot was a man to be reckoned with.

What was that saying? Fool me once, shame on you; fool me twice, shame on me.

Well, she was suitably shamed.

Regardless of all that, Ford—this chameleon of a man, whom she barely knew and couldn't possibly hope to understand—was the father of her child. She had no way of anticipating how he would react if he were to learn the truth.

She clearly took too long to formulate her question, because Jonathon leaned forward. "If you've got a question, you should ask now. He might not be on the phone with his family much longer."

Suddenly, she was struck by an awful thought. Her skin went clammy as panic washed over her. Dear God, what if the reason Jonathon didn't want to talk about Ford was because he was married? Choking down her dread, she asked, "By family, you don't mean wife, do you?"

Jonathon laughed, a rusty uncomfortable snort of

derision. "Ford? Married? Hell, no. He's that last man on earth who would cheat on a wife."

She clenched her jaw against her innate dislike of being laughed at. "Well, I hardly know him. How am I supposed to know that?"

Jonathon's smile faded. "Ford's father kept a mistress for the last fifteen years of his life. He had a whole other family he had set up in a house one town over. While he was alive, he kept all those balls in the air himself. But when he passed away, he'd named Ford executor of his will. All of sudden Ford had to find a way to make peace between these two families."

"My goodness. What did Ford do?" She asked the question almost without realizing she'd done it.

"Ford did what he always does." Jonathon's expression had turned from icy to grim. "He smoothed things over."

Okay, so she wasn't exactly an expert on women, seeing as how most of her friends were men. She could only imagine how she would feel if she found out that the man she'd loved had had another family secreted away somewhere. She'd be pissed. No amount of "smoothing things over" would make that all right. And yet, if anyone could do it, she believed Ford could.

"They must just hate each other," she murmured.

"Surprisingly, they don't." Jonathon shrugged as if to say he didn't get it, either. "They resented each other for a long time, but now they're friends, strange as that sounds. Ford's younger sister—his full sister, that is—

Chelsea is about the same age as Beatrice. Ford managed to convince both Suzanne and Patrice that the girls all needed each other. Of course, it helped matters that his dad had died practically broke. So Ford was pretty much supporting everyone."

"How old was he?"

"Twenty-three or so."

She'd read somewhere that he'd made his first million by the time he was twenty-two. If he was supporting five women not long after that, he must have been highly motivated indeed to keep making money. From what he'd told her, his sisters were only now in college.

She glanced toward the door to her office through which Ford had disappeared. "This kind of thing, with the constant phone calls. This happens often?"

"Only when there's some crisis they want him to solve. They tend to…um, disagree a lot. When they do, they all call Ford to sort it out for them."

"So he solves all their problems, but he never lets them get too close, does he?"

Jonathon sent her a piercing look. "Why do you say that?"

"Because it's what I would do."

# Seven

From where she sat, she could see Ford through the open door of her office. He stood with his back toward them. Tension radiated from him. She could see it through the lines of his shoulders, in the way he shifted them as he spoke, as if he were trying to stretch out the knotted muscles. But she could hear the tone of his voice, as well. Not the words, the tone. Quiet and soothing.

She wondered, did his family know he was lying to them? If not with his words, then with his intent.

She was watching Ford so closely that Jonathon surprised her when he said, "You say that because you think you're so much alike."

There was the faintest hint of condemnation in his

voice. It made her chuckle. "Oh, God, no. Not at all."
Finally she looked back at Jonathon. "He's so
charming, isn't he?"

"I don't know what you mean."

"I saw it in Texas. The way he can manipulate
people. Talking them into things. Get them to do things
they normally wouldn't."

"You're saying he charmed you into bed with him."

She slanted a look at Jonathon, tilting her head to
the side as she studied him. "Do you always do that?
Willfully misunderstand what people are saying?"

"I've found most people say things they don't really
mean. And mean things they're not willing to say
aloud. I've found it's best to make sure everyone is on
the same page."

She nodded. "Very well, then, maybe he did charm
me into bed with him. But I certainly wasn't unwill-
ing, if that's what you were asking. No, what I meant
was that he has the ability to charm everyone. But I
don't think he lets many people close."

No, like her, he kept everyone at arm's length. His
charm was as much a weapon as her sarcastic quips. She
couldn't say exactly why she knew that to be true, simply
that she understood it on a gut level. The same way she
knew that if fate hadn't thrown them together again, she
never would have seen Ford after that one night in Texas.

Somehow the thought made her sad. Ford wasn't
hers to keep, but she was glad she'd had this chance to
see him again. To get to know the man he really was.
Even if that man wasn't someone she could let too close.

Jonathon didn't respond, but studied her with that same steady gaze she found so disconcerting.

"Have I satisfied your curiosity?"

Kitty flashed him a cavalier smile. "You've certainly answered all of my questions."

More to the point, he'd told her everything she really needed to know about Ford. If he found out he really was the father of her child, he'd do everything in his power to take care of her. But he'd never really let her or the baby in. He'd never love her or the baby the way she wanted to be loved. She'd just be another burden to him.

And wasn't that just the last thing she needed? Another man to coddle her. Yippee.

Ford couldn't tell how much progress he and Jonathon had made on convincing Kitty to accept their offer, but he sensed something had changed while he'd been on the phone with his sister. He'd come back to the table to find Kitty looking pale and withdrawn. To make matters worse, not much later, Jonathon had gotten a call, as well, and had to leave the meeting.

Now half a day had passed and they were no closer to signing papers. Kitty had vanished after lunch, leaving him to go over the quarterly financial statements with Marty, whose eager nervousness reminded him of a puppy with ADD.

To make matters worse, he'd wandered over to Kitty's office. He hadn't planned on coming there. That's just where he'd ended up. As if he no longer had any control over where his feet took him.

A quick glance in her office told him it was empty. She better not have left early. He'd already turned to leave when he heard a noise from the other side of the office. The door to her bathroom was open.

"Kitty, are you there?" he asked, crossing her office.

He was a few steps from the bathroom when the door slammed closed. "Go away," said her muffled voice.

He should have taken at her word, but he made the mistake of hesitating just long enough to hear the recognizable sounds of someone throwing up. He cringed.

"You okay?"

"Go a—" More retching.

That sounded bad. Not that hurling ever sounded good. He should definitely leave. He'd almost made it to the door when a voice in his head stopped him in his tracks. *She's obviously sick, and you're running for the door. What kind of jerk are you?*

But she'd told him to go.

*Of course she did. No one likes puking. You think she's going to ask for your help? No way. But you can't just leave her there.*

He walked back to the bathroom, praying the door would be locked. That would be the perfect excuse to just turn and walk away. He tried the knob. And the damn thing wiggled.

He opened the door to see her wiping her mouth with the back of her hand. Thick strands of dark hair had fallen down from its twist to hang in her face. Her gaze blazed with anger.

"I said go away." But her hands trembled as she lowered herself to sit on the ground beside the toilet.

He'd done the right thing.

Shutting the door behind him in case anyone came in, he said, "You don't have to be so proud."

"Great. A lecture. Thanks." She pressed her cheek to the tile wall. "Next time you're throwing up, I'll fly out to California to razz you."

"Yeah, I'll give you a call," he shot back. He pulled a paper towel from the dispenser and ran it under the faucet before handing it to her. "Here."

"Thanks." She wiped carefully at the corners of her mouth, then folded that edge to the center and pressed the damp cloth to her forehead. A sigh of relief escaped her lips.

The sound stirred something deep within his belly. Some primitive urge to care for and protect. To possess.

Okay, she should not look sexy right now. That was just wrong.

He looked around for something else to do and saw a mug sitting on the ledge under the mirror. After rinsing it carefully, he filled it. He squatted by her side and held it out.

After a second, her eyes flickered open. She stared at him for a moment. If she saw the heat in his gaze, she didn't comment, but the tension seemed to stretch between them as she sipped the water. He half expected her to come back with one of her customary jabs. Instead she said merely, "Thanks."

"You're welcome. Can I get you anything else?"

"One of my lollipops. Top drawer of my desk. Right-hand side."

Glad to have something to do, he headed straight for her desk. The first thing he saw when he pulled out the top drawer was an artist's sketchbook. A large pencil drawing dominated the page. In the bottom left-hand corner was a scared little girl in a pinafore dress, with black curls and huge eyes, like a cross between Shirley Temple and Betty Boop with just enough Kitty Beidermann thrown in to make the character unmistakable. She clutched her hands in front of her in exaggerated terror. Behind her loomed an enormous monster, all pointy teeth and glistening drool. Its arms arched over her head, wicked claws gleaming. The monster's body was formed by the letters *F, M* and *J*. The overall effect was both humorous and compelling.

So, she fancied herself an artist, did she?

He grinned as he picked up the sketchbook and flipped the page. However, the other pictures weren't cartoons but rather sketches of jewelry. It was the same tongue-in-cheek, gothic sensibility, but applied to intricate drawings of necklaces and earrings.

"Find one of the yellow ones, if you can," she called out from the bathroom.

He looked back in the drawer and saw a pile of lollipops. After digging through for a yellow one, he headed back to the bathroom, flipping through the sketchbook as he went.

When he reached the bathroom, he tucked the book

under his arm to pull the wrapper off the lollipop. He held it out to her. "These help?"

She plopped it in her mouth and rolled her eyes at him, either in relief or at his obvious doubt. After several strong sucks that caved in her cheeks and worked her throat in a way that was alarmingly erotic, she nodded.

"They're specially formulated." She spoke between sucks. "High in Vitamin C. Sour flavor. Helps with the morning sickness."

This was morning sickness? Undeniable proof of the baby growing in her belly. The baby that was maybe his, maybe not his. But she was definitely making herself known. He felt as if a hand reached into his chest and gave his heart a squeeze.

Kitty swayed a bit, apparently still feeling wobbly, and he automatically reached out a hand to steady her. Her touch on his arm felt weak and trembling. That hand squeezing his heart tightened to a fist.

Before she could protest, he wrapped one arm around her shoulder and gripped her arm with the other, guiding her out of the bathroom to the sofa in her office.

They'd just left the bathroom when her door opened and Marty strolled in. He stopped dead in his tracks, looking from Kitty and back to Ford, then to the open bathroom door through which they'd obviously just walked. Together.

Marty's gaze narrowed and his cheek muscles twitched into a frown. "I'm glad with all the work we have to do that you two are finding ways to amuse yourselves."

Ford waited for Kitty to explain her morning sickness. Instead she pressed her body against his side and slithered her arm around his waist. With exaggerated slowness, she pulled the lollipop from her mouth and smiled. Then she slanted him a look meant to turn men rock-hard.

"Me, too," she murmured with the faintest wink.

Marty gave a disgusted squawk and fled the room, apparently imagining that they were about to go at it again right in front of him.

As soon as the door shut behind him, Kitty sprawled on the sofa, stretching her legs out in front of her indelicately and popping the lollipop back in her mouth with absolutely no artifice.

"Oh, thank God he's gone. Like my nausea wasn't bad enough without having to listen to him."

"You could have explained."

"Trust me. The last thing I need is Marty feeling sorry for me." She shuddered with mock disgust, closing her eyes again to concentrate on her lollipop.

Her hand rested on her belly, her fingers absently toying with the swatch of knit that covered the exact spot where he imagined her baby growing. The way she'd stretched across the sofa, her belly appeared perfectly flat with only the gentlest slope to her stomach. No one would guess she was even a day pregnant. She must not be very far along. More than a month, since she'd already taken the test, but not much more. Maybe two.

The recesses of his brain started doing a little involuntary math, but he shoved the thought aside. She'd said it wasn't his. She was letting him off the hook. That was enough. He didn't want to be a dad and he sure as hell didn't want to inflict himself as a father on any poor kid. It wasn't just him she was letting off the hook. It was all of them. Until she was far enough along to get proof one way or another, he had to take her word for it anyway.

To distract himself from those disconcerting thoughts, he pulled the sketchbook out from under his arm and started flipping through it again.

"What is this?" he asked.

She opened a single eye to gaze at him. When her gaze fell on the sketchbook, she tensed for a second. Then she closed her eye and forced a breath that almost sounded relaxed. "Just doodles."

"They don't look like doodles. They look like jewelry designs."

He held up the page to reveal a sketch of a necklace and earrings. The set was full of intricate curlicues and elaborate swirls in a style that managed to reference Victorian styles while still looking modern.

"It's just something I drew up. It's not even very original."

"What do you mean?" He turned the page to look at the next design.

"I modeled it after some of my grandmother's old jewelry. The ones I had to sell. Most of the drawings in there came from pieces of my grandmother's. A swirl here, a flower there. Just bits I combined together from one piece or another."

He looked up from the drawings. Her free hand still rested on her stomach, but her fingers had started tugging at the knit. Normally Kitty's innate confidence bordered on arrogance. If he didn't know better he'd think she was fidgeting.

He flipped to the next page, staring at the image for a moment before turning the page ninety degrees to get a better angle. "Is this a case for an iPhone?"

She pulled in her legs, straightening. "You know not everyone likes their gadgets to look like gadgets."

It was the same scrolling design as one of the earlier pictures, but this time the perfect size and shape to enclose a cell phone. The page held three drawings, one of the back; the second depicted elegant, tiny, clawed feet, which wrapped around the front of the phone; the third showed the delicate hinges along the side. He could imagine it in gleaming sterling. The overall effect was a brilliant merging of gothic Victorian and geeky tech. Between the clawed feet and the ghoulish tiny gargoyle face on the back, the piece almost had…a sense of humor.

Like the drawing of FMJ gobbling up Kitty.

"Did you think of this?" he asked.

"It's similar to my great-grandfather's cigarette case."

"Wait a second." He flipped back a few pages to the drawing of the earrings and pendant. He squinted at the scrawled writing he'd dismissed initially. In tiny letters he saw the words *Bluetooth?* and *ear buds?* "This isn't jewelry, is it? These are gadgets. This isn't a necklace, it's a case for an MP3 player."

She reached to pull the sketchbook from his hands. "You don't need to poke fun at me."

"I'm not." He held the book just out of her reach. "I think it's brilliant."

Her gaze narrowed in suspicion as she stepped closer to him, still reaching for the notebook. "It's completely unrealistic."

"Says who?" he asked.

"Everyone I've ever showed it to."

"Which is?"

"My father. The board of directors. No one's gonna buy geeky jewelry."

He scoffed, dismissing her concern. "Let me guess. Your father was one of those guys who thought iPhones would never sell, either."

She set her jaw at a stubborn angle. "Besides which, Biedermann's *sells* jewelry, we don't make it." Once again she reached for the notebook. "We don't have the means or the experience to even do a mock-up of that kind of thing, let alone manufacture it."

"Biedermann's doesn't." He thumbed through the pages until he returned to the first image that had caught his attention. He flipped the book around to display the picture of FMJ. "But FMJ does." He grinned. "Sometimes it's good being the evil monster."

She blinked in surprise, then chuckled for a second. But then she studied his face, finally pulling the sketchbook from his grasp. "It's too risky."

"No, it isn't. Matt has a whole electrical engineering department that would love to take a whack at this. Let me just fax him a couple of the pages."

"No."

"But—"

She turned on him suddenly. "Biedermann's is practically hemorrhaging money right now. The absolute last thing we need to do is venture into something like this. If we took a risk like this and it failed, we'd never recover."

"Then the trick is not to fail."

"That's so easy for you to say. Everything you touch turns to gold, right? Buy a company, sell a company. It's all the same. You make millions in your sleep. Besides, if you're wrong, and Biedermann's dies off completely, you can still sell off chunks of us to recoup some of your losses. FMJ could probably use the tax write-off anyway. It may not matter to you whether or not Biedermann's flounders or flourishes, but it matters to me."

As gently as he could, he said, "You know, Kitty, for someone who claims to be desperate to save Biedermann's, you're sure not willing to take many risks to do it."

"I am willing to take risks. I'm just not willing to risk everything."

A second later, she'd snatched her purse out of the desk and was gone. And, damn it, she'd taken her sketchbook with her. He was going to have to find a way to get it back, because he was going to send those drawings to Matt. This could be the key to everything. The niche market Biedermann's was looking for. Not just upscale jewelry, but high fashion accessories for the gadgets nearly every American owned.

*Biedermann Jewelry. It's not just for engagements anymore.*

He nearly chuckled at his own little joke. This could really work. Between Matt's electronic genius and Kitty's artistic brilliance, they could hit a market that no one else had tapped. Biedermann's would be back on top. And best of all, Kitty would be responsible for that.

He could do this for her. He could fix her professional life.

God knew there wasn't much he could do for her personal life.

# Eight

From the blog of New York gossip columnist Suzy Snark:

> Fiddling while Rome burned. Polishing the brass on the Titanic. Both phrases imply great negligence in the face of disaster. New Yorkers may want to add a new idiom to that list: Getting a massage while your company is being bought out.
>
> I know, we usually eschew the nitty gritty business details for outright gossip, but this tidbit was too salacious to keep to myself. Besides, the business geniuses at FMJ have scheduled a press conference for this afternoon to announce their acquisition of Biedermann Jewelry. I thought

you might want something to consider while they're trying to convince their stockholders it's a good thing they're squandering their own resources to bail out Ford Langley's girlfriend.

Readers will be shocked to learn that while Biedermann Jewelry stock prices continue to plummet, heiress Kitty Biedermann continues to receive daily spa treatments. Sources say she spends upward of two thousand dollars a week on mani-pedis and facials. In a time when her personal finances must be taking a hit, that's got to hurt.

Is the heiress addicted to pampering? Is she simply careless? Or is there something else going on here? Perhaps she sold all her Biedermann stock back when it was still worth something. Too bad she didn't see fit to tip the rest of us off, as well.

"Is any of this new blog true at all?" Ford asked.

She glanced at the image on his iPhone. Her stomach clenched at the sight of the scarlet swirl at the top of the screen. Another Suzy Snark blog. Just what she needed.

"Ah," she quipped, trying to sound completely blasé. "Suzy Snark. What fun."

"Have you read it?"

"I don't read trash."

He held out the iPhone. "You need to read this."

Panic clutched her stomach. Her gaze darted from the phone to his face. She wanted nothing to do with any of that rubbish.

"Why don't you try to sum it up for me?" she suggested in her best spoiled-brat voice.

"It accuses you of negligence." Ford continued to hold out the phone as if he expected that to be all the encouragement she needed.

Though her heart seemed to stutter in her chest, she didn't reach for the phone. What exactly had Suzy Snark discovered?

Ford continued, his tone full of exasperation. "She says you've been spending your days at the spa. Getting massages and pedicures when you should be working."

"Is that all?" Her heart started thudding again, a rapid tattoo she was sure Ford would be able to hear.

"What do you mean 'is that all?' Is there more?" he demanded. "Is there something you're not telling me?"

Instead of answering, she tried to sidestep the question. "It's just a stupid gossip blog. You and Jonathon place entirely too much importance on what this woman writes. What does it even matter?"

He shoved his phone back in his pocket. "It matters. It may just be a gossip blog, but who knows how many people read it. This woman maligns you every chance she gets. Has it occurred to you that Suzy Snark may be the reason Biedermann's stock is in free fall?"

She sucked in a breath. "No. It hasn't."

"I did some preliminary research. Every time she posts about you, the stock price dips. Starting with today's press conference, we're going to defend you against this woman's lies. Now why don't you—"

But he must have seen the truth in her expression,

because Ford broke off. He studied her in silence for a moment before slowly shaking his head. "She's not lying, is she?"

"I wouldn't know. I didn't read the blog."

Ford ignored her comment. "Is she right? Have you really been spending hours of every workday at the spa?"

"I'm not going to defend myself to you."

"You're going to have to defend yourself to someone. The fact that you haven't denied any of this makes me think it must be true."

"What is it you want me to admit to? Going to the spa sometimes? Fine, I do that. Every woman I know gets regular manicures and pedicures. Most men I know, too. It's not a crime."

"No. But if you're doing it during office hours, every day, then it looks bad. It looks like you're not doing your job. It looks like you don't care about the company. And if you don't care about it, then why should anyone else?"

"Is that what you think? That I don't care about Biedermann's? I would do *anything* for Biedermann's."

"So you keep saying. But, frankly, I'm not seeing it."

"Are you kidding me? Since I took over as CEO, I've poured everything I have into this business. I've spent every waking moment trying to educate myself on how to be the best CEO I can. I've listened to every damn business book published in the last decade, from *Barbarians at the Gate* to *The 4-Hour Workweek,* none of which have been remotely helpful, by the way. I've worked eighty-hour weeks. I've abandoned my social life completely.

"None of that made any difference. The stock price just kept going down. So I decided to buy whatever stock I could in hopes of keeping the price up. I liquidated all of my assets. Sold everything I had. Furniture, art, jewelry. Things that had been in the family for generations. I quietly auctioned it off piece by piece. A year ago, I moved out of the townhouse where I grew up, where Biedermanns had lived for over a hundred years. I sold it and moved into a *walk-up*."

To her embarrassment, her voice, which had been rising in pitch steadily, broke on the word *walk-up*. She knew where she lived was the least of her worries, but somehow it signified all the things wrong in her life.

Knowing she was being ridiculous didn't make it sting any less when he said, "Come on, you make it sound like life without a doorman just isn't worth living. Surely it's not that bad."

"Have you ever lived without a doorman?" she asked.

"I live in a craftsman remodel down by campus in Palo Alto," he deadpanned. "I've never had a doorman in my life."

"Well, I now live on the fourth floor in a building without an elevator. I grew up with staff, for cripes sake. Our housekeeper worked for my family for forty-five years. After I let Maggie go, she couldn't even afford to pay the tuition for her granddaughter's college."

Maggie had been like family. No, more than that. To a girl who'd never known her mother, Maggie *had been* family. And Kitty had had to fire her. Sweet Maggie had tried to comfort her, made her hot tea and murmured

optimist platitudes like, *I've always wanted to travel.*
Maggie had been too proud to accept a handout once
she was no longer employed, so Kitty had done the
only thing she could do. She'd tracked down Maggie's
granddaughter and hired her at Biedermann's.

"Then why did you sell the house?" Ford was
asking her. "And if you had to sell it, why not move
someplace nicer?"

At his question, she bumped her chin up defiantly.

"Because," she shot back. "When the stock price
started to drop, I couldn't just stand by and do nothing.
So I bought as much as I could. And then when it kept
dropping, I couldn't even pay the taxes on the townhouse. Selling the house was the only option."

"You should never have invested your personal
assets in—"

"I know that, okay?" she snapped. "I was trying to
help Biedermann's and I made a stupid mistake. I'm
really good at making stupid mistakes, thank you very
much."

It was just one of many, many stupid mistakes.
Sometimes she felt buried under the weight of them.

"I'm just trying to—" he began.

But she cut him off with a belligerent glare. "I don't
need your help."

He talked over her protests. "If Biedermann's really
does go under, you'll have lost everything."

What could she say to that? All she could do was
shake her head and blink back the tears. "If Biedermann's
really does go under, then I've lost everything anyway."

But that wasn't entirely true anymore, was it? She'd have the baby. She'd have the family she'd always wanted. It was a small consolation that was turning into everything.

"So tell me this," he said. "If you're so desperate to keep Biedermann's afloat, why this elaborate act? Why don't you want anyone to know what you're doing? Why spend your days at the spa getting massages and facials? You've got to know how bad that looks."

She met his gaze. "I can't—" she began before breaking off. Then she swept a hand across her forehead, pushing her hair out of her face. "I can't explain that."

"Well, try. Make me understand what's going on here. Give me something, anything, that makes this make sense."

"This is just what I do."

Whenever the influx of written material got too much to handle, she took Casey, went to the spa and had her assistant read aloud to her. The paperwork was so overwhelming. Business documents were the worst. She just couldn't wrap her head around the pages and pages of words. Listening to them read aloud helped. But what kind of CEO had her assistant read everything aloud? Christ, it was like she was a preschooler at story time. How could she explain that to Ford?

Instead she said, "It's like a…a coping mechanism or something."

"You mean the massages are a way of relieving stress?"

She all but threw up her hands in frustration. "No. I mean, I was raised never to reveal my weaknesses. You always have to keep up appearances."

"I don't understand."

"No. Of course you wouldn't. My mother died when I was young. My father was completely loving and indulgent, but Biedermann's always came first, so he wasn't around a lot. I was raised by my grandmother, who was already well into her sixties when I was born. It…"

She struggled for words. Finally she finished with, "It made for an unusual upbringing. I grew up in the 1990s, but really, it's like I was raised in the 1950s. To my grandmother, appearances were everything. I know she loved me, but in the world she lived in, you never let anyone see your weaknesses. You never aired your dirty laundry."

And a child with a disability—a child who was imperfect—was the ultimate dirty laundry. She'd been such an embarrassment to her whole family. Such a disappointment. How could she stand disappointing anyone else?

"So, going to the spa is your way of whistling in the graveyard? Of pretending everything is okay when it obviously isn't? You're not fooling anyone."

"I fooled you, didn't I?"

"You didn't fool me so much as make me doubt your sanity." His words were like a slap. He must have regretted them, because he sighed and scrubbed a hand down his face. "Look, you've got to defend yourself against Suzy Snark's allegations. Whoever she is, you've got to let people know she's wrong about you."

"And tell them what? That I was completely unprepared to take over as CEO? That I have no discernible leadership skills? That I have nothing to offer the company at all? How would admitting any of that help matters?"

"At least people would know you cared," he said finally.

Then she sighed, suddenly exhausted by the conversation. "My pride is all I have left."

For someone who'd lived her life in the public eye, Kitty seemed surprisingly nervous during the press conference. He doubted that anyone in the press noticed.

They stood side by side, along with Jonathon and Marty, a united front against the questions of the press. After he'd made the initial speech about FMJ's decision to acquire Biedermann Jewelry, Jonathon had stepped forward to outline the basis of FMJ's financial plan for Biedermann's.

As Jonathon spoke, Ford stopped listening. It was all stuff they'd discussed before. Instead he focused his attention on Kitty. She stood beside him, dressed in a gray pin-striped dress that wrapped around her waist. It managed to mimic the feel of a business suit, but its curve-hugging lines looked outrageously feminine. Her hair fell in dark, glossy waves, shadowing one side of her face. Bright red lipstick highlighted the bow of her lips. She looked like she'd stepped out of a Maxim photo shoot. A teenage boy's idea of how a woman should look in the workplace. A sexpot in a business suit.

Probably every man in the audience was mentally undressing her.

Hell, he wasn't a teenager and even his body had leaped in response to the sight of her. He'd had to battle some primitive urge to drape his jacket around her shoulders and bundle her back to her office, where he could strip her dress from her body and worship her like an acolyte.

At least until he'd noticed how nervous she was. Outwardly, she seemed fine. More than fine, actually. The press no doubt saw the confident, beautiful—if a little overblown—woman that she intended for them to see. That he'd seen at first glance.

It was only at second glance that the illusion began to slip. Her smile, though open and alluring, was a little stiff. It was too unwavering. There was no play about her lips.

This wasn't just nerves. This was perfectly contained, well-schooled nerves. This was someone who spent a great deal of time and energy learning to hide her panic.

The idea that Kitty—so composed, so polished and poised—might be fighting panic knocked him off balance. So off balance, in fact, that he let the press conference go on much longer than it should have.

Before he knew it, there was a blond reporter who looked about twenty-two saying, "Ms. Biedermann, when your father died unexpectedly last year, you were obviously woefully unprepared to take over as CEO of

Biedermann Jewelry. Can you explain why you insisted on serving in a position you have neither the skill nor the training to hold? And furthermore, how do you answer allegations that it's your gross incompetence that has led to Biedermann's current predicament?"

Ford kept waiting for Kitty to interrupt the reporter. Sure, Kitty was obviously nervous. But he'd seen the subtle signs of nervousness from her on other occasions in which she'd gone on to cheerfully lambaste him.

From what he'd seen, Kitty never backed down from a fight and never took crap from anyone. So he was blindsided when the reporter made it past the phrase "woefully unprepared" without getting the verbal equivalent of a body slam. Why wasn't Kitty defending herself?

By the time he heard the phrase "gross incompetence" he was done waiting for Kitty to don her own boxing gloves. He stepped up to the microphone. "If there are any signs of gross incompetence, I haven't seen them. FMJ would not have invested this kind of money in a company whose leadership we questioned."

"Then is FMJ merely investing in Biedermann's?" a different reporter asked. "Or can we expect you to do your signature restructuring and complete overhaul?"

"We'll be announcing some very exciting things for the stores soon." He flashed his best charming smile. "I promise you this, within a year everyone in this room will be shopping at Biedermann's."

"And about rumors that this acquisition is fueled by a romantic relationship between you and Ms.

Biedermann?" This question was again from the annoying blond.

Ford shot Kitty a glance to see if she was finally going to light into the woman, only to see Kitty still had that deer-in-the-headlights look.

So he ducked his head and gave the reporters his most boyishly mischievous smile. "Well, you found me out. This is all just a ruse to ask Kitty Biedermann out on a date. I figured a techie geek from California like me wouldn't have a shot with a blue blood like Kitty Biedermann. Hell, I couldn't even get her to return my phone calls before." A chuckle rumbled through the audience of reporters. "But seriously, my relationship with Ms. Biedermann is purely professional. On my first night in town she took pity on me and allowed me to accompany her to the Children's Medical Foundation fundraiser. We attended as business colleagues."

"So you're not the father of her baby?"

"Ms. Biedermann's personal life is a private matter. Let's keep this about business."

And with that, Jonathon took the cue to wrap up the press conference. A few minutes later, Ford guided Kitty out the room and whisked her up to her office. By the time he had her alone, his shock had given way to anger.

"What the hell was that?" he asked even as he slammed the door shut behind them.

She spun around, her eyes wide. "What?"

"The way you behaved out there with the press. That's what."

"I don't know what you mean," she stammered.

She pressed a palm to her stomach as if to still the fluttering in her belly. He grabbed her by the wrist and held her hand out between them. "Look at you. You're shaking."

She jerked her hand away and thrust it behind her back. "So what if I am? Those things make me nervous."

"Yeah. I noticed. But that's no excuse for letting that reporter walk all over you."

Kitty glared at him. "What was I supposed to do?"

"You were supposed to defend yourself."

"How could I defend myself? She was badgering me with questions. There was nothing I could do."

"Kitty, I've watched you go toe-to-toe with a drunken rancher twice your size. Hell, every time we meet you try to rip me a new one. You know how to hold your own in a fight. That ninety-pound reporter shouldn't have had a chance."

She turned away, obviously searching for an explanation that would placate him. Finally she said simply, "That reporter was telling the truth."

"About us?" he asked. "We agreed what happened between us is nobody's business but our own. If you had a problem lying in a press conference, you should have told me that before—"

"Not about us," she interrupted. "About me." Again she turned away from him, but this time he sensed it was because she couldn't bring herself to meet his gaze. "All those things she said about me were true."

"Kitty—"

"About me being 'woefully unprepared.'" There was a disparaging sneer in her voice. "About my gross incompetence. It's all true."

He stared at the stiff lines of her back, barely comprehending her words. She looked like someone waiting to be hit.

For a moment he could only stare at her while he sorted through his confusion. "What do you mean? You're not incompetent."

"You only think that because I do such a good job hiding it. But I don't know what I'm doing. I wasn't prepared to run Biedermann's. The board never should have named me CEO."

"Kitty, being a CEO is a difficult job. People are rarely prepared for it. In your situation it was worse because your father's death was so unexpected and you were grieving for him. I'm sure it feels overwhelming. But that doesn't make you incompetent."

She glanced over her shoulder, sending him a watery smile. Where those *tears* in her eyes?

"You're not listening to me. No amount of preparation would have been enough. I'm just not smart enough."

And then he made his biggest mistake. He laughed.

She flinched. Exactly as if she'd been slapped. She was facing the windows again, so he didn't see her expression, but he would bet those tears were spilling down her cheeks by now.

He wanted to cross the room to her, take her in his arms and offer her comfort, but he knew that stubborn pride enough to know she wouldn't want him to see her crying. He wouldn't add insult to injury by making her face him.

"Kitty, I'm sorry, but the idea that you're not smart is ridiculous."

"Ford—"

"I've listened to you verbally skewer just about everyone you talk to. You can work a crowd like no one I've ever seen. Anyone who can hold their own in a room full of wealthy socialites could not possibly be stupid. If you weren't smart, believe me, I'd have noticed by now."

She shot him an exasperated look. "Why are you arguing with me about this? When my father and grandmother were still alive, they protected me the best they could. When my father died unexpectedly, I should have had the sense to step aside. But I was selfish. I love this company more than anything. I thought that would be enough. But I only made a mess of things."

She seemed so dejected, so unlike her normal self, he reached out a hand to her, but she deftly slipped out of his reach.

"You mentioned at the press conference that you'd be doing some restructuring. If you really intend to do everything in your power to ensure Biedermann's is financially viable, then you'll fire me."

# Nine

"What the hell is up with Kitty?"

Ford cornered Casey looking for some answers. Casey glanced up from the pot of coffee she was making just as Ford shut the door to the break room.

Casey slanted him a look from under her shaggy bangs. "Do you mean, like, today? Or ever?"

The previous times he'd spoken to Casey, she'd impressed him as being little more than a surly reprobate. He'd wondered how such a girl had gotten a job at Biedermann's, let alone kept it. Nevertheless, the best way to get the dirt on someone was through his or her assistant. Besides, she seemed to be the only person Kitty might confide in.

So Ford flashed Casey a sympathetic smile. "Kitty must be pretty tough to work for, huh?"

The girl's characteristic frown darkened to a full-fledged glower as she shoved the coffeepot onto the heating element and flicked the on/off toggle. "If you're just looking to talk trash about Kitty, you'll have to find someone else. I'm not into that kind of negative bonding. This job's too important to me."

He held up his hands in a gesture of innocence. "I was just trying to be sympathetic."

"You were just trying to dig for information," Casey said shrewdly as she pulled a clean coffee mug from the cabinet.

"Maybe I was," he admitted, more than a little surprised by Casey's show of loyalty. Since the negative bonding Casey had accused him of obviously wasn't going to work, he decided to take a different tack. "Kitty's not always the most forthcoming person. I'm trying to figure her out. That doesn't make me the enemy."

Casey shot him a suspicious look, but said nothing as she poured cream and then sugar into the mug. She sent an equally dark look at the coffeemaker, which was gurgling slowly. Poor girl was obviously torn between her need for caffeine and her desire to storm out in a huff.

"I'm trying to help her. But I can't do that unless I understand what's going on. Something's—"

"You're trying to get her fired."

"I'm not." Hell, that was the last thing he wanted. Keeping Kitty employed and well taken care of would at least minimize his guilt. "I'm trying to save her job. But she's not giving me anything to work with. She's—"

"She's too proud," Casey said quietly, without meeting his gaze.

"Exactly." Encouraged by the lack of belligerence in Casey's tone, he pressed on. "Do you have any idea why she would think I should fire her?"

"She said that?" Casey's voice held a note of panic.

Wasn't that interesting. "You're really worried about her losing her job."

"Hey, I know what people around here think. That she's such a b—" Casey broke off and seemed to be considering the hazards of cussing in front of the man who was ultimately her boss. "Such a witch—" she corrected "—to work for that I'm the best she can get. But it's not like that."

Ford said nothing. He'd wondered himself how exactly a surly, semicompetent girl like Casey had landed a prime job like the assistant to the CEO of a major company.

"She's the best boss I ever had," Casey continued. "And if I lost this job, I'm guessing I'd lose the scholarship, too."

"The scholarship?"

"Yeah. The scholarship that pays tuition for community college for all Biedermann employees. 'Cause there's no way I could pay for college on my own. I'd have to drop out of HCCC."

"Oh. That scholarship."

He'd read just about everything on Biedermann company policy, and he'd never heard of an employee scholarship. Which made him think Kitty was paying for this girl's college out of her own pocket. Kitty, who'd had to sell her home and had auctioned off family heirlooms, was paying the tuition of this ill-mannered, unskilled girl.

Was Kitty…*softhearted?* It was easier to imagine the Dalai Lama sponsoring an Ultimate Fighting match.

But what other explanation was there?

He shoved a hand through his hair. Damn it, why did she have to be so full of contradictions? Why did she have to be fragile one moment, all bristly defenses the next? Why couldn't she just be the manipulative witch that everyone thought she was? That would make his life so much easier.

If he ever wanted to be free of Kitty and all the complicated emotions she stirred up, he was going to have to find a way to save Biedermann's. And save Kitty's job.

And apparently Casey's job, too.

"Look," he said to Casey. "I'm trying to do the right thing here. Not just for the company, but for Kitty, too. If you help me out, if you help me understand what's going on here, I'll make sure you don't lose your job. Or your scholarship."

Even if he had to start paying the girl's tuition himself. And wouldn't that be just great. 'Cause all he needed in his life was one more woman dependent on him.

Casey pursed her lips and studied him. "What do you want to know?"

"Kitty told me her father never expected her to run Biedermann's. Do you know why?"

Casey shook her head. "No. I never met the old man, 'cause I was hired after he died. But office gossip is he always wanted her to marry someone who'd take over as CEO. You ask me, it's why that skeezie Marty is so mean to her."

"You think Marty expected to be made CEO?"

She shook her head, pouring coffee into her mug now that the maker had finally stopped dripping. "Haven't you noticed that icky way he looks at her? Like she's his golden lottery ticket or something. I think he wanted to marry her himself." Casey jabbed her coffee with a spoon and gave it a brisk stir. "That guy creeps me out."

Ford felt a sucker punch of jealousy. He struggled to bury it. Kitty's love life wasn't his business. Or so he kept telling himself. Still, he found himself asking, "Did she and Marty ever go out?"

That was not him giving in to his curiosity. If Marty was smarting from a broken heart, that might be motivation enough for him to make things unpleasant for Kitty. He might even be leaking information about Kitty to Suzy Snark.

"Naw." Casey waved her hand, dismissing the possibility. "Kitty wouldn't stoop that low." But then Casey tilted her head to the side, considering. "But Marty isn't, you know, smart about women. And you know what Kitty's like. Marty might have thought she was hitting on him."

Ford had to stifle a groan. Yes, he did know what Kitty was like. She used her beauty and sensuality like a defensive shield. Whenever someone got too close, she'd turn into Kitty the vamp. Had she accidentally hit Marty with that overblown charm of hers? Had she crushed his expectations, and somehow turned a man who should have been her friend into an enemy?

"Ah, Kitty," he murmured half under his breath. "Maybe you really are stupid."

Beside him, Casey stiffened. "Hey, that's just mean."

"No, wait," he jumped in to correct her. "I didn't mean—"

"She's not stupid, she's dyslexic, and if you don't know the difference then you're the idiot."

"She's dyslexic?" Ford barely heard Casey's words as shock spiraled through him.

*Dyslexic?* Kitty was *dyslexic?*

"She hides it well, right? I guess when you have a disability like that, you're used to dealing—" Casey broke off and did a visible double take. "Wait a sec. You didn't know?"

Guilt flashed across Casey's face, but then she turned and scurried from the room, cupping the mug in both hands, shoulders hunched defensively.

What did he even know about dyslexia? He'd gone to high school with some kids with dyslexia, one of whom had gone on to become a rather famous jazz musician. Ford hadn't kept in touch with Steve, but they'd been friends in school and he remembered how much trouble Steve had had learning.

Suddenly Ford remembered things Kitty had said or done that hadn't made sense before now. In all the meetings they'd been to together, whenever someone handed out information, she'd never even look at it. Proposals, contracts, synopses, whatever. She'd just slip it into her leather folio without so much as a glance. Her behavior gave the impression of careless disregard for the work of others. But that wasn't it at all.

And what was that she'd said once? Something about listening to books about business. Not reading them. Listening to them.

If she had trouble reading, her job would be nearly impossible. Add to that the possibility that she may have inadvertently offended her CFO.

He thought about his own relationship with Jonathon. At FMJ, he, Jonathon and Matt functioned more as a triumvirate than their titles would imply. Still, he'd be unable to do his job as CEO without Jonathon. Their relationship and their success stemmed from their absolute trust.

No wonder Kitty was floundering as the head of Biedermann's.

Ford broke into a quick jog to chase after Casey, who was now halfway down the hall. "Hey, hold up."

Casey rounded on him, her expression hardened into protective defiance. "You can't say anything to her about this."

"Of course I'm going to talk to her about it."

"You can't," Casey pleaded in a whisper. "If she finds out I told you, she'll fire me! She's totally crazy about hiding it. I'm not even supposed to know."

"Then she didn't tell you herself?"

"No way." Casey sent a furtive glance down either end of the hall as if she expected corporate spies to be lurking around every corner.

"So you figured it out on your own."

"Yes." Casey started walking again, apparently satisfied that no one was listening in on their conversation. "Like, my interview for the job was a dead giveaway. She didn't care if I could type or use a computer or anything. She just had me read aloud. And that's pretty much my whole job. Every time she goes to get her nails done or to get a massage, she has me come along to read to her."

Which explained why Kitty spent so much time at the spa. What had she called it? A coping mechanism.

He remembered what she'd said about how appearances were everything. No wonder she didn't want anyone knowing she had a learning disability. Unfortunately all the things she'd done to protect herself ending up making things worse.

Casey sent him a pleading look. "You're not going to tell her all of this, are you?"

"I have to."

He felt like he finally understood her. He only hoped it wasn't too late to help her.

Just when Kitty thought her day couldn't get any worse, Ford showed up at her apartment. Again.

She stood with her hand on the edge of the door,

glaring at Ford through the foot-and-a-half gap between the door and the jamb. "Let me guess, some idiot in the building let you in again."

"It was a different guy this time. But he'd watched the press conference and I convinced him we really were in love and just didn't want anyone to know it."

"What is it with you sneaking into my building?"

"It's nothing personal. I just didn't think you'd let me up."

"I wouldn't have. Probably because I didn't want to see you. Funny how that works, isn't it?"

She couldn't really blame her fellow tenants for being unable to keep Ford out of her building when she couldn't keep him out of her mind. He was a charming bastard, that was for sure. She'd always thought of herself as an expert at manipulating men. So why was it none of her tricks worked with him? Worse still, why was his persistence so appealing?

That was the real problem. Not that he wouldn't leave her alone, but that she didn't want him to. She moved to shut the door in his face, wishing she could block out her feelings as easily.

But he blocked her with his foot in the door. "Why didn't you tell me you were dyslexic?"

Her stomach clenched at his words as a wash of chilly panic flooded her. How had he found out? It was a secret she'd kept her whole life. The one she'd done everything to protect. She'd been prepared to resign from Biedermann's rather than talk about it. And he'd found out anyway.

Damn him. Why couldn't he just stay neatly in her past the way one-night stands were supposed to? She shoved aside all her emotions, burying them deep in her belly, pretending they didn't rise up in the acid of her sarcasm.

"Why didn't I tell you I was dyslexic?" she repeated. "The question is, why would I? It's completely irrelevant and frankly no one's business."

He reached out a hand as if he were going to pull her into his arms, but she deftly avoided his grasp. She'd been staying one step ahead of intimacy her entire adult life. Why should he be any different?

He clenched his jaw, staring her down with his hands propped on his hips. His very body presented a formidable line of offense. "You should have said something."

"I hardly even notice it," she lied, moving to the far end of the room before turning and circling back. "You have a birthmark on your shoulder. We've never talked about that, either."

"I wasn't about to resign over my birthmark."

"Well, maybe you should," she said glibly. "It's hardly your best feature."

"Stop it."

She stilled, taken aback by the edge in his voice as much as his words. Glancing around, she realized she'd made a complete circuit of the living room and now stood before him once again. She was back where she'd started.

Sometimes her whole life felt like that. As if she was

going in circles, always moving, always pretending she was making progress, but never getting anywhere.

Tears burned her eyes as she felt her throat close off. God, she would not do this. She would *not* cry in front of him.

It was bad enough when she'd done it at the office. When she'd had the excuse of the stress of the press conference to fall back on. She wouldn't do it again.

She tried to move past him, to just keep moving. As she always did. Because moving in circles was better than standing still, even if she wasn't getting anywhere.

But he snagged her arm as she walked by. He turned her to face him. "You don't have to pretend this doesn't matter to you. You don't always have to be so tough."

She laughed; it sounded bitter and unpleasant even to her ears. "You can't possibly understand what my life has been like. Do you have any idea how many people would love to see me fail?"

He studied her for a minute, clearly considering her words. "Have you ever considered that there might be just as many people who'd like to see you succeed?"

She blinked, surprised by his words. But he was wrong. Stubborn, but wrong. "You don't know what you're talking about."

"I know enough," he continued, "to know that people with dyslexia aren't stupid. And that there are plenty of dyslexic people who are very successful."

"There may be. But I'm not one of them." He looked like he wanted to say something, but she glared at him defiantly. "Don't."

"What?"

"Don't try to sugarcoat this. You never would have before you knew about my disability."

"I wasn't about to—"

"Yes, you were. I could see it in your eyes. You were about to tell me that it's not my fault that Biedermann's is in this situation. Or worse still, that things aren't as bad as they seem. Because I know better. *You* know better. If Biedermann's wasn't circling the drain, FMJ wouldn't be here, offering to buy us out. If things weren't desperate, you wouldn't be here at all. And trust me, the last thing I want is for you to treat me differently now that you know I have a disability."

"Okay," he said slowly. "I won't lie to you. Things are bad." He stroked a soothing hand down her arm. It was a gesture that was benignly gentle. Paternal, almost. "But that doesn't necessarily mean you're responsible. Businesses fail for a variety of reasons. You're not—"

"Yes, I am. I'm the company's CEO. That means I'm responsible. Biedermann's has thrived for five generations. Until I took over. And for the past four quarters we've released negative earnings and our stock is plummeting. If FMJ were in the same situation, you wouldn't flinch from taking responsibility yourself."

"Maybe you're right." He stroked her arm again in that maddening way. The touch was generically tender. As if he was gentling a horse or comforting a child. As if knowing she was dyslexic made her less desirable. "If you don't think you can serve as CEO, then we'll find something else for you to do. Your sketches were amazing. You could launch your own line of jewelry."

His words stirred up a long-buried yearning. Her own line of jewelry. It was what she'd always wanted. Her barely acknowledged greatest dream. His words might have even placated her, if she didn't know just how impossible that dream was. He was leading her on just to appease her vanity. Worse still was the way he stroked her arm.

His touch was so completely innocent, so totally sexless, it sparked her anger. She was more than her dyslexia. She wasn't a child. She wasn't a spooked animal. She didn't need to be comforted or soothed or reassured.

"Stop that." She jerked away from his touch.

"What?"

"That thing you're doing where you stroke my arm. With that calming, gentle touch." She propped her hands on her hips and glared at him.

"What is it you want from me, exactly? You want me to admit how hard this is on me?"

"That would be a start." There was a note of surprise in his voice. As if he hadn't expected her to cave so easily.

"Of course, it's hard. Biedermann's is ingrained in my family. My father and grandparents always took so much pride in the company. This is what people in my family have been doing for five generations. Ever since I was a child, running Biedermann's was all I ever wanted to do."

"Surely it wasn't what you always wanted."

"Of course it was," she snapped; for an instant her irritation edged out her softer emotions. "My father brought me to work with him from the time I was a toddler. You know, I never missed having a mother." She turned away, embarrassed by the confession. Afraid that it made her sound heartless. Or worse, that it was a lie. That she truly *had* missed having a mother. That if her mother had lived, Kitty might have been a completely different person. More lovable. Her natural defensiveness kicked in and when she spoke her tone was bitter with resentment. "My father loved me enough for two parents. I had the best of everything. I went to the best schools. And when those weren't good enough, I had the best tutors. He coddled me all my life. Maybe that's why it was so shocking when I found out the truth."

To her surprise and embarrassment, her voice broke on the word *truth*. She brought her hand to her cheek and felt the moisture there. She brushed fervently.

Before she could hide them, he was suddenly at her side. With a gentle touch of her shoulders, he turned her to face him. She swallowed past the lump in her throat, resisting the urge to turn away from him.

"What truth?" he asked gently.

"That I'd never be able to run Biedermann's. That I'd never be more than just a pretty accessory." Through the sheen of her tears, she saw the flicker of disbelief. "He'd taken me out of school and hired private tutors. He carefully regulated everyone I came into contact with. He was only trying to protect me, but it meant I had no idea what I was capable of. Or rather incapable of. I was in college before I knew how odd my upbringing was. Before I realized I was reading at a third grade level and I'd never graduate. In *college*." She let out a bitter bark of a laugh. "I hate to think how much money he had to donate to get me in in the first place."

Tears streamed down her face. She looked up at him, fully expecting to see the panic most men displayed when faced with tears.

But there was no panic. No terror. And he wasn't running away. Instead, he leaned down and brushed a gentle kiss across her lips before he pulled her close and wrapped his arms around her.

She sank against him, relishing his strength, even as it annoyed her. She didn't want to want him. She wanted nothing more than to be left alone with her misery. But apparently he wasn't going to let her do that. And she wasn't strong enough to make him go away. Not when she had such a short amount of time with him anyway.

When he leaned down to take her mouth in a kiss, she met him, move for move. She pressed her body against his, needing the feel of his muscles moving beneath her palms.

His hands moved over her body, peeling away layers of clothing as easily as he'd stripped away her emotional defenses. He swept her up into his arms and carried her to the bedroom as effortlessly as he'd swept back into her life. His every touch heightened her desire.

She needed him. She needed this. Here, in the bed, they were equals. A perfect match.

With him, she could be herself as she could with no one else. But as much as she wanted this moment to last forever, she knew it couldn't. Her heart filled with bittersweet longing, even as he made her body soar. Even as pleasure shuddered through her nerve endings, she knew it was the last time they'd ever be together.

She had to tell him the truth about the baby and once she did, everything between them would change forever.

# Ten

"This wasn't what was supposed to happen," she murmured.

Boy, she'd said a mouthful there.

"Ain't that the truth?" he muttered.

She pulled back just enough to look up at him. Through a sheen of dried tears she gazed into those liquid brown eyes of his and felt some cold icy part of herself melt.

Finally he asked, "What was supposed to happen?"

"You were supposed to leave." She ducked her head back to his chest.

"I was?" He tipped her chin up and studied her expression. "Is it so bad that I stayed?"

She let out a sigh that was part tearful shudder, part

exasperation. Her lips curled in a wry smile as she answered. "Yes, it is."

"I don't get it." His smile held both humor and something darker. "I know why I *shouldn't* stay, I just don't get why you don't want me to."

"Think highly of yourself, don't you?" She stretched as she said it, arching against the wall of his chest, relishing the feel of his strength. "But I can't argue with that at all," she continued. "In bed we're great together. It's out of bed that we're a disaster."

As easily as she'd slipped into his arms, she pulled herself free. The tears were gone, but her eyes felt dry and scratchy, as if she'd bawled for hours.

"You think we're a disaster together only because this thing with Biedermann's is between us," he pointed out.

"Not only because of that," she murmured, grabbing her clothes, but didn't explain.

"Not only. But mostly."

She bumped up her chin. "Even with only Biedermann's between us, that would be enough. The company is my whole life."

"True," he admitted. "But we're not on opposing sides here. You keep treating me like the enemy, but I'm not. FMJ is here to help. We're here to fix things for you."

"That's just it. You don't see anything wrong with that, do you?"

"With what?"

"The fact that you want to fix things for me." The fact that she had to explain it at all was only more proof of the problem. "That you want to help."

"No, I don't. It's what we do at FMJ. It's what *I* do."

"Exactly. If I let you, you'd swoop in and take over everything for me. FMJ would manage Biedermann's and I'd never have to make another decision in my life. Just sit back and live off my stock dividends and never worry about anything ever again."

"Most women wouldn't be complaining about that," he pointed out wryly.

She thought of what Jonathon had told her about his mother and sisters. Maybe they were content to live like that, but she never would be. "I think you're wrong about that."

"Look, you said yourself you were raised to find a rich husband, marry him and let him run Biedermann's for you. How is what I'm proposing any different?"

"For starters, you're not actually proposing, are you? It's different when people are married. You're suggesting a business arrangement. Out of pity, no less."

"Fine," he said, an unexpected bite of irritation in his voice. "You want to get married? We'll get married."

For a second, she just stared at him in shock. What did he expect her to do? Leap with joy? Instead, she let out a bark of laughter. "You want to marry me so I'll feel better about accepting money from you? That's ridiculous."

"Why? Because you're too proud to accept help?"

"No. Because people should get married because they love each other, not out of some misguided sense of…" She searched around for the right word, before finally pinning him with a stare. "Why exactly did you propose again? Was it pity?"

"It was *not* pity." He returned her gaze steadily. "Did you love Derek?"

"I…" That had been different. With Derek, it had been all business. Not this crazy mixture of business, lust and emotion. "That was different."

"How?"

"I could trust him." At least, she'd thought she could trust him. More to the point, she could trust herself with him. She knew how she felt about him. She admired Derek's business sense and his ambition, but she never could have loved him. When he dumped her, he'd wounded her pride, but her heart hadn't felt the slightest hiccup.

Quite simply, she'd never loved Derek, but she did love Ford. With him, it would be totally different. She'd be so vulnerable. She'd be at the mercy of her own emotions. And he would treat her just like he treated everyone else. He'd be charming, thoughtful and solicitous. Without ever actually caring about her at all.

Of course, she couldn't say any of that aloud. So instead she said, "And I understood his motives."

"I just thought—" Ford broke off, struggling to put into words what he could barely understand himself. "Look, you're pregnant. The single-parent thing is really hard. I watched Patrice struggle to do it for years. And Mom, after my dad died. It's a tough gig." He must have read the absolute horror on her face, because he let his words trail off before finishing lamely, "I don't know. I thought, maybe I could help out with that."

"Wow," she began with exaggerated disbelief. "You thought that *maybe* you could 'help out' raising your own—" And then she stopped dead as she realized what she'd just said. "You should just leave."

"What was that you were going to say? Raising my own *what?*" He grabbed her arm as she reached for the doorknob. "My own what? My own *child?* That's what you were going to say, wasn't it?" He searched her face, but she'd quickly schooled her expression to reveal nothing. "Wasn't it?" he demanded.

She yanked her arm from his grasp. "I misspoke."

"No, you didn't. You know that baby is mine. Tell me the truth."

Kitty met his gaze, chin up, eyes blazing. "I have no idea who the father of this baby is. Yes, I slept with you, so it could be yours. But I sleep with a lot of men. It could be anyone's."

He just shook his head. "You little liar."

"You don't believe me?" she asked coolly.

"Not for a minute. Saturday morning, when I was worried because we didn't use a condom, you told me you'd been tested when you got back from Texas. But we had used a condom in Texas. There was no reason for you to think you might have picked something up from me. Unless you were just being incredibly careful. Which you wouldn't be unless what happened in Texas was rare. Like, once in a lifetime rare."

An odd mixture of frustration and relief washed over Ford. *Why the hell hadn't he thought of this earlier?*

It was so obvious now that he'd thought it through. No one else could be the father of her child, because there was no one else. For Kitty, there was only him.

And he didn't even want to think about how much better that made him feel. How that strange pressure in his chest started to ease up. All he knew was this: he was the father of Kitty's child. Now she had to marry him. There was no reason not to.

"We're getting married," he announced. "That's final."

"That," she sneered, "is the stupidest thing I've ever heard. Getting married because I'm pregnant may actually be more stupid than getting married because you feel sorry for me."

"I'm not going to fight with you about this."

"Good, because I'm not going to fight with you about it, either. You can't make me marry you. You want to support the baby. Fine. Send a check. If you even want to be a part of the baby's life, I'm okay with that. We'll negotiate custody or something. But I'm guessing you won't even want that."

Fury inched through him, slow and insidious. Because she was right. He couldn't make her marry him. And, damn it, he wished he could.

"You can't keep me from my child," he warned her.

"I won't even try. I'm betting I won't have to."

"What's that supposed to mean?"

"Ford," she said, shaking her head. "You go through life keeping everyone at arm's length. You don't let anyone close to you. And you're so charming most people don't even notice."

"But you did," he muttered.

"Well, I consider myself something of an expert at holding people at an emotional distance." She flashed him a smile. If he didn't know her so well, he might not have seen the sadness in her gaze. "So I recognized the signs. You have a mother, a step-mom, or whatever she is, and three sisters. Sure, you support them financially. You fix problems for them, but that's the extent of your relationship with them. You don't let them choose. If they're too much of an emotional burden for you, then I'm guessing a baby is way more than you're ready for."

He wanted to argue with her, but the best he could come up with was a grumbled "This isn't over yet."

What could he really say? He *didn't* let anyone close to him. Not even his family. What kind of husband would he make? What kind of father?

Kitty and the baby would be better off without him. The best thing he could do for them was show himself out.

She'd always considered her active social life a part of her job. She didn't have much formal training and had not even graduated college. She wasn't the kind of woman who could inspire the confidence of the board or the stockholders. But there was one area of business in which she excelled. Schmoozing.

For that reason, dinner parties and gala balls

weren't mere social engagements. They were work. Tonight's gallery opening was no different, with one exception. Normally, when she worked a room, it was with the intent of making contacts and keeping her ear to the ground for useful information. But today she wasn't looking for information. She was looking for a spouse.

She may have scoffed at Ford's proposal of marriage, but she had to agree he had a point. Being a single mom would be tough.

But she certainly couldn't marry Ford. She was far too emotionally involved with him. Oh, who was she kidding? She was in love with him. He made her feel things no other man had ever made her feel. But for now, she was hoping that was a temporary condition.

Surely all she needed was some time away from him. Time for her feelings to fade and her heart to heal. And that would never happen if she married him.

And if he asked her again, she might not have the strength to say no.

Her only hope was to go back to her original plan. Find a husband who could help her run Biedermann's. Once she was safely engaged, Ford would leave her alone and she could start the long, arduous process of getting over him. What she needed now was a husband who would care about her baby, but never press her for a truly intimate relationship. Luckily she knew Simon Durant would be the perfect man for the job.

She moved through the crowd, her gaze shifting as she looked for a head of artfully tousled black hair.

Finally, she saw him at the back of the room, his arm draped over the shoulder of a whippet-lean man a good decade younger than he was.

Simon's face brightened when he saw her. "Kitty, darling! With all that nonsense in the news, I didn't think you'd make it."

Simon greeted her with double air kisses to her cheeks. Cosmo, the pretentious young artist whose show this was and whose shoulder Simon had recently been draped over, merely nodded before turning his attention elsewhere. But then, Cosmo had never liked her.

Kitty squeezed Simon's hand in greeting. She nodded in Cosmo's direction as she asked, "Do you think he'll notice if I steal you away for a few minutes?"

"He's talking to an art critic, so I doubt it."

Simon linked his arm with hers and guided her toward the open bar.

"So you've been following the stories in the news?" she asked.

"Mostly no, but the gossip has been hard to avoid. I don't suppose the delicious Mr. Langley is…"

He let his voice trail off suggestively.

"Gay?" she supplied. "Unfortunately, no." But wouldn't this all be much easier if he were? She certainly never would have found herself in her current situation. "I have a problem, Simon, and I think you might be able to help me with it."

They'd reached the bar. Kitty ordered a bottled water and Simon ordered a mango mojito. "You know I'll do anything for you."

She waited until they'd received their drinks and were out of the range of nosy ears before leaning close and saying, "Okay. Then marry me."

Simon choked on his drink, spewing a froth of orange liquid a good three feet. "Marry you? Honey, you're not exactly my type. And I didn't think I was that subtle or you were that dumb."

She smiled. "I'm not. And, for the record, neither are you."

"In that case, why would we get married?"

She sipped her water. "Simon, you're a brilliant businessman, but your family doesn't appreciate you." The Durants owned a chain of hotels. It was a business that had been around almost as long as Biedermann's. However, the Durant family tree was massive, sprawling and loaded with acorns of brilliant businessmen. Unlike her own family tree, which had been winnowed down to her one scrawny branch.

"You're not reaching your full potential at Durant International. You're too far down in the line of succession. Right now you're stuck as—what is it?— junior VP of public relations?"

Simon cringed.

"We both know you're capable of so much more." Kitty leaned forward, her zeal showing just a little as she sensed his interest being piqued. "Marry me, take over as CEO of Biedermann's and we'll kill numerous birds with one stone. You'll get a job you can be proud of and you'll come into your inheritance."

He quirked an eyebrow. "My inheritance, eh?"

"Rumor has it your very conservative grandmother is withholding your inheritance until you marry and settle down."

Simon's eyebrows both shot up. "The rumor mill has been active indeed."

"Is it true, then?"

"Let's just say Grandmother Durant has never approved of my lifestyle, but I have plenty of other sources of income. And I don't care about the money."

"Ah, but you do care about her. And I suspect it bothers you that you've never lived up to her standards. She'd be very pleased if we married. You could even provide her with a great-grandchild."

Emotion flickered across Simon's face, barely visible in the dim lighting of that gallery. Something dark and a little sad. She knew in that instant that her instincts about Simon had been right.

While he was decidedly gay, he regretted some of the things his lifestyle had cost him: his family's respect and the chance for a family of his own. She might just be able to tempt him onto an easier path. They'd never have a real marriage, but they were friends at least. Which was more than some couples could say.

Simon frowned as if he were seriously considering her offer. Hope surged through her. Maybe this would actually work. If it did, it would all be so simple. Such a fine solution to all of her problems.

"And what would you get out of this marriage?" he asked.

"I'd get a talented CEO. With you at the helm, Bie-dermann's stock would start to climb again. I'd keep the company out of the hands of FMJ. It's so perfect, I almost wonder why I didn't think of it before."

Simon studied her. "I was wondering that myself. After all, you haven't gone to lengths to hide the fact that you've been looking for a husband to bail you out."

She nearly laughed. "Don't tell me I've offended you by not propositioning you before now?"

"Not at all. I'm just curious why you're suddenly so desperate." Simon gave her a piercing look. "You know I'd never be the kind of husband you deserve."

She nodded. "Of course I know that. But we're friends. I think it would be very easy for us to settle into a marriage of sorts."

He cocked his head to the side and asked, "If you're serious, why come here? Why not just call? Why ask now? It's not often a man gets tracked down in the middle of his lover's art show and propositioned."

She had to laugh at that. "It seemed like the kind of thing to discuss in person. And I'm in a bit of a hurry."

"You make a very tempting package, my dear, but—"

"But you're not tempted?" she asked with a sigh.

"It's more that I think you'll regret it later. In my experience, when someone propositions you late at night, on impulse, it's because they're running away from someone else."

"I'm not running away from Ford." But the panicked note in her voice alarmed her.

Simon leveled his gaze at her. "Really? Why don't you tell me what happened?"

"Nothing happened," she insisted, determined to leave it at that. However, she kept talking, seemingly unable to stop the flow of words. "That man is impossible. He's insulting and rude. And he..." She struggled to regain the composure she felt slipping. "And he asked me to marry him."

Before she knew it, she'd told Simon the entire story. From the unplanned pregnancy to her incompetence as a CEO to Ford's offer of marriage.

When she finished, she looked at Simon, fully expecting a flood of sympathy. Instead he gazed at her in that penetrating way of his.

"What?" she asked.

"I'm just trying to figure out why you need me to be your husband and your CEO, if Ford has already offered to do the job."

"I can't accept his proposal. He only offered because he feels sorry for me."

"Sorry for you?" Simon asked.

She fumed. "I think he sees it as a point of honor."

Simon laughed at her. "Sure there's pity sex. But there's no such thing as a pity marriage. No man is that honorable."

Humiliation burned her cheeks as she asked, "Then why would he offer to marry me?"

Simon shrugged. "You'll have to ask him. Maybe he offered for the reason most men ask a woman to marry them. Maybe he loves you."

Shock coursed through her body. Love? Ford might love her? For one awful moment, her heart leaped into her throat, then sanity returned. "That's impossible."

"Are you sure?" Before she could answer, he pressed on. "Do you love him?"

"I don't—" But she could only shake her head. Not in denial, but in confusion. Was what she felt really love? Not a temporary blip of imaginary love, but real love. The kind strong enough to sustain an actual marriage? "I don't know."

"Then you better figure it out." Simon pulled her close and leaned down to brush a kiss across her cheek. But before his lips made contact with her skin, someone yanked him away from her and punched him soundly in the face.

"You didn't have to punch him."

Kitty sat beside Ford in the back of a taxi, but she'd crammed herself as far against the door as she could. Her arms were crossed over her chest as she gazed belligerently forward, her legs crossed away from him so that as she tapped her foot in irritation it scraped against the door. The cab driver kept glaring at her in the mirror, but she ignored him. Occasionally, the driver sent him a pleading look for backup, but Ford ignored him, too. Hell, he had bigger problems. Much, much bigger.

"What were you thinking?" she demanded.

What was he supposed to say to that? He hadn't been thinking. When he'd walked into that gallery and seen another man leaning down to kiss Kitty, he'd simply lost it. Never mind that the man doing the kissing was gay. Ford hadn't known that until after he'd punched him, when a pint-size, flamboyant man had shrieked and run across the room to kneel beside the fallen man. A lot of drama had ensued. Ford figured he was lucky the police hadn't been called, because an arrest was the last thing he needed to add to his humiliation.

To make matters worse, he'd obviously been set up. He'd gone to that art gallery in the first place because half an hour earlier he'd gotten a picture e-mailed to him of Kitty snuggling up to that guy. He'd been furious. It hadn't mattered that the e-mail had been from someone claiming to be Suzy Snark. He'd deal with that issue later. For now, he had more pressing issues.

Kitty shifted in her seat so she was almost facing him. "Do you have anything to say for yourself?" she asked in slow, baffled tones. "Any explanation for why you'd do that?"

There was a note of expectancy in her voice. Was there some answer she wanted him to give? Did she understand his actions? Because he sure as hell didn't.

He glanced at her only briefly before looking back out his window. He didn't know what to say. Because the truth was, he *did* have to hit him. When he'd seen Simon kissing Kitty, the need to hit him had been so strong it had almost been a compulsion.

In that moment, all the heightened emotions of that past week—all the anxiety, all the desire, all the frustration—all that emotion had crystallized into pure, blinding fury.

"Do you have anything to say for yourself? Anything at all?"

"I don't want to talk about it."

She threw up her hands in a *what the hell?* gesture. She snorted, turning toward him. "Of all the stupid—"

"I know. Shut up." He turned to face her, too. "You think I don't know what I did was stupid? I know. I'm thirty-two years old—damn it—I know better than to punch a guy just because he's kissing my woman. I. Know. Better."

Her eyes widened slightly at his words. She looked as if she wanted to turn and run, but in the tight confines of the taxi, there was nowhere to go. And since she wasn't saying anything, he kept talking.

"I'm not a complete moron, despite all evidence to the contrary. I don't fight. That's just not who I am. Back when we were kids, Jonathan got into plenty of fights. Matt, too. But not me. I was always the one talking the other guy into backing down. I've always been too smart to fight." He scrubbed a hand through his hair. "I guess you just bring out the idiot in me."

Her gaze narrowed slightly. "That's all you have to say for yourself?"

"What else do you want me to say?"

"Nothing. Nothing at all." Then she leaned forward and tapped on the glass separating them from the cab driver. "Pull over here," she ordered.

"Come on, Kitty, you can't get out here. It's late and you're a twenty-minute cab ride from your apartment."

"I'm not getting out. You are."

# Eleven

Kitty watched Ford climb from the cab with a sinking stomach. If she didn't know it was too early for her to feel the baby moving, she'd have sworn the little bugger was giving her a swift kick in the gut. And not in a good way.

She'd given Ford the perfect opportunity to tell her he loved her. And all he'd come up with was "You just bring out the idiot in me."

That was the best he could do? Not "I love you." Not even "I couldn't stand the sight of another man touching you." Geesh, she would have settled for "I was jealous." But oh, no. That's not what she got. She got "You just bring out the idiot in me."

Well. What could she have said to that? "Gosh, I'm so glad I could help"?

Simon had been wrong.

Ford didn't love her.

But she did love him.

Something she hadn't known for sure until she'd been sitting there beside him in the cab, heart thudding away in her chest, waiting to hear his answer. Praying for a declaration from him.

And the instant he'd made that stupid idiot comment she'd known that she'd been kidding herself until now. She wasn't immune to Ford. He had the power to crush her very soul.

How could she even see him again? How could she risk falling even more in love with him?

No, she needed some distance. Not to mention some time. She had never backed down from a fight in her life, but she knew Ford. He wouldn't leave her alone. He'd never give her heart time to build up calluses. Which meant she had to go into hiding.

A few minutes later when the cab pulled to stop in front of her building, she leaned in the window as she paid. "Can you wait? I'll be down in just a few minutes."

It didn't take her long to pack a bag and return to the waiting cab. It was risky, leaving just now, when the deal with FMJ was still up in the air, but she just couldn't stay. She'd always thought losing Biedermann's was the hardest thing she'd ever have to go through. Turned out she was wrong. Losing Ford was so much harder.

By morning, Ford was ready for some answers. And, frankly, he figured he had them coming. Unfortunately, Kitty was nowhere to be found. She wasn't at work, she wasn't at home. She wasn't even at any of the spas he could think of calling.

In the end, he decided to check with the one person he least wanted to see. Simon Durant.

He tracked Simon down at the other man's apartment on the Upper West Side.

When Simon opened his front door sporting an already bruising black eye, Ford didn't waste any time. He figured the man was seconds away from throwing him out already.

He tried to contain his anger, but it crept into his voice as he asked, "What the hell did you say to Kitty?"

Simon's eyebrows shot up as he gestured for Ford to follow him into the living room. "Why do you assume I said anything to her?"

"Because she's gone."

"Gone?" Simon dropped onto the sofa, stretching out his legs along the seat.

"Yes, gone. As in, she's not answering her phone, she's not at home, and no one can tell me where she is."

"Ahh. I see." Simon nodded sagely, but didn't offer anything else. Then he looked meaningfully at the chair across from him.

Ford sat begrudgingly. This wasn't a social visit, but Simon clearly enjoyed toying with him. "So what did you say to her?"

"Hmm, let me think." Simon tapped his forefinger on his upper lip as if deep in thought. "First she asked me if I would marry her."

Ford had to repress the urge to leap across the coffee table and wrap his hands around the other man's throat. But hitting Simon last night obviously hadn't helped anything, so Ford sat, drumming his fingers on his knees, and prayed that Simon would reach the end of the story before he reached the end of his patience.

"And what did you say?" Ford gave Simon a verbal nudge.

"Well, no. Obviously." Simon sent him a look that seemed to ask, *Are you always this dumb?*

"Obviously."

"And then she told me that you had asked her to marry you. It's all very *Midsummer Night's Dream,* don't you think?"

Ford ignored him and asked, "Then what happened?"

"Then she cried a little." Simon's flippant tone vanished under the weight of this accusation. "And you know, Kitty never cries."

Ford could only swallow and nod.

"Do you know she's under the impression you asked her to marry you because you pity her?"

"That's absurd," Ford said automatically.

"I'm glad you think so." Simon flashed him a wane smile. "That's what I said. I told her I thought you were in love with her."

Ford felt like his stomach dropped out of his body as his mind went wheeling.

"Well?" Simon asked after a minute.

"Well, what?"

"Are you? In love with Kitty, I mean."

"No" was his automatic response, but even as he said the word he felt a pang deep in his heart.

Kitty was probably the most amazing woman he'd ever known. Smart, sexy as hell, and so damn pretty it almost hurt to look at her. None of which was even half as impressive as her pure strength of will. Her independence. In her lifetime, she'd managed to overcome challenges he couldn't even imagine. And she was so damn determined to do it all on her own.

It was kind of ironic. For the first time in his life, he wanted to help someone. He wanted to shoulder all the burdens or to stand by her side when she shouldered them herself. He wanted to be there for her no matter what. Not just for her, but for the baby, too. He wanted to try his hand at being the kind of father he'd never had.

If only she'd let him. Of course he was in love with her. Who wouldn't be? "Yes," he said finally.

This time, the smile Simon sent him was beaming. "Well, then." He straightened. "We have some work to do, don't we?"

If Kitty had any illusions that Ford would come rushing after her to sweep her off her feet, they faded quickly. As one week passed into the next, she faced the possibility that he wasn't coming for her. True, she'd made herself difficult to find, but not impossible. After all, the hotel was just a few blocks down from Biedermann's headquarters.

At first, she mostly just sulked. It wasn't so much that

she expected him to find her, but rather that she hoped he would. In her mind she replayed scenes from all the classic romantic movies she'd watched growing up. The ones where the man chases down the heroine on New Year's Eve or at the Empire State Building to declare his eternal love. She wanted their story to have that kind of ending, even though she knew it was impossible.

When she wasn't entertaining romantic fantasies about Ford, she ate and slept, the two activities her doctor most approved of. She was surprised how tired being pregnant made her feel, but thankful that lots of rest and near constant eating kept the nausea at bay.

As far as work was concerned, she turned over the negotiations with FMJ to Marty. Following Ford's advice, she came clean to Marty about her dyslexia. He was shocked, but far more sympathetic than she'd imagined he'd be. He called daily with updates about the acquisition, but she found it hard to care.

Still, she knew the negotiations had not yet been finalized. So when Casey came by for a visit and mentioned that Ford had scheduled another press conference, she was immediately suspicious. If Ford was ready to talk to the press, it could mean only one thing. If he wasn't going to announce that the deal was finalized, did that mean FMJ was pulling out?

Whether she was ready to face him or not, it was time for her to come out of hiding.

Staring out at the sea of reporters, Ford had to swallow down his nerves. He'd done dozens of these things in the past, hell, maybe hundreds, and they'd never bothered him at all.

But he knew if he had any chance of winning Kitty back, it would be right now. And she was out there somewhere, just waiting to see what he had up his sleeve.

He'd known—of course—that the one sure way to guarantee she came to the press conference was to tell Casey to keep her away.

He didn't have long to worry about it, because before he knew it, Matt was giving him the nod that it was time to begin.

"Acquiring Biedermann Jewelry was quite the departure for FMJ. Up until now, we've been known for pioneering green technologies. However, we were confident that with the right leadership and creativity Biedermann's could once again become a leader in the industry.

"Though our agreement with Biedermann's hasn't been finalized, we're so enthusiastic about the new direction we're taking things we wanted to give everyone a sneak peek at what we're doing.

"Casey there is passing out swag bags, and if you'll look inside, you'll see what I'm talking about. We're launching a line of stylish accessories for personal mobile devices."

A murmur went through the crowd as people began digging through the bags. Each of the twenty bags contained the Victorian-inspired iPhone case and the gothic Bluetooth earpiece. The earpiece had taken the most work, but luckily Matt had figured out a way to retrofit an earpiece FMJ was already manufacturing.

"These are all just beta versions," Ford continued over the whispers. He smiled broadly. "So go easy on them. The final versions will be in stores within a few months, along with the rest of the line. All of which, by the way, are designed personally by Kitty Biedermann herself."

Kitty could not have been more surprised than anyone else in the audience. She sat in the back row, feeling a little like Jackie O. hidden under sunglasses and a hat. So far, no one had recognized her.

When she'd opened the bag Casey had handed her with a wink, she'd actually gasped aloud. Thankfully her gasp was one of many exclamatory noises, so she didn't think anyone had noticed.

She dumped the two boxes on her lap and then carefully opened the first, unwrapping the tissue paper that surrounded the iPhone case. Her hand trembled as she held it. It was something she'd never dreamed she'd see. Her design come to life, strange and a little absurd though it was, with its Victorian curlicues and its gothic clawed feet.

After a lifetime of dreaming of it, she was finally holding one of her creations in her hands. Even better, the people on either side of her were murmuring excitedly. Her father had been wrong. There was a market for her work.

And Ford had given it to her.

By the time she returned her attention to the press conference, Ford was answering questions.

"Will Ms. Biedermann continue to design the line?" one reporter asked.

"I certainly hope so. As you can see, her designs are very original."

"Does this mean she won't be serving as CEO of Biedermann's?"

"Ms. Biedermann is extremely smart and talented. Like many other people who are dyslexic, she's shown tremendous resilience in overcoming her disability. Needless to say, FMJ will be happy to have her in whatever capacity she chooses to fill."

Kitty's head snapped up as panic poured through her body. He'd just casually dropped her dyslexia into the conference like it was nothing. What was he *doing?*

Ford had paused as shock rippled through the crowd, but now he continued. "Her learning disability has made her job as CEO extremely difficult, as you can imagine."

"So then she won't be continuing on in her current position? FMJ is going to replace her?" one of the reporters asked.

Ford's gaze sought out Kitty where she sat in the back of the room. He'd seen her trying to blend in when she'd first arrived. Not that Kitty could disappear in a crowd. Her intrinsic style and grace made her stand out.

When he'd made the announcement about her dyslexia, she'd near leaped to her feet. She yanked off her sunglasses and was glaring at him through the crowd. Was she anxious to hear his answer or sending him a telepathic message to explode? He couldn't tell. For now, all he could do was answer the reporter's question as honestly as he could.

"On the contrary. FMJ is going to do everything in its power to support her in whatever she decides. Biedermann's is still her company. However, the position she holds within the company will ultimately be her decision."

After that, he answered a few more questions and then wrapped up his part. He neatly handed the podium over to Matt to talk about the specs just as they'd planned. He wanted to slip out quietly. The last thing he wanted now was to get waylaid by some nosy reporter. No, there was only one person he wanted to talk to right now. And only one question he wanted answers to. Now that he'd revealed her biggest secret to the world, would she still want to talk to him?

She caught up with him right outside the conference room, falling into step beside him as if it hadn't been nearly two weeks since he'd seen her. As if there weren't repeated marriage proposals hanging in the air between them.

Finally the tension got to him and he broke the silence. "They seemed enthusiastic about the new line."

She slanted him a look, but the sunglasses were back on and he couldn't read her expression. "It was a big risk announcing it this early."

"It was. But Biedermann's stock price has been

climbing steadily since I scheduled the press conference. It had been fluctuating based on the Suzy Snark blogs. No matter what happens, Biedermann's is no longer in danger of being delisted."

After today, she would be fine even without him, if that's what she chose.

She stopped him, placing a hand on his arm. "Why did you do it? If our stock prices are climbing then theoretically I don't have to accept your buyout offer now. You made it easier for me to walk away from you."

"That's one way to look at it." He grinned wolfishly. "But all of Matt's Bluetooth stuff is proprietary technology. If you want Biedermann's to actually sell those gadgets of yours, now you have to sign the papers."

"So it was a trap?"

They'd reached the hotel lobby by now, and she stopped cold. He turned to face her. He'd been wondering when they would get to this part of the discussion. The part where she ripped him a new one for spilling the beans about her dyslexia.

But instead of the blazing anger he expected to read in her expression, he saw only shattering vulnerability.

"You can't honestly expect me to trust you after this. After you—" Her voice broke. Without meeting his gaze she pushed past him to walk briskly through the hotel lobby.

He caught up with her in a few steps. Grabbing her arm, he turned her to face him. "I brought up your dyslexia in the press conference to prove you can trust me."

"That makes perfect sense. Betray someone's trust to prove that they can trust you." She tugged on her arm, glaring at him. "Except I hadn't even trusted you enough to tell you about my dyslexia. You wheedled that information out of my assistant."

She used the word *wheedled* with relish. Obviously she remembered he'd objected to it the last time.

"No, you're right," he told her. "You didn't tell me. But then you didn't tell Casey, either. I can almost excuse you not trusting me. But Casey? That kid would do anything for you." He shook his head in exasperation. "Have you ever wondered what all this deception has cost you?"

She stared at him blankly, as if she didn't understand his words, but at least she was listening.

He tipped her chin up so she was looking full at him. For a second he studied her face, taking in the lines of strain around her mouth, the clear green intensity of her eyes. Her perfectly kissable bow of a mouth, painted a tempting scarlet.

His heart seized in his chest. He may have royally screwed this up. If she didn't forgive him, this may be the last time he was this close to her. But he couldn't think about that now.

"Kitty, your family made you believe your dyslexia was something to hide. Something to be ashamed of. But it's not. It's—"

"Don't try to tell me it's no big deal. That it doesn't make me different than anyone else." She twisted her chin away. "Because it is a big deal. It makes everything harder."

"Which is exactly why you need to be able to ask for help. You need to surround yourself with people you trust." His frustration crept into his voice. "No one does everything on their own. The rest of us mere mortals need help all the time. Why shouldn't you?"

But she just shook her head. "You don't get it, do you? This was my secret. It wasn't yours to tell."

"Exactly. And you were never going to tell it. You would have let people go on thinking the worst of you forever rather than have even one moment of vulnerability. So I made the decision for you. I did it because it was the right thing for you.

"For once in my life, I did the right thing, not just the easy thing." He laughed wryly. "I could have just left things as they were. I probably could have even talked my way back into your bed." He waited for her to protest, but she didn't. They both knew he was right on that account. "Instead, I did that one thing that I knew would piss you off, because I knew it would make your life better."

"So you did it because you wanted to piss me off?"

"No. I did it because I love you."

Kitty's heart, which had been racing with fury and fear, seemed to stop in her chest. She squeezed her eyes shut for a second as emotion flooded her.

He *loved* her?

When she opened her eyes he was still there. Watching her expectantly. "Look, neither of us is any good at this. We're both slow to trust. Neither of us let other people close. And it would undoubtedly be easier on both of us if we walked away right now. But I don't want to do that, and I'm betting you don't want to do that, either."

She opened her mouth to speak, but her throat closed off and all she could do was shake her head mutely.

"So I say we decide right now. We stick with this and make it work."

She wanted to believe him, but her heart didn't know how to trust what her mind heard.

"Biedermann's—" she began.

His hand tightened around her arm. "This doesn't have anything to do with Biedermann's. This is about you and me. And the baby we're going to have." He paused, his gaze dropping from her eyes to her belly. "I love you, Kitty. And I want to be a father to our baby. The only question is, do you trust me enough to let me?"

Her heart stuttered in her chest. Did she trust him? The question had barely flitted through her mind before she knew the answer. Of course she did.

An unexpected bubble of laughter rose up in her throat. Ford cocked an eyebrow at her giggle, his expression still expectant. But before he could ask why she was laughing, she threw her arms around his neck.

"Of course I trust you. Which is so silly because just a few minutes ago I didn't think I did."

She felt his arms wrap around her and tighten, felt his face nuzzle into her hair. Only when she felt the shudder of his deep breath did she realize how nervous he must have been.

She pulled back to meet his gaze. "You know I love you, too, right?"

His lips quirked into a half smile. "I thought my chances were pretty good."

"What would you have done if I'd have said no?"

"I'm not the kind of guy who takes no for an answer."

"Meaning?" she asked.

"Meaning, I would have pursued you until you said yes."

Just a few weeks ago, that answer would have infuriated her. Now she knew it was just exactly what she needed. *He* was just exactly what she needed.

She forced a mock frown. "You know, that was pretty gutsy. Asking a jewelry heiress to marry you when you didn't even have a ring to offer."

To her surprise he smiled broadly. "Hey, this I have covered." He reached into his pocket, pulled out something small. When he opened his palm, he revealed a single earring shaped like a bird.

"My earring," she gasped. She picked up the earring and let it dangle between her fingers. "I thought it was lost forever. I can't believe you kept it all this time."

He cupped her cheek in his palm. "Maybe I was just waiting for the right time to give it back to you."

As he pulled her into his arms one more time, she thought back to the first night they'd met. Maybe part of her knew even then that he was the perfect man for her. Or maybe she was just very, very lucky.

Either way, she was smart enough to hold on tight to this wonderful man and never let him go.

# Epilogue

From the blog of New York gossip columnist Suzy Snark:

Faithful readers of this column have no doubt been disappointed with the lack of drama in Kitty Biedermann's life. Ever since her springtime wedding to hunky business magnate Ford Langley, her life has been dreadfully dull. But that is all about to change. Late last night, with all the theatrics one would expect from Kitty's daughter, Ilsa Marie Biedermann-Langley made her first appearance.

The tiny diva will be living at her family's full-time home in Palo Alto, California, but you can expect frequent visits to the city. After all, Kitty's new line of accessories are the must-have items of the season, once again putting Biedermann Jewelry at the top of the fashion food chain.

"Ilsa made the Suzy Snark column," Ford said, looking up from his laptop.

Kitty's head snapped up. "She did?" Her gaze narrowed. "That Suzy Snark better watch it. If she—"

"Don't worry, it's all good stuff." Still, he chuckled at his wife's fierce reaction. It was their first morning back from the hospital. He and Kitty were sitting quietly at the table, him with his laptop, her with her sketchpad. Baby Ilsa slept quietly in the bassinet they'd rolled into the kitchen. For the moment, all was peaceful and quiet. Not that it would be for long. He could already tell that Ilsa had her mother's sassy temper. Which was just the way he liked it.

* * * * *

**Gabe was a planner. But nowhere in his plans had he made allowance for an *unplanned* pregnancy. And now fatherhood was being thrust upon him.**

And he hadn't even gotten to sleep with the woman.

Not that he wanted to.

Gabe quelled a bitter smile even as his fingers curled into fists, his anger rekindled. Of course he wanted to. But that was a purely physical desire. And physical desires had nothing at all to do with reality. A woman like her did not fit into his plans.

His first priority had to be to get her to trust him. He wanted rights that only she could give him. He would use what little he knew of her to his advantage. And as she began to trust him he would find out what —or how much—she really wanted.

# THE MAGNATE'S
# PREGNANCY
# PROPOSAL

BY
SANDRA HYATT

Published in Great Britain 2011
Harlequin Mills & Boon Limited,
Eton House, 18-24 Paradise Road, Richmond, Surrey TW9 1SR

THE MAGNATE'S PREGNANCY PROPOSAL © Sandra Hyde 2010

ISBN: 978 0 263 88093 9

51-0211

Harlequin Mills & Boon policy is to use papers that are natural, renewable and recyclable products and made from wood grown in sustainable forests. The logging and manufacturing processes conform to the legal environmental regulations of the country of origin.

Printed and bound in Spain
by Litografia Rosés S.A., Barcelona

For Wendy, who read everything right from the very
beginning, and who was there with friendship
(and wine) well before then.
You make my world a better place.

After completing a business degree, travelling and then
settling into a career in marketing, **Sandra Hyatt** was
relieved to experience one of life's eureka! moments
while on maternity leave—she discovered that writing
books, although a lot slower, was just as much fun as
reading them.

She knows life doesn't always hand out happy endings
and figures that's why books ought to. She loves being
along for the journey with her characters as they work
around, over and through the obstacles standing in
their way.

Sandra has lived in both the U.S. and England and
currently lives near the coast in New Zealand with her
school sweetheart and their two children. You can visit
her at www.sandrahyatt.com.

Dear Reader,

Welcome to my second book for Desire™.

Things and people aren't always what they seem—
and that's very much the underlying idea of this book.
Chastity Stevens's situation isn't what she at first
believes it to be, and Chastity herself is not the woman
Gabe Masters thinks he knows.

Throughout the book, Chastity and Gabe are forced to
work through their issues (and their attraction), so that
by the end of the story, Gabe is the one man able to see
beneath the façade Chastity presents to the world, to the
woman she is on the inside.

The first glimmer of an idea for this story came when
I read a magazine article about a man trying to adopt
a child who was biologically, but not legally, his.
The circumstances of that case were complex (I think
a surrogate was involved), but it gave me the start I
needed—that first "what if" question, which for me is
often the beginning of a story idea.

I had a lot of fun with the setting of this story, basing
Sanctuary Island on a jewel of an island I once stayed
on as a parent helper for my daughter's school camp,
and adding some convenient alterations of my own.

I do hope you enjoy Gabe and Chastity's story. Please
e-mail me at sandra@sandrahyatt.com and let me know
what you think.

*Sandra Hyatt*

# One

The boardroom door of Masters' Developments Corporation thudded against the wall. From his seat at the head of the oval table, Gabe Masters looked up sharply to see *her* standing there. Her blue gaze sought and fixed on him. The shock of her sudden appearance registered through every cell of his body. Only years of sitting around this very table, maintaining the bland expression that served him so well in negotiations, kept him in his seat and his shock hidden.

How dare she?

Julia, his PA, appeared breathless at her side. The wildly misnamed Chastity Stevens, with her coiffed honey-blond hair, wearing a figure-hugging black suit as though she was still in mourning, managed to make his elegant PA look downright frumpy. Her perfectly shaped lips were a glossy red, as were her vertigo-inducing shoes and her small elegant bag. Her white-knuckled grip on that bag was the only indication that she wasn't utterly composed.

It was no consolation for her intrusion.

"I'm sorry." Julia shot him a look, her eyes wide. "I couldn't stop her." She reached for Chastity's arm. But with a subtle sidestep, Julia's hand was left flailing in the air.

"It's fine, Julia. I'll handle this." He nodded for his PA to leave.

The gazes of the other men at the table, which had at first flicked to him, were now all fixed on Chastity, noting the porcelain skin, the baby-doll eyes framed by long, dark eyelashes and the seductive curves accentuated by the fitted suit. Curves. He knew just how much those curves had cost. Hadn't his brother, Tom, paid for them, and kept on paying?

Till the day he died.

Gabe fought for composure, fought to keep his voice calm. It was a struggle he'd win. He always did. He stood. "I'm afraid now's not a convenient time, *Ms.*—" he put emphasis on the title "—Stevens." She had never taken Tom's name and he was glad of it. "If you'd like to follow Julia, she'll set up an appointment for you."

"Don't pretend you don't know I've been trying for weeks to make an appointment to see you. It gets old quickly, and infuriating soon after." Her frustration gave Gabe a savage sense of satisfaction. But it wasn't one he could indulge. Not here. Not now.

"I've been a little busy lately." He shared a conspiratorial smile with the men around the table, heard their muted chuckles in response. They'd all been putting in long hours negotiating the purchase terms for his next resort.

That was part of his reason, but he'd also not attached any importance to seeing the gold digger who'd driven a wedge into his family. That damage, now Tom was dead, could never be repaired.

"Excuse me one moment, gentlemen." Gabe strolled toward her. "Leave now," he said in a lethally quiet voice, "and Julia will make an appointment. You have my word." With one hand he held open the door, and with his other gestured for her to leave. She'd made enough of a scene, he needed her gone. A multimillion-dollar deal was at stake here, riding in part on his reputation. It had been difficult enough getting the other men here when so many businesses had wound down for New Zealand's traditional slow, summer month of January.

This deal needed to be signed today. He was not going to have it compromised by her.

He caught her subtle trademark scent of spring flowers—incongruously innocent. What little color had been in her cheeks leached away as she held his gaze for several thudding heartbeats. And even if he'd wanted to, he couldn't have fathomed the expressions that chased one after the other through those wide eyes. Anxiety, he would have said if he'd had to put a name to the predominant emotion. But that made no sense at all. She was the one who'd barged in on his meeting.

Finally, she turned and stepped out of the room.

Gabe nodded to Marco, his second in command, trusting him to take over, before he followed Chastity out.

"You don't seriously expect me to place any faith in your word," she said as he closed the door behind them.

"I don't have time for this. I've asked you to leave. And I meant the building, not just the boardroom." She opened her mouth to speak, but he cut her off. "If you don't, I guarantee you won't get to see me at all, won't get whatever it is you've decided you want from me." He saw her stiffen, saw the flare of delicate nostrils.

Her blue eyes filled with a steely resolve he hadn't seen before. "And if you don't see me right now," she said, "then I guarantee you won't ever get to see the child I'm carrying. Your own flesh and blood."

Gabe could only stare at her as he processed her outrageous claim.

"My office." He spoke through clenched teeth. "Three doors down on the left," he added, though she knew perfectly well where it was. After all, she'd worked here until two years ago, first briefly for him and then for Tom. Till she'd decided that becoming Tom's wife was a far more lucrative position than being his PA.

Chastity, paler than ever, paused outside his office door. Instead of going in, she glanced frantically around, then veered toward the reception area, breaking into a run as she neared it, pushing through the swinging doors and past the trio of poinsettias on the glass coffee table. His last sight of her was with one hand clamped over her mouth as she raced into the women's restroom.

He was waiting, seething, at the doorway when she reappeared a few minutes later, face still pale, but her head held high. A single damp tendril of hair clung to her jaw, the only sign anything was amiss.

She knew better than to look for any sympathy from him as she preceded him into his office. The one time he had asked anything of her—that she not stand between

Tom and his family—she had coolly denied having any influence in the matter. Gabe shut the door behind them, then leaned against it. And waited.

But now that she'd presumably gotten what she wanted, his attention, she seemed reluctant to speak. She lowered herself unsteadily onto one of the leather swivel chairs before his desk, her shapely legs pressed together and angled out to the side, one ankle tucked behind the other. She turned to him, opened her mouth, closed it again and looked toward the window. He followed her gaze. The Auckland sky was a clear, bright blue, but whitecaps dotted the distant harbor and low on the horizon, gray clouds gathered, threatening a storm that might finally break the humidity oppressing the city.

Gabe looked back at Chastity. Moisture beaded at her hairline and her hands were clenched around the armrests of the chair. He expelled a harsh sigh and strode over to the hidden bar on the far side of his office. He poured water into a glass, crossed back and held it toward her. Her gaze flicked up, not quite meeting his, before she stretched out a manicured hand and wordlessly took the glass. Gabe moved away, resumed his position at the door, arms folded against his chest.

Chastity wanted to speak, but couldn't as she fought back another surge of nausea. *Please. Not in front of him.* She'd thought she was beyond caring what he thought.

Apparently not. He was the last person on earth she wanted to humiliate herself in front of.

The Masters family, and Gabe in particular, wouldn't take her news well. He'd thought their connection with her was over. Just as she had.

For the last month she'd been agonizing over how to break the news to him. But day after day, week after week when he hadn't returned her calls, her angst had given way to frustration and then anger. Enough anger that she'd stormed in here determined to fulfill her promise to Tom before any more of the year slipped by. Unfortunately the strength the anger had given her seemed to have vanished with her last hasty trip to the bathroom. She took a sip of water then set the glass down on the edge of his desk.

Last night, before her bedroom mirror, she had rehearsed what she planned to say. She'd thought she had it down pat. Brief, informative and above all emotionless, like the man standing in front of her. And yet here she was, in the understated luxury of his enormous office, unable to get even the first word out.

"What do you want? And make it quick." So, maybe he wasn't emotionless. He despised her. It infused every word he uttered. "I have a meeting to get back to."

She forced herself to speak calmly. "If you'd seen me when I asked, I wouldn't have had to do this."

"And what is *this* precisely?"

She'd known it wouldn't be easy, but she'd forgotten the sheer potency of six foot two of angry man. Chastity drew in a deep breath. "I'm trying to do the right thing." Finally, she looked up and met a gaze as dark as bitter coffee. So similar and yet worlds apart from Tom's.

"As much as that would make a refreshing change, I find it *very* hard to believe."

She couldn't entirely blame Gabe for his cynicism. Tom had used her as an excuse for all but severing contact with his family, initially without her knowledge. And then once she found out, she hadn't protested, she had cared only that her presence gave Tom the space he had said he needed. The fact that the distance suited her, too, was an added benefit.

She looked at Gabe, the high-achieving golden boy of the family. All she had to do was give him her news and then leave. "I'm pregnant." The quiet words fell from her lips.

Before she could continue with her carefully planned explanation of the circumstances, Gabe's gaze dropped to her almost flat abdomen, the slight thickening of her waist concealed by her jacket, and then tracked back up. "Now *that* I can believe."

And just like that, the sustaining anger was back. His brother had been dead for three months, and Gabe was implying that she'd slept with another man. Without conscious thought she launched herself from her chair and drew back her arm. His callous insinuation had brought flooding back the humiliation she had thought she'd left behind her years ago.

Gabe's stance changed, ready, eager to intercept her blow. She didn't know what she'd intended, but as her glare locked on his, she caught herself, lowered her arm and sat back down. She wouldn't give him the satisfaction of having her thrown out and bringing assault charges.

And she couldn't afford to indulge her own satisfaction in having at least tried to wipe the smug superiority from his face.

For long seconds a tension-filled silence electrified the air between them.

"How in the hell do you think you're going to convince anyone that a child of yours has anything to do with me or my family?" He paused, his features sharpened, the panther about to strike a lethal blow. "Tom was sterile."

Chastity stood. She didn't have to take this. She'd told him she was pregnant, like she'd promised. It wasn't her problem that Gabe chose not to believe her. "If you'll step aside, please, I need to leave." She walked toward the door, toward Gabe, who remained unmoving. In a few moments she'd be gone, giving them both what they wanted. If only he'd move. Finally she was one step away from him. Contempt burned in his eyes.

Slowly, he shook his head. "I thought you'd sunk as low as you could go. Clearly I overestimated you." He opened the door wide.

Her nails dug into her palms. She'd made her choices in life and she stood by them. He had no right to judge her. She stepped past him, fixed her gaze on the elevator doors beyond the reception area, and, ignoring the blatantly curious look of the receptionist, headed straight for them.

It wasn't till she stood waiting for the car to reach the top floor that she became aware of someone behind her. She glanced over her shoulder. Gabe stood there, arms folded across his chest, feet planted apart like a bouncer at a night club. He was seeing her off the premises.

The elevator pinged, the doors slid open. Chastity stepped in and turned to face him. Granite Man, Tom had sometimes called his older brother. It wasn't hard to see why. But against her will, she also remembered a time when she'd first worked here, when he had at least always been fair.

But most importantly, she reminded herself, there were

two parts to her promise to Tom and she'd only fulfilled the first. She had vowed to tell Gabe not only that she was pregnant, but also how the baby had been conceived. If she didn't do it now she'd only have to come back.

As the doors started to close, Gabe lowered his arms and turned away. Chastity sucked in a deep breath, put out her hand and the doors stopped. Gabe swung back. "What—"

"Things aren't always what they seem, Gabe. And the world won't always fall into place according to your rigid rules." She held his stony expression. Tension arced between them. "Before he died, Tom and I tried IVF." She spoke quickly, just needing to get the words out. "We used the sperm he banked before his radiation therapy." She lowered her hand, and as the doors closed between them, she had the grim satisfaction of seeing Gabe Masters's smooth, chiseled jaw drop open.

# Two

At the ground floor, Chastity stepped out into the building's light-filled atrium and, taking deliberately slow, deep breaths, tried to admire the fountain she'd once found both beautiful and soothing. She stared at the glistening play of water, but in her mind's eye could see only a pair of dark, accusing eyes. It would take more than a fountain to erase that image. She should feel relief that she'd kept her promise to Tom. She could now move on. Instead, she felt only a chilly foreboding.

"Explain it to me again." The deep voice, so close, startled a gasp out of her. She whirled to face Gabe, his gaze deadly serious. He stood between her and the exit.

The hope that fulfilling Tom's wishes meant this was over had been futile. Even hoping for a few days to fortify herself after this afternoon's confrontation had been pointless. Of course he would want more. And he'd want it now. But still she tried to delay the in-evitable. "Don't you have a meeting to get back to?"

A muscle jumped in the smooth line of his jaw. "Marco's taken over now. He can handle things for another five minutes." He glanced at his watch before looking back at her, waiting for her response.

"I've said all I need to. We can go back to dealing through our respective lawyers. Just like we have since Tom's death." She stepped around him, focusing on the revolving doors of the exit, on the freedom of the world outside. And yet she knew this would be different.

Death was an end. A baby was a beginning.

Within seconds he was beside her, his long, easy stride effortlessly keeping pace with her hurried steps. They entered a section on the revolving door and she had to slow down to follow its ponderous progression. "I'd like you to explain it properly." Gabe spoke calmly, quietly, but Chastity heard the note of urgency that lay just beneath the surface, felt the tension radi-ating from him.

Together they stepped into the stifling heat. She knew enough about Gabe to understand that if there was something he really wanted, he allowed nothing to stand in his way.

"There's a bench in the park across the road." He made the remark both a suggestion and a command. Chastity considered her options. Her car was only a block away. She didn't have to do this. The afternoon had been harrowing enough as it was. All she wanted was to go home, get out of the confining suit and the tor-turous shoes and go for a walk, a very long walk, along the beach. She opened her mouth to refuse him.

"Please?" He spoke before she could, his tone quiet and reasonable.

It wasn't a word that would come easily to him, at least not when addressed to her. "All right. Five minutes." She could hold herself together for that long.

She paused when they got to the park bench over-hung by the branches of an oak tree. Gabe looked at her, then sat first as if conscious that the way he towered over her made her uneasy.

Chastity lowered herself beside him, keeping a careful distance. She drew in a deep, deliberate breath. He still used the same cologne he had when she'd worked for him, a scent that somehow seemed uniquely his, one that in her mind she equated with utter, im-movable, unreasoning strength. It wasn't the scent of a brick wall, but it might as well have been.

She undid the two buttons of her suit jacket. The suit had been fine for his air-conditioned offices; it defi-nitely wasn't ideal for midafternoon heat and humidity, despite the shade of the oak. Dropping her hands to her sides, she ran her palms along the wooden planks of the bench. "I used to sit here sometimes when I worked for you and Tom."

"I know."

She glanced sharply at him, then looked away, watched a team of gardeners weeding a distant flower bed. It made sense. Acutely observant, he was one of those men who seemed to know at all times what was going on with everyone.

"Explain your pregnancy again." Gabe clearly didn't need or want small talk or preliminaries.

It was probably for the best. She could deal in facts

and keep the emotion out of it. He'd angled himself toward her, one elbow resting on the seat back in what she recognized as a deliberate posture of openness. Chastity folded her arms across her chest and watched the gardeners. The sound of their easy laughter carried to her. Their lives surely weren't as carefree as she wanted to believe, but she envied them even the imagined simplicity.

"Tom knew the risk of sterility was high, so before he had his treatment he banked some sperm." Clinical, but she had to be, she couldn't let herself pause or stumble. "Surely you knew that?" Tom's illness had happened several years before she met him. And it was, according to Tom, when he'd still been on good terms with his family and in particular his brother.

Gabe nodded. And waited.

From the corner of her eye, she saw his hands clench into fists. "Several months ago we decided we'd try for a child."

"You went back to the original clinic?"

"Yes. My pregnancy was confirmed a week before Tom's accident."

"He knew?" Gabe's voice was quiet.

She looked up and met the espresso-brown of his gaze, saw the lines that furrowed his brow. Chastity nodded and those lines deepened.

Gabe stood and took a few steps along the path. He lifted a hand to the back of his neck and she heard his muttered curse. She'd never seen Gabe anything other than utterly calm. Never seen him betray that he was as rattled as he clearly was now.

Beyond him tree branches swayed in a gathering

wind that did little to ease the humid oppression of the afternoon. Distant blue-black clouds continued to build on the horizon, threatening, promising, a thunderstorm. A trickle of perspiration ran down between her breasts.

She studied Gabe's back, noted the broad shoulders and the fisted hands now shoved into the pockets of his dark pants. After what felt like an eternity, he turned and walked back to her. His skin had paled and anger and frustration burned in his eyes.

"Thanks to you, Tom all but cut himself off from the family since the day you moved in with him. Why are you telling me this now?"

"Because he asked me to. As soon as the pregnancy was viable, he made me promise that if anything happened to him that I'd tell you about the child, and specifically about how it was conceived." She had agreed only because Tom was finally in excellent health. But excellent health had provided no defense against a rain-slicked road, a sweeping bend and a power pole.

"And what is it you think you want from me?"

"I don't want anything from you. Things can go on just as they have been."

He shook his head. "That's not going to be possible."

"Why on earth not?"

"Because if you're telling the truth, you're carrying a Masters child. And we look after our own."

Chastity stared at him, willing the breath back into lungs that felt like they no longer functioned properly. "*If* I'm telling the truth?"

Gabe lifted one nonchalant shoulder. "You have to admit there are other possibilities."

Chastity stood and started walking. She didn't care where, as long as it was away from him.

She sensed him beside her. "Go away."

"I need the truth."

"As if you'd believe the truth. You only ever believe what you want to hear, see what you want to see."

He kept pace with her.

Unable to shake him off, Chastity stopped and whirled to face him. "All right. The truth is I was never faithful to Tom and I certainly haven't been faithful to his memory. I have no idea who the real father of my baby is, it could be one of dozens of men, so I thought I'd try to convince you it was Tom's, because I'd so like your family's continued involvement in my life. Obviously you're not that easy to fool, so I give up, and now you can go. You won't hear from me again." Her eyes welled with indignant tears and her breath came in shaky gasps.

Gabe didn't move. And neither would she.

He closed his eyes for a moment, opened them again. "I'm sorry if my question hurt you."

His apology was even less expected than his accusation. Gabe Masters never backed down.

Chastity stood frozen.

"We need to talk." With an open palm, he gestured back toward the bench. "Would you rather sit or walk?"

Neither option appealed. As far as she was concerned, she'd kept her promise to Tom. So she should be free of Gabe. "We don't need to talk."

Those searching brown eyes held her immobile. "I need to know what you want, what you're thinking."

"I told you already. All I wanted was to let you

know…the situation. Like Tom asked me. If you or your family want to see the child sometimes as he or she is growing up, we'll work something out."

"My parents will want more than occasional visits at Christmas and birthdays." He paused, then added quietly, "And so will I."

"Really?" She made no effort to hide her surprise or her own cynicism. His family's demands for perfection were what had driven Tom to draw a veil between them and, according to Tom, were what had turned Gabe into a workaholic perfectionist, always striving for bigger and better deals. She'd thought, hoped, they'd be content to carry on pretending she—and by default her child—didn't exist.

"Yes." His conviction was absolute.

A long silence fell before he spoke again. "How are you placed for raising a child?" His gaze swept over her.

"I don't need money, if that's what you're asking." Though quite probably he was questioning whether she had the necessary standards to raise a Masters child rather than the necessary funds.

He nodded once and she wished she knew what was going on behind his serious assessment, because the only thing she could be certain of was that *something* was going on. His brows drew together the way they did when he was working on a problem. And it filled her with foreboding. Gabe Masters didn't make rash decisions. He pondered problems in private and when he'd reached a conclusion, he implemented it. It didn't make him a good team player, but it had made him a phenomenally successful businessman. That, along with a talent for surrounding himself with equally capable and astute colleagues. Most of whom *were* good team players.

Out of nowhere another wave of heat and nausea roiled through her. She looked frantically around but they weren't near the park bathrooms.

Cool hands suddenly framed her face. "Breathe," he instructed, calm and sure. His eyes held hers, calm and sure. With gazes locked, she breathed, slow and controlled, and gradually the nausea, the heat, subsided as though he'd willed it.

"I'm fine now…thanks."

He lowered his hands. She still felt the imprint of his touch, of each long finger against her skin.

She took a small step back. Oh, the indignity of it all. "They call it *morning* sickness. Unfortunately my stomach appears to be synchronized for morning in any number of time zones."

"It's been bad?" He sounded almost concerned.

"Not really. It occasionally ambushes me. It's worse if I'm tired or stressed." Both of which she'd been lately and both because of the prospect of facing Gabe. Now at least that was over. "Look, Gabe. I really need to go. You've had your five minutes."

He glanced at his watch, his frown deepening. "I'll drive you home."

"No." She wanted Gabe seeing and knowing as little as possible about her life. She had her space carved out and it was a comfortable, safe space. It was hers and she got to say who came into it. That list of people was a short one. And Gabe Masters definitely wasn't on it.

"I *am* walking you to your car."

She shrugged. "I don't suppose I can stop you?"

He shook his head. "Not until I'm certain you're okay. And given how pale you are, that's not yet."

They walked in silence. Outside his building he stopped long enough to buy a bottle of ginger ale from a vending machine. "It's good for nausea," he said as he opened it and passed it to her.

Chastity took a grateful sip of the cold beverage, sliding a wary glance in his direction. She didn't quite know how to react to a Gabe who was being…considerate.

She stopped at the small, blue, four-wheel-drive Toyota and beeped it unlocked. Even her car was more of an insight into her life than she wanted Gabe to have.

"What happened to the Mercedes coupe?"

She lifted her chin a fraction. "I traded it."

He clamped his lips together. Ahh, there it was, the familiar cynicism, the slow burn in his dark eyes. As though she had pocketed the cash difference for some nefarious purpose, perhaps a gambling addiction or a drug habit. Chastity showed no reaction. She would be impervious. But it hurt, it always did, no matter how much she pretended to the world, or herself, that it didn't. But that pretense was her only defense. Her armor.

Gabe opened her door for her, closed it as she fastened her seat belt. Finally, with the prospect of escape so close, her tension started to ease. She rolled down her window. His assessing eyes remained steady on her as though searching for something. She turned the key and the engine rumbled into life.

Grim determination settled over the already harsh planes and angles of Gabe's face. His brows drew together. His problem-solving face again. He leaned down, rested his hands on the window frame. "This is not going to work the way you thought it would."

# Three

Gabe was only mildly surprised when the doorman called to say he had a visitor, a Ms. Stevens.

After watching Chastity drive away, he had gone back to the negotiation, by which time it was all but signed, and he had let Marco continue to run the show. He'd sat in the room, pretending nothing was out of the ordinary, even commenting a couple of times, nudging things in the right direction when needed. But he was dialing it in.

His thoughts were with her.

With her baby.

With his brother.

As soon as possible after the deal was closed, he'd left. He'd needed time to think, something he did best on his own. So he'd gone to his gym to swim and run and sweat his way through his options till finally he narrowed them down to one.

Then he'd come back to his apartment. It had been little more than an hour since he'd phoned her. He'd known the message he left on her voice mail would get a reaction. He glanced at his watch. He just hadn't expected it to be quite this swift. She hadn't taken any time to consider his offer. He'd purposely phoned late, hoping that she would at least sleep on it and preferably take the weekend before she reacted.

What did surprise him, as he carried his Scotch to the elevator to wait for her ascent, was the curious mix of emotions her pending arrival stirred. The anger and frustration he was used to; it was the charged anticipation that was new. The kind of anticipation he used to feel before going into a negotiation or pulling together a major deal.

It had to be the blond bombshell's bombshell.

In less than a day his carefully ordered life had broken up like a jigsaw puzzle thrown against a wall and he was still determining how best to reassemble it.

He couldn't believe what Tom had done. How he had deceived him. His relationship with his brother, though good in their younger years, had been strained of late. Part of that strain was due to the woman he currently stood waiting for, and the impact she'd had on his family. But if he was honest, there was more to it than just that. Whatever it was, it was far too late to rectify. Tom was gone and he wouldn't be coming back. Ever.

And now there was the child his dead brother's wife was carrying. A complication he would never have foreseen and could still scarcely accept.

On cue the elevator doors slid open. Chastity's blue eyes widened, her chest beneath the white silk of her blouse rose and fell along with her audible intake of breath. She really wasn't any good at hiding her emotions—those eyes were far too expressive.

She was stunningly beautiful. His first sight of her years ago had been like a blow to the solar plexus. It was a reaction he'd learned to manage. He liked a little more substance in his women, something beneath the glossy exterior.

This evening she wore a sleek, black, tailored pantsuit with perilously high-heeled shoes, her face flawlessly made up. Had she been out since he'd last seen her, with someone else? Another man? The thought twisted his insides. Despite the aspersions he'd cast on her character earlier, he didn't really want her to live down to them.

"You're looking lovely." He knew she'd hate the blasé compliment, but there'd always been something about her that made him want to upset her composure. "I didn't expect to see you so soon."

"If you'd left me your phone number along with that obscenely ridiculous message, I would have called and saved us both this inconvenience."

She was still so cool, so remote. He'd always sensed there was more going on under the veneer than she allowed the world to see. In that one way they were perhaps similar. "I'll give it to you now," he said, matching her detachment.

"I'm not expecting to need it ever again." Along with the coolness, the steel he'd witnessed in her this afternoon in his boardroom was there again. "Tell me," she continued, "that the *solution* you suggested I consider was just a sick—" her gaze dipped to the Scotch in his hands "—alcohol-fueled joke."

She searched his face and he let her see just how serious he was before he spoke. "I've just poured this. And I don't joke."

"I don't see how it could be anything other. The very idea of you with any baby at all is ludicrous. But to suggest that you—*you*—adopt mine…" She shook her head in disbelief.

He'd been planning to offer money, enough to keep her in luxury for the rest of her life, wondering if despite her earlier assertion, that was what she was truly after. But her vehemence, the righteous anger sparking in her eyes, was more warning than he needed that that offer, at least right now, would be the wrong one to make. Instead he took issue with her use of the word *mine*. "It's not just yours. It takes two to make a baby."

"And this child's father is dead."

Tom. If he were still alive, Gabe might well have throttled him for this stunt. When he didn't say anything further she drew herself up and squared her shoulders.

"You may think—" she jabbed a manicured finger at his chest "—that because you're a Masters, because you were brought up with privilege and you've got money and power, you can do whatever you want. That you can look down your nose at me and push me around till I fall in with your plans." She jabbed again. "Well, I've got news for you, buster. All the money and power in the world doesn't change the fact that this baby is now mine and mine alone."

He caught her surprisingly fragile wrist and drew the jabbing finger away from his chest. His action silenced her words and for a fraction of time they stood there, facing off, inches apart, her hand trapped by his. "It's not money and power that change that fact," he said quietly.

She twisted her hand from his grip. The expression on her pale face tilted up toward him managed to be both mutinous and wary. "What are you talking about?"

Unexpected sympathy for her welled. From this point on, everything she thought she knew would change irrevocably. He probably should have played this differently, prepared her better for what was to come. But then there really was no way to prepare her for it. "Why don't you come in and sit down?" For the first time that he could remember, he was stalling and he wasn't sure whether it was for her sake or his own.

The course of his life was about to change, too. It was up to him to control it.

"No."

He raised an eyebrow. It was a look that had quailed more than one man before.

It had no discernable effect on Chastity. "We have nothing to discuss. I'm only here because I needed you to be very, very clear on that point. And now that I've made it, I expect any and all future communication to be between our lawyers."

Gabe felt a flare of purely objective admiration at her strength and clarity and at the sparks of passion that lit her eyes. A reluctant smile tugged at one corner of his lips. "Tom should have had you as a member of his negotiating team."

"If I need a reference, I'll know where to come." She pivoted on her very high heel.

He'd broken another rule in getting sidetracked from the point at hand. "Wait." She paused at his command, tension in the straight line of her spine, but didn't turn back. "There's something you need to know. Something Tom would want you to know." He tried to make his voice conciliatory.

After several seconds she slowly turned, her gaze wary.

"It's not news you're going to enjoy." That surely qualified as the understatement of the year.

The first fat drops of rain hit the window in his living room. Gabe turned and walked across the marble-tiled entranceway, stepping down into the sunken living room and crossing to stand in front of the floor-to-ceiling window. The raindrops on the glass refracted the light, making the city blur and shimmer in the night. When the full enormity of her—their—situation had first crashed down on him it had stolen the breath from his lungs. An alien and ungovernable tension still hummed within him.

He turned back to see Chastity hesitating at the edge of the tiles, unsure whether to take the next step, or, judging by the way her wide eyes darted from side to side, whether she should run.

"You're here. You may as well listen to what I need to tell you. Besides," he explained as he gestured to the window and the rain that now lashed it, "you don't want to be out driving in that."

If he knew anything about her at all, she probably considered the storm preferable to time with him, but she lifted her chin and took three small steps closer. "What is it you think I need to know?" she asked, skeptical, almost accusatory.

Gabe turned back to the window. He watched her reflection in the glass, saw the defiance in her stance, in the arms folded across her chest as though that could protect her from what he had to say. He met her gaze in the reflection, spoke just loudly enough that he knew she would hear. "The sperm Tom deposited before his radiation therapy was destroyed, by fire, along with almost the entire clinic."

"No." The word was clipped and adamant. She shook her head, her blond hair brushing over her shoulders. "I don't know what game you're playing. Tom and I went back to that very clinic."

"They replaced the clinic. They couldn't replace the… stock."

"No." She was still furiously shaking her head. "Tom told me it was his. 'True blue Masters stock,' he said. He wouldn't lie."

Droplets of water ran down the windowpane like so many tears. "That much is true," Gabe said quietly and saw her confusion.

A flash of lightning split the sky and for a second illuminated the city. "You're contradicting yourself." She spoke quickly, her voice high and tight, discomposed at last and yet he found no satisfaction in it. "You can't even keep your own story straight—a sure sign of lying."

He turned, held her gaze. "I'm not contradicting myself. Tom was only twenty when his sperm was destroyed. He was still recovering physically and emotionally from the cancer and he was devastated." He shrugged. "I wanted to help him. We came up with a solution of sorts." Gabe saw panic building in her eyes. He took a deep breath. "The child you're carrying *is* a Masters. But it's not Tom's child. It's mine."

Chastity didn't know how she did it, but she made it to his couch and sank onto it. "No." She spoke the word quietly this time. Gabe offered no contradiction as he watched her warily, probably wondering whether the cream leather was safe from her rebellious stomach. But there was no nausea, only numb disbelief.

She thought back to her visits to the clinic, to how Tom had been so protective of her, filling in all the forms they needed so all she had to do was sign her name where he had showed her to. And how he had insisted that, should anything happen to him, Gabe know how the child was conceived.

The ultimate deception.

She dropped her head into her hands. And now she was the one paying the price, carrying the child of a man who despised her, who clearly didn't want her as his child's mother. But who did want her child.

She looked up to see that Gabe had turned back to the rain-lashed window and stood motionless in front of it. His hair was slightly disheveled as though he'd run his hands through it more than once.

He didn't joke. He'd said it himself. So hysterical laughter, which would undoubtedly turn into hysterical tears, would be entirely inappropriate. Chastity pushed herself to her feet. Home. She needed to go home. Maybe she'd go to sleep and wake to find this had been just a nightmare.

Her legs were a little unsteady beneath her, but at least the thick carpet muffled her steps. She'd be able to slip out unnoticed. Fixing her gaze on the exit, she took another step. Sudden heat suffused her and the room tilted and started to spin…and then her legs were scooped out from beneath her and she was floating. Disoriented, she pressed her face into the shoulder she was cradled against and for a moment caught that scent of strength and had the fleeting sensation this was indeed all a dream and that everything would be all right.

The sensation passed as she was set back down precisely where she'd been a few seconds ago. The only difference being that now Gabe was at her side and gently guiding her head down between her knees. She lowered her head and tried to breathe calmly, deeply. Thank goodness she was wearing pants rather than a skirt. And now she really did want to laugh. Of all the irrelevant thoughts to have.

Feeling steadier she pushed against the resistance of Gabe's hand and sat up. The hand slid lower, lingered between her shoulder blades and then withdrew altogether.

"Can I get you something to eat or drink?"

"No. I'm fine now, thanks." She tried again to stand. Only to find she didn't even make it to her feet before he grasped her hand and pulled her unceremoniously and, she suspected, effortlessly back down.

"Sit." His tone brooked no argument.

"I'm fine." She tried to inject more conviction into her voice. "Honestly. And I really, really, need to go home."

His grip on her hand stayed firm. "You're not going anywhere yet." He spoke almost kindly, as though it was a fact he regretted as much as he knew she would. "There's a storm outside, you're pregnant, you've had a shock and you just fainted."

There was only one of those four facts that she could even begin to argue with. "I didn't faint."

"If I hadn't caught you, you would have hit the ground."

She'd known it was a weak argument to begin with,

but that didn't make her happy about it. "I've never fainted before."

"Ever been pregnant before?"

"No," she said on a sigh and sagged into the couch. She'd thought she had everything so well sorted out. Well, at least as much as was possible in the circumstances. She was grieving for Tom, but she was financially secure, she had her own house, and if she ever needed anything more—for the baby—she had the shares and other assets she'd inherited when Tom died. An inheritance she'd not even assessed properly yet. But she knew, because Tom's lawyer had told her, that it was substantial.

Finally, Gabe released her hand. "I know how much of a shock this is for you."

She slid her hand in close to her side, away from his touch. "I guess I do." It was probably the only thing about her he really could understand.

Gabe's baby. She was carrying Gabe's baby. Two people who had nothing in common, who wanted nothing to do with each other, were now inextricably bound.

Gabe eased back, as well, and with a barely audible sigh tipped his head back and closed his eyes. Chastity took the opportunity to look at the man who had just turned her world upside down. He shared some of Tom's features, but on Gabe the strong jaw, the dark, straight eyebrows and the liquid brown eyes were somehow different enough to make what on Tom had been charming good looks seem harsher and uncompromising.

Not wanting to get caught studying him, she looked away and surveyed his apartment instead. It was a distraction technique, she knew, but it beat dealing with her current reality. She'd never been here before. Social calls between the two brothers had ended when she had moved in with Tom.

Here again there were similarities and differences with Tom. Both men had a taste for quality but Gabe's was less showy, more masculine. And here at least a person wouldn't have to worry about accidentally knocking over a priceless glass sculpture. Gabe's couch, though cream-colored leather, was deep and soft, the sort you could curl up on with a good book. She thought of her own largely unfurnished home, where she needed to get going to.

"Stay here the night," he said, as if reading her thoughts. And though his words were quiet, they held an implacable ring. He wasn't asking or suggesting. "I have a guest room. Everything's made up."

"No." It seemed to be all she was saying tonight.

"Why not?"

"I can't. I don't want to. And…it wouldn't be right."

"Right?"

"To stay here. In your apartment."

"What are you worried will happen?"

"Nothing. Trust me, I know that. I just don't belong here." *In the home of a man who thinks so little of me.* "I want to go back to my own home." *And bury my head under my blankets to shut the world out.*

"You don't belong out there, either." He gestured to the window as another bolt of lightning split the sky. "At least lie down for a little. You're paler than the couch. Then, when the storm passes, I'll take you home."

She didn't want to admit that he was right, but though she was sometimes stubborn she was generally sensible. "All right. Just for a while," she finally conceded.

He stood and held his hand toward her, but she ignored it as she pushed herself off the couch. She wouldn't let herself need him in any way. It was bad enough that she was giving in to his insistence that she stay. She caught the single raised eyebrow before he turned and motioned for her to precede him in the direction of what had to be the apartment's bedrooms. He kept close, within touching—or catching—distance, as they walked.

"In here." He pushed open a door on their right and Chastity caught her gasp before it escaped her throat. A four-poster bed, piled high with pillows and draped in a lacy white coverlet, dominated the room. To one side sat an old-fashioned armchair and in front of it in the center of a small table, stood a vase overflowing with pale pink tulips. Soft drapes hung at the window.

She walked in and ran her fingers down the closest of the bed's carved wooden posts. It was the kind of room and bed she'd imagined when she'd read fairy tales about princesses late at night in the damp, draughty room she'd shared with her half sisters. Back when her sisters had bothered sleeping at home.

She turned to find Gabe still standing at the entrance, studying her, his expression inscrutable.

"Bathroom's through there." He tilted his head in the direction of an adjoining doorway.

"Thanks." She stepped out of her shoes, and sat on, or rather sank into, the bed. "Am I supposed to be able to feel a pea under this mattress?"

He smiled—actually smiled—straight white teeth showed, the brown eyes crinkled and softened. "It's a little over the top, I know, but I told the decorator this was the one room she could do what she wanted with. It's the only one I never use myself." His smile faded.

"Get some rest. I'll wait up." Was that sympathy, kindness, she heard in his gentler tone?

She considered telling him not to wait up, to get some sleep himself, but that would be like saying she intended to spend the night here. She dropped her gaze to her toes and wriggled them experimentally. At least the shoes hadn't killed them. "Thanks."

She heard the soft click of the door closing.

Reducing the mountain of pillows on her side to one, she stretched out on the bed and closed her eyes. But instead of sinking into the blissful sleep the bed promised, she was assaulted by the recollection of Gabe's information and the implications that would surely have.

Her baby was his baby.

He was her child's father.

And she knew he spoke the absolute truth when he said that visits at Christmas and birthdays were never going to be enough.

Chastity shouldn't have been surprised when sunlight on her face woke her. She'd known she was tired, had known she would sleep—eventually. During the night she had taken off everything but her underwear and slipped between the sheets.

She lay for a moment savoring the big bed, the crisp cotton and the billowy canopy above her. But it was Gabe's bed, even if it was a guest bedroom, and she couldn't help but feel exposed and vulnerable to him here. She rested her hands over the gentle swell of her abdomen. Gabe's bed. Gabe's baby. It was all so very wrong.

She showered quickly, taking just a moment to be impressed by the array of luxury toiletries provided, and had no option but to get dressed in the pantsuit she'd worn last night.

Gabe stood facing the window as she stepped into the living room. Beyond him, sunlight shone on the high-rises of the city and in the distance the harbor sparkled. No trace of last night's storm. He turned. He, too, wore the same clothes as last night. Tiredness lined his face and his dark hair was tousled. A rumpled throw lay on the couch.

"I'm sorry. I slept right through."

He shrugged. "I'd hoped you would."

She didn't quite know how to deal with a Gabe who still sounded concerned for her. It was oddly comforting when really she knew it should make her suspicious. "I thought the pea would keep me awake, but I guess they don't make them like they used to. Or maybe they just make the mattresses better."

His smile was a shadow of the one she'd seen the previous evening.

"And last night, it wasn't just a bad dream, what you told me?"

He shook his head as he walked toward her. No such luck. More like a waking nightmare.

What was he planning? What did he really want? She hadn't forgotten his suggestion that he adopt. He had to have known she wouldn't accept that, but he would likely have a fallback position already planned. Her best move was to get away from here, and him, as quickly as possible.

"By the way," he started quietly.

"Gabe?" The high, cultured voice emanated from the direction of what she guessed to be the kitchen, and filled

Chastity with dread. As if she'd needed another reason to get gone. "I'm sure I left the silver cake knife here after you hosted that soiree before the opera."

"My mother's here," he finished, stating the obvious.

"I'll go." She started to turn, but he grasped her wrist.

"Running won't achieve anything."

She looked up into those serious eyes. "What about hiding? I could survive in that guest room for days. You could slip food under the door."

He shook his head, one side of his mouth tilting up, surprised amusement in his eyes. "Won't achieve anything, either."

"Yes, it will," she hissed. "It'll mean I won't have to face your mother."

"She's going to find out sooner or later. And in my experience sooner is generally better. Everyone can move forward."

"Well, in my experience later, much later, is better. It delays the shouting, the accusations, the pain."

He searched her gaze and then abruptly looked past her.

"Gabe. Why didn't you tell me you had a visitor?" Cynthia's voice carried that falsely bright note that Chastity dreaded.

She turned slowly and watched the older woman's eyes first widen in surprise and then narrow on her. "Good morning, Cynthia." Chastity kept her own voice as even as she could.

"You." Cynthia's gaze dropped to where Gabe's clasp had slid down Chastity's wrist to wrap around her hand. "Gabriel. What's going on?"

Chastity tried to free her hand, but he held firm. He probably thought she'd still try to run.

He'd be right.

"Chastity and I needed to talk last night. She stayed because it got late and because of the storm."

"What could you possibly have to say to that woman?"

Chastity looked at Gabe, imploring him not to tell his mother. Not yet at least. Not while they were in the same room together, preferably not while they were on the same planet.

He gave the smallest nod of his head before turning back to his mother. "Her name's Chastity." His defense surprised her, partly because she was fairly certain that everyone in the family, apart from Tom, referred to her as "that woman."

"My friends call me Chass." She fired one of Cynthia's bright fake smiles back at her, half expecting to hear an angry hissing noise in response. Cynthia, of course, was far too well-bred to make any such noise. But her lips did tighten into an impressively thin line.

"And what is it you needed to talk about?"

Chastity held her breath. After far too long a pause Gabe said calmly, "It was a private conversation."

She squeezed his hand in thanks. He squeezed back before releasing her fingers from his clasp.

Chastity seized her opportunity. "Anyway, I'd like to say it's been lovely seeing you again, Cynthia, but I don't suppose that's been true for either of us. And now I have to go or I'll be late for my…thing that I don't want to be late for." She didn't run, she didn't even walk fast as she made her way to the elevator—but that didn't mean she didn't want to.

A masculine hand reached in front of her to cover the call button. "Can I persuade you to stay and have some breakfast first?" he asked gently.

"I think you know the answer to that one. It goes something along the lines of, *not in a million years.*"

He pressed the button for her. "She has another side."

"I'm sure she does."

The doors slid open. Chastity stepped in and turned around. Gabe was studying her, a frown creasing his brow. He tossed something toward her. Reflexively, she caught it. She turned the glossy red apple in her hands. "One bite, deary," she said in a frail, wheedling voice, "and all your dreams will come true."

She looked up to see the raised eyebrow. Oops. "Thanks."

"I'll be in touch."

"I suppose you will."

Making good on his promise, Gabe stood waiting for her in the shadows of a liquidambar tree as she stepped out of the glass-fronted office block where she now worked and into the midday sun. Stunning. Not a hair on her head was out of place. Her lips were the color of ripe plums. A soft cream-colored blouse crossed over her front, revealing a pale vee of skin before hugging her waist. A black skirt clung to her hips, the subtly rounded abdomen, and skimmed her knees. Shapely calves. Slender ankles. Killer heels. And toenails the exact shade of her lipstick.

She was an island of fresh, untouchable beauty in a sea of harried office workers jostling and rushing to make the most of their lunch breaks. Just as he had that morning a week ago in his apartment, he felt the urge to stand between her and the world, or as the case had been then, her and his mother.

Even though she was more than capable of protecting her own interests. Hadn't she proved it with Tom? Find a rich man, marry him and all your problems are solved. She was also astute and intelligent. He'd seen evidence of that in the brief time she'd worked for him.

Before he'd transferred her to Tom's department because of his attraction to her. An attraction that he wouldn't allow himself to have for someone who worked for him. He'd sensed, too, that it was reciprocated.

Or so he'd thought. But after scarcely two months as Tom's PA, they had come back from a business trip to Las Vegas and announced their engagement.

His mother placed the blame for the haste squarely at Chastity's feet.

Gabe had hidden his own quiet fury—at Chastity, at Tom, but mostly at himself. When the fury ebbed, he was able to congratulate himself on his lucky escape.

Their engagement had stretched on for eighteen months, not a day passing that Gabe didn't hope his brother would see that Chastity wasn't right for him and call it off. But then one Monday, as Tom sauntered by his desk at work, he'd thrown out the cocky aside that he and Chastity had gotten married on the weekend.

She caught sight of him now and he schooled his face into a neutral expression. He sensed rather than saw her hesitation. For a moment he thought she might turn. She didn't. Her step slowed as she approached him. Beneath her flawless makeup and the impossibly long eyelashes, he detected a hint of tiredness about her eyes.

Was it her pregnancy that did that, or was it specifically the news that it was his child she carried? News that had seen him, too, losing sleep.

Gabe was a planner. Yearly, five-yearly, longer term. Backup strategies for if things didn't go as he visualized. He set goals. He achieved them. But nowhere in his plans had he made allowance for an *unplanned* pregnancy. He was always careful. Always. And now fatherhood was being thrust upon him.

And he hadn't even gotten to sleep with the woman.

Not that he wanted to.

Gabe quelled a bitter smile even as his fingers curled into fists, his anger rekindled. Of course he wanted to. But that was a purely physical desire. And physical desires had nothing at all to do with reality, or what was good for him. Or even what was right. A woman like her did not fit into his plans.

Except she had to now. He had to find a way forward.

Chastity didn't look at him, just kept heading down Queen Street, eyes straight ahead. The strange harmony of a week ago, those hours when they had been almost united by their common shock, had gone. He fell into step beside her.

His first priority had to be to get her to trust him. He wanted rights that only she could give him. Today would be the first step in that direction. He would use what little he knew of her to his advantage. And as she began to trust him, he would find out what—or how much—she really wanted.

"You're lunching alone?" His gaze slid over her again as he looked for answers. He only found more questions. Questions he didn't like. Was this woman who carried his child dressed to impress someone at work? He felt the razor-sharp slice of unexpected jealousy. Caused only, he told himself, by the very fact that it was his child she carried.

She said nothing.

He wanted to get under her skin the way she so effortlessly got under his. "Not meeting a rich, smitten client?" So much for his first priority. Instead of building trust he was antagonizing her, responding to an almost schoolboy urge to rile her and ruffle that flawless perfection.

She flicked a glance at him then looked away and quickened her stride, her heels tapping out her frustration at his presence. "If you're done insulting me, you can go." In the instant before her cool dismissal, he'd seen the flash of hurt in her eyes. Was it feigned or real? For someone with such an icy veneer, it shouldn't be so easy to wound her. He expected, needed, her to be tougher, to have an inner hardness that matched the flawless exterior.

She kept walking. Her legs were long, but his were longer and he kept pace effortlessly. "Tom left you enough money?"

"You know he did."

"And as executor of Tom's will, I also know you haven't touched a cent of it yet. Why is that?"

They reached an intersection and she stopped and turned to him, her gaze cool and distant. "Now's not a convenient time to talk."

The lights signaled permission to cross and a crowd of shoppers and workers surged around and past them as they faced each other. She was clearly well aware of the power she held. Her body, her baby. She would be no pushover. He could almost respect that. Almost. He stepped a little closer. She held her ground. "I thought we could have lunch. There's a place nearby. Down at the marina." A light breeze feathered through her blond tresses. And suddenly, as he caught the scent of spring flowers, he regretted the proximity he'd initiated.

Chastity tilted her face up. "Why?" Blatant distrust infused the word and the blue eyes that searched his.

Which was precisely where their problems lay. The distrust was a little rich coming from her. He wasn't the one who'd married someone he didn't love. But he didn't draw attention to that detail. "I want to know the woman who's having my baby."

The words hung in the air between them.

"I can't." Her gaze slid away. "I…uh…don't have long for lunch."

She was a lousy liar. Gabe raised an eyebrow in query and that was all it took for guilty color to climb her cheeks.

Chastity expelled an exasperated sigh. "You know my schedule, don't you?"

He lifted a shoulder. "I like to be in full possession of the facts." He watched her expectantly, curious to see which way she'd jump now. Her wide-eyed gaze met his then tracked away. "Lunch?" he asked again.

The gaze came back, remote and resolute as if she'd called up some reserve of strength. "No." No explanation. No justification or apology.

Gabe didn't think he'd ever been turned down so summarily by a woman before. Clearly she didn't know how much he relished a challenge.

# Four

Resisting the temptation to relax and let her guard down, Chastity kept her arms folded across her chest. She turned her face to the sun and wind, felt some of the tension ease that Gabe's presence inevitably caused. She still wasn't quite sure how or why she'd let him talk her into this. She kept most men, most people even, at a distance. That was how she felt safest. But Gabe casually disregarded the barriers she worked so hard to maintain.

He kept challenging her and something told her to challenge right back, that it was imperative to not let him see how deeply he unsettled her.

She chanced a glance at him, standing at the helm, feet spaced wide, hands resting on the large wheel. His suit jacket and tie were lying where he'd tossed them on a seat in the cabin below. The top buttons of his white shirt were undone and the sleeves rolled up. He was missing the eye patch, but with his wind-ruffled hair, broad shoulders and strong tanned forearms, there was a definite air of the pirate about him. Helped by the fact that she felt almost like she was being held hostage. Pirates, she reminded herself, were after treasure. And in this case she knew full well the treasure was not her but the baby she carried. She was not about to let him lay claim to it for himself.

If she wanted him to back off she needed two things. First, she needed him to trust that she would be a good mother and second to understand that she knew what her rights were, and more specifically, she knew what *his* rights were *not*.

"When you said we'd be eating at the marina, I thought you meant at one of the harborside cafés or restaurants."

Gabe looked her way. "Did you?"

"You know I did. So I can only assume that we're on your yacht because a) you don't want to be seen with me, b) you don't want anyone overhearing our conversation, or c) you don't want me to be able to leave whenever I want."

Gabe looked beyond her to the expanse of the ocean. A gull cried out as it wheeled high overhead. "Or d) because I thought you might like it."

"You can have your d) if it makes you feel better, but don't expect me to buy it."

He glanced at her. "It won't make you nauseous, will it? Being on a boat?"

"No," she said honestly, "the breeze helps."

His gaze returned to the horizon. "Tom told me once that you loved the sea. That you'd grown up near it."

"He told you that?" And Gabe had remembered? Of

course he had. He'd have stored the information away in the steel trap of his mind in case one day it came in handy for his own purposes. Like today. Thank goodness she'd never told Tom the full story of where and how she'd grown up. That would only have given Gabe more ammunition, more reason to not want her raising his child.

"It was in the early days."

"Before you stopped talking to each other?"

His brow darkened and she almost regretted having dimmed his obvious pleasure in being on the ocean. From what she knew of Gabe, he didn't do much other than work, devoting his life to the Masterses' empire. Even today he'd taken two phone calls since she first saw him on Queen Street. That he considered their situation worthy of his time and his effort—he'd gone to the trouble of ascertaining the hours she worked—worried her.

His gaze dropped to her. "Can we try starting from this point and moving forward? I won't bring up the past if you don't. At least for this afternoon."

"Does that mean you'll stop insulting me?"

"Yes."

"We could try." She couldn't quite keep the skepticism from her voice.

"Would you rather eat at a restaurant?" he asked, facing her.

"Are you offering?"

"If it would make you more comfortable."

She hadn't expected that and was grateful for it. "No, this'll be fine." She tried to sound conciliatory. The truth was she did love the sea. She had, as he'd said, grown up near it. Not as he might imagine, in a plush beachfront home, but in an isolated, poverty-stricken community, with a family that no one considered upstanding. But the ocean and foreshore had been first her playground and then her sanctuary.

"If it makes you any happier, we're not going far. There's a bay I know that'll be sheltered from this westerly. We'll be there in twenty minutes."

She shrugged her acceptance then turned her focus back to the ocean. It took more of an effort than she would have expected. There was a secret part of her that could have kept watching Gabe and how he handled the boat, how he, too, lifted his face to the sun and wind, just as she liked to. If, as he'd said, this was a beginning and she didn't already know him, she could almost be captivated.

In fact, she had been once.

When she'd worked for him, she'd gotten a secret pleasure from his company, from just being around him. But when she'd inadvertently let her attraction show, he swiftly transferred her to Tom's department. A clear signal that he wasn't interested in someone like her. A man like him wouldn't be. But it had still hurt.

So when Tom made his offer of marriage later, it seemed like a good one. As good as she could expect. Better even.

Lost in thought about choices made, she watched the ocean until they anchored in a small bay surrounded by forested hills. Gabe brought up a hamper from the galley and spread the contents—which looked like they'd been prepared by one of the restaurant chefs— onto the table. They ate in a silence that she wouldn't exactly call companionable but at least it didn't resonate with animosity. Every now and then she caught a glimpse of Gabe, sitting just a couple of feet across from her—his jaw as he chewed, tanned fingers as he tore a bread roll in two.

Finally, Chastity swallowed her last mouthful of sweet strawberry tart and allowed herself to look up and properly meet his gaze. "So, you know about my work?" What else did he know?

"The four mornings a week you work for Knight Architectural? Yes. Jordan told me the week you started."

"Jordan told you?"

His gaze was steady on her. "Seeing as how I regularly send millions of dollars of business his way, it wouldn't pay to do anything to piss me off."

"It always comes down to money, doesn't it?"

"I'm not sure it does with Jordan," he said thoughtfully. "He didn't ask me if he could hire you. He just told me you'd started. He said he thought it was better I hear it from him rather than find out accidentally, as I undoubtedly would."

"You didn't tell him to fire me?"

"Who he employs is his decision."

"And you didn't threaten to pull your business?"

"No. I like the work they do, but I did tell him I didn't want you having anything to do with my account."

"I told him the same thing."

Gabe nodded. "I like to keep business and personal affairs separate." He looked away, lifted his bottle of ginger ale to his lips and took a swallow. There had been a definite insinuation in his statement, a subtle emphasis on the word *I,* an implication that unlike him, *she* did not keep them separate.

Chastity put her fork down. "I didn't set out to snare

Tom, as you and your family believe." Their engagement had been Tom's idea, one she'd given in to in a moment of lonely weakness, but it had turned out to be an arrangement that worked surprisingly well for both of them. Their marriage had been the same. Her two years with Tom had been the happiest of her life and she missed him constantly.

"Of course not."

She ignored his obvious skepticism. The last thing she wanted was to be drawn deeper into a discussion about her relationship with his brother.

"And you and Jordan?" he asked. "I saw the photo of the two of you at last month's gallery opening."

Chastity reeled. She'd just recently buried her husband. And Gabe was all but accusing her of having a relationship with a man who was both her boss and her friend. A man who'd been trying only to cheer her up by insisting she go to the opening. It was that easy to catapult her back to the bleak teenage years when the taunts that were true of her half sisters—and her mother—had also been leveled at her. "So much for refraining from the insults." She pushed her plate away. "It's about now that I'd leave if we were at a restaurant."

"It was a question not an insult. You're remarkably quick to misinterpret."

"Don't blame me. It was an insulting question with an underlying accusation. 'Why would Jordan hire her,'" she mimicked the voices of her tormenters, "'if she's not putting out.'" Chastity cupped her breasts, lifted them up and together, revealing the swell of her cleavage. "'She couldn't possibly have any brains or any skills.'"

Gabe leaned back in his chair. "I'm not apologizing to you because I did *not* say any of those things."

She dropped her hands to the table, clenching them as she leaned toward him, her nails digging into her palms. "Tell me you weren't thinking them."

"I wasn't thinking them," he said quietly. How did he look for so long without blinking, just keeping those brown eyes steady, searching, on her? "I hired you, remember. Not because you *put out,* but because of your brains and your capabilities."

It was Chastity who looked away then. He was right. It had been Gabe who'd first hired her, and he'd expected only that she do her job and do it well. She'd respected him for that. For a time she'd had his respect, too. And the respect of a man like Gabe Masters had meant a lot to her. Which made it all the more painful when she'd lost it.

"I want to know how things stand in your life at the moment, so we can figure out how to move forward," he said.

"You don't need to do any figuring out."

"Yes, I do. This child is mine, too." His dark eyes challenged her.

She met that gaze and played her ace. "Not legally. Sperm donors give up any and all rights." He would know that. He needed to be clear that she knew it, too. Only that fact let her sleep at night.

His jaw clenched and she saw the frustration in his gaze. He'd known all right. "But biologically and morally," he said slowly, "you can't deny that."

Chastity looked over the railing at the water lapping against the side of the boat. Even though the law was on her side, he was right and he'd keep pushing till she acknowledged that. "I'm not denying it, but it means nothing to me."

"Liar." He said the word quietly. "Look me in the eye and say that."

She couldn't. For better or worse—and she was guessing worse—he was her baby's father. That meant something to him. And it meant something to her. Just what that was she still had to figure out. But she had other arguments in her arsenal. "It's a girl," she said.

"Pardon?"

She looked up from the water. "*My*—" she used the word deliberately "—baby is a girl."

A sudden frown marred his brow, drawing his eyebrows together. She was both relieved and disappointed.

"They monitor everything very closely with IVF pregnancies."

If anything, the frown deepened. "You're telling me this because…?"

Suddenly she didn't feel so sure of her ground. His frown wasn't masculine disappointment that would diminish his interest in her child, but anger. Directed at her. "It makes a difference to some people."

"You think…? You seriously think…?" For a moment he was lost for words. "Does it lessen the child's worth to you?"

"No, of course not, but some people…"

He turned away from her, but she'd heard the barely suppressed fury and could see it in the rigid set of his shoulders. And she knew that somehow she'd lowered herself even further in his opinion. The exact opposite of what she was trying to achieve. It was minutes before he turned back to her. "Who?"

She didn't answer, pretended she didn't know what he was referring to, that he hadn't straight away cut to the heart of her assumption.

"What sort of man wouldn't want a child because she was a girl? Other men you've dated?"

"That's not your business. Nor is it relevant."

"Your father?"

"What father?" She snapped the question and the bitterness that tinged those two words surprised her. She never thought about the man who'd fathered her. It must be the pregnancy that had her drawing comparisons, and the contrast with the joy she felt.

Gabe nodded slowly, then spoke through clenched teeth. "I'm not other men." A fact she was well aware of because there was no other man she felt this unsure of herself around.

Gabe pressed a button and the rumble of the anchor chain being drawn up reverberated through the boat.

She'd offended him with her assumption, but given the insults he'd leveled at her, she wasn't going to feel bad about that. Or, at least, she wasn't going to let it show. Because if he sensed any weakness, he'd exploit it.

Gabe stepped back from Chastity's front door and waited. Of course she wasn't home. She would be spending the day with friends, the high-flying crowd she and Tom used to run with, or perhaps family. But not her father.

That she had thought, hoped, that he, too, might ever turn his back on his child had initially angered him. Did she really see him as that inhuman? But yesterday, after he'd walked her to her car in a silence that was far from pleasant, he'd wondered what about her life had taught her to expect others to turn their backs on her? The absent father, of course, but who else? He'd made a mental note to find out more about her, specifically her family. He needed to know what made her tick. Which was why he was here.

He knocked again. This house had surprised him, as far too many things about her were doing lately. He didn't like surprises—they meant he wasn't in full possession of the facts, that he was forced to react.

The weathered cedar home, perched on a remote spot on the craggy west coast, was nothing like the harborside apartment she'd shared with Tom. It wouldn't have been cheap—coastal property never was—and it still had a view of the water, but that was all the two residences had in common. The apartment had been the epitome of inner-city sophistication. Manicured gardens had graced the building's entrance and elegant potted palms dotted the marbled interior lobby. He looked about him. The few trees that had the audacity to establish themselves on the sloping ground here had been punished by the salty wind for it, growing permanently stooped and windswept.

Gabe turned back to his Maserati. The trading of her coupe for the four-wheel-drive made a little more sense. If she was driving the hilly, winding road regularly, she'd need something more practical.

Beneath the distant pounding of the surf, he caught another sound, a quiet clang. He changed direction and made his way around the side of the house.

In a sheltered corner of the garden, a woman with Chastity's face and figure knelt geisha-style on the ground by a small, freshly planted shrub. The impostor's blond hair was pulled carelessly into a high ponytail. She wore knee-length shorts that looked like they'd once—a very long time ago—been a pair of jeans, and a faded red T-shirt. He realized then that he'd only ever seen her dressed in black and white, mainly black. Even before Tom's death. A shovel lay on the ground beside her and she grasped a trowel loosely in her hand, but her gaze was directed toward the pounding white surf and the sparkling blue of the ocean beyond.

She looked fragile and forlorn. A hollowness welled somewhere in the region of his chest. Gabe felt a weakness in his legs that could see him kneeling beside her and an ache in his arms that he could ease by filling them with her.

She swung her head and her eyes widened in her pale face. As she scrambled to her feet, she wiped at her clothes, succeeding only in smearing traces of dirt down her T-shirt. "What are you doing here?" She looked beyond him, checking to see that he'd come alone.

The weakness passed. He made it pass. He was here with the intent of softening her attitude to him, not vice versa. He held up the slim gift-wrapped package in his hand. "A birthday present and a peace offering all in one."

"Oh. Thank you," she said hesitantly. "How did you know?"

"It's the same day as Dad's."

"But," she tilted her head and looked at him suspiciously, "that doesn't explain how you knew it was mine, too."

"It was the reason you and Tom couldn't come for dinner last year, remember?"

She nodded slowly. And though that would ostensibly indicate agreement, he got the feeling she didn't in fact remember and that she wanted nothing more than to send him packing. But she couldn't. Not when he'd brought her a present. Not when she needed him, too, even if she wasn't ready to admit that.

He nodded at the freshly planted shrub. "Interesting way to spend your birthday." He strolled closer. Where were the family and friends he'd envisioned? Why was she here alone?

Chastity followed his gaze and turned back to the shrub as he closed the distance between them, stopping when he stood by her shoulder.

"My cat died yesterday. I planted this for him. It's about the only thing I think will grow here."

"I didn't know you had a cat."

"He wasn't mine really. He came with the house. But he was nice to have around. He helped—" She realized who she was talking to and stopped as she looked abruptly at him. "I'm not even really a cat person." She glanced again at the freshly turned earth. "And I'd only had him a couple of months."

Was she trying to convince him or herself? Because if she could see the tear tracks through the dirt smudges on her face, she'd know she had to work a lot harder before he was even close to being convinced.

"I suppose I should invite you in?"

He should say yes, give her no choice. But he felt like he was intruding here. He shrugged. "Not if you don't want to. I don't want to spoil your day." And maybe it would be better for him, too, if he didn't, if he just turned around and went home and banished the image of a woman alone on her birthday, burying her cat.

She thought for a good long while as he waited, curious to see which way she'd jump, and he worked at persuading himself that it didn't matter to him either way. Sunlight glinted on her earrings which, if he wasn't mistaken, were made of tiny shells and tinsel. A remnant of the recent Christmas? These looked like they'd been made by a child, certainly not a Tiffany's jeweler.

"Hard to spoil it," she finally said with a shrug. "You may as well come in."

Gabe didn't quibble over the fact that the invitation was being extended only because she didn't think even he could make worse what was clearly a lousy birthday. In fact, he felt a surge of relief. Not surprising, he told himself. After all he was here only to establish a rapport with her. He needed her to accept the fact that his name should be on their child's birth certificate, because then he'd have rights. A father's rights. He would do whatever he needed to achieve that. Because whether she liked it or not, he intended to be a significant part of his child's life.

A low timber deck spanned the width of the house, and they crossed the lawn and walked up the two steps that ran along its length. Bifold doors were pushed wide open so that the outdoor area blended seamlessly into the indoors.

The first thing he saw, standing on the kitchen counter, next to a card clearly made by a child, was a black-and-white photo of Tom. In the picture his brother was laughing. It had been a long time since Gabe had seen that particular smile of Tom's. The one that was a combination of joy and mischief, as though he'd just told some shocking but hilarious joke at the dinner table.

Sorrow and regret, for all those things unsaid, the bridges unmended, lanced through him.

He glanced at Chastity, who had stopped by his side. She was looking at him rather than the photo. Her face was turned up to his, her eyes clear, and he read her sorrow, but there was something else there, something that looked like…pity? For him? She broke the gaze. "I'll just clean up." She held aloft her grubby hands between them. "Help yourself to a drink. There's soda in the fridge."

Gabe watched her disappear, followed the sway of her hips, the stride of her long, slender legs. His jaw tightened. Frowning, he turned deliberately and surveyed the room. The almost bare room. His frown deepened. Where was her furniture?

Just like the flow between outdoors and indoors, the open kitchen with its polished hardwood floors blended seamlessly into a dining and living room. Bold, bright, indecipherable artwork hung on the walls and a bookcase brimmed with books stacked two deep. But the dining area held only a small round table with a single chair. And in the living room there was a blue two-seater couch. No TV, no stereo system that he could see. Though in the far corner, incongruous in its ostentation, stood Tom's lacquered, cream-colored grand piano. An affectation because Tom hadn't played. But sheets of music now rested on the stand. Gabe crossed the room, his footsteps echoing in the empty space, and stared at the music—Beethoven—with penciled notations in a neat hand he recognized as Chastity's made in the margins and between the lines of music.

In another corner stood a five-foot-tall piece of

branching driftwood that had been painted silver. Sea-shells, some natural, some painted silver or gold, dangled from the bare branches. Her Christmas tree? Gabe thought of the tree at his parents' house, ten feet tall and professionally decorated, this year's theme colors being silver and blue. He shook his head, not understanding Chastity. And wanting not to want to understand her. Back in the kitchen he found the soda she'd mentioned, and stood looking out at the sea while he drank it.

He turned at the sound of her footsteps and took a few seconds to absorb the blow to the solar plexus. Not only was she fully made up, she'd brushed out her blond hair and now wore a black and white, designer sundress with a fitted bodice and strappy high-heeled sandals. This was an altogether more beautiful woman.

He preferred the other. "What did you do with her?"

"With who?" She tilted her head.

"Your evil twin, or maybe she was the good twin. What cupboard or basement have you locked her up in? I should rescue her."

This Chastity's perfectly painted lips stretched into a smile—a real smile—one that had amusement spar-kling in her clear eyes, one that seemed to make the day itself brighter while it stole some of the oxygen from the room.

He raised his can of soda to her in a toast. "Happy birthday." She looked away from him to face the sea, and he felt the loss of that brief warmth. He hadn't meant to make her smile fade so quickly.

"Thank you," she said quietly.

He closed the distance between them, too aware of

the pale bare shoulder next to him, too aware of the scent of spring flowers. "No family today?"

She tensed. "No." The single word was clipped, a warning to avoid the topic. Nothing fragile or forlorn about this woman. "What about you? Shouldn't you be with your father?" She quickly turned the subject.

"I've just come from the family lunch."

She glanced at his soda. "You'd probably like something stronger then."

He felt a grin tug at his lips.

It had been a predictably awful formal meal, with Tom's absence—the fact that he'd never again be with them—hanging over them. The broken fences would stay that way always. His father usurped Tom's customary role and drank too much; his mother stayed true to form in bitterly and repeatedly pointing it out.

Gabe had been glad to escape, had enjoyed the solitary drive out here. But if his family's day had been marred by Tom's absence, then so must Chastity's have been, and to a far greater extent. As much as he'd doubted that she'd truly loved his brother, or married him for anything other than his money, he hadn't doubted that they'd had a good friendship and an understanding that he had no insight into. Tom had seemed less edgy in the last two years and Gabe attributed that to Chastity's presence. "If I'd known you were alone, I would have invited you."

"To share in the bitterness and accusations, to be treated like something someone stepped in? Gee, thanks."

"We're not that bad."

She didn't answer. She didn't need to. Even today when they'd talked about Tom, his mother, despite

Gabe's corrections, had referred to Chastity, when she'd been unable to avoid it altogether, as That Woman. Maybe being alone really was preferable. It certainly appealed to Gabe. Alone—no responsibility for anyone else's happiness, no bearing the brunt of their bitterness, no tiptoeing around the taboo subjects.

The silence grew heavy, oppressive with memories and, on his part at least, regrets.

"Why are you here?" she finally asked.

"To give you your present." The lie rolled surprisingly easily off his tongue. "I tracked down your address yesterday. You didn't make it easy."

"Maybe because I'm not keen to be found."

"Anyway, I was intrigued."

"Gathering information on the opposition?"

"We're not opposition. We're on the same side."

"Not if you think you have any more rights than an uncle with regard to my child."

He quashed the anger and the arguments that rose. "I didn't want to talk about that today." Not till she was less wary of him.

"Hard to avoid when it's the only reason you're here."

Clearly she hadn't bought the gift reasoning. Smart woman. "Maybe I was worried you were alone."

"And you think your company is preferable to being alone?"

"Good point," he said, unfazed.

She hesitated. "Sorry. That was unkind."

"But true. As far as you know." Funny, she actually looked as though she regretted having said something she thought might hurt him. The remark hadn't even registered on his scale of insults.

"Not entirely. Do you remember the corporate team building? We managed all right then."

The last thing he'd expected was for Chastity to defend him to himself. And with that particular incident.

He remembered too well the session his HR head had convinced him would be a good idea. He had no time for that nebulous touchy-feely sort of thing, but knew that others sometimes got benefit from it. Or so he was told.

So he'd held his tongue and sent his executive team off for several days of making bridges and scaling walls and blindfolding each other or whatever else it was they did on those things. He'd avoided it for the most part, but put in an appearance on the final day.

Chastity, back then his efficient PA, had only been with the company for a couple of months. He was put onto the same team as her, and somehow the two of them ended up spending three hours on a riverbank waiting for their teammates, lost somewhere on the other side, to find the river and build a raft so they could cross and "rescue" them. When he'd accepted it was not going to be a quick process, and ascertained that the quiet, glamorous Chastity was surprisingly relaxed about the whole situation, he'd had no choice but to relax, too. They talked, about nothing in particular, and even told a few corny jokes.

The afternoon had lived for some time in his memory as one of the pleasantest he'd spent in a long while.

When their teammates did eventually turn up with the remains of a raft, it was Gabe and a surprisingly competent Chastity who'd lashed the barrels and bits of wood back together to enable them all to return to shore.

There was no sign of that woman now. He needed to get back something of that rapport. "What are you doing for the next week?" He knew that Knight Architectural practically shut down for the first half of January and that Jordan encouraged all his staff to take their leave then.

"Why do you want to know?" She was guarded, suspicious.

"I'm going to Sanctuary Island to look at the lodge. The deal was finalized just the other day." At the meeting she'd interrupted.

"And?" she asked, her eyes narrowed.

"I want you to come with me."

Those eyes widened with shock and something like fear. "I don't think that's a very good idea."

The fear bothered him. "Because you don't like me?"

She half smiled, but there was no humor in her expression. "Or because you don't like me?"

"I'm trying to like you," he said quietly.

"Against every instinct."

"There's more at stake here than our past…difficulties. Like you said, the team-building exercise, before there was any history, showed us that we can get along." He tried not to think of the night after that afternoon, when they'd all sat around a bonfire talking and singing. Chastity's voice, sweet and crystal clear, had twined inside him, her eyes had glittered in the firelight and he'd been hit with the knowledge that he wanted her.

In a way he most definitely shouldn't.

A few weeks later, when the attraction still hadn't abated, when he thought he'd seen it reciprocated but repressed, he'd had her transferred to Tom's department. And when, a few weeks after that, the desire for her had only grown, he made the decision to ask her out—as soon as she got back from Vegas.

But by then she already had her rich man.

She squared her shoulders and the fear on her face disappeared, replaced by challenge. He couldn't help thinking the bravado was an act. "Face it, Gabe. For once I hold the power. And you don't like it. Admit it."

"I have no problem admitting it. But we have to move forward from here. And you know what's right. That I'm right—about this." He gestured to her abdomen, the slight swelling disguised by the fall of her dress.

She hesitated.

"The lodge isn't finished yet. The original developer went bust on it. There'll be no other guests. You'll have your own chalet right on the edge of the bay. I'll be working. There'll be no pressure."

"You won't try to influence me about the baby, or even talk about it?"

He considered her request. They *would* be talking about the baby. But for that to happen he first had to get her there. "Ultimately we will have to." He gave her that much honesty. "But I won't until you're ready."

"I'll think about it."

Gabe was good at reading people and her *I'll think about it* was a no; she just didn't want to come right out with it. But time was ticking and this was the perfect opportunity. It was a slow period, the first few weeks of the New Year always were. He could use the time to work on her. He'd been considered charming once, back in the days when he'd had to use charm. Of recent years, his wealth and power had been enough to ease the way. He wanted his name on that birth certificate, he wanted rights, because despite what the law said, her child was his. He hadn't planned on being a father anytime soon, but now that he was going to be, he wasn't about to let her cut him out of his child's life.

A young voice called Chastity's name, startling him. Gabe turned in time to see a waif of a girl, all scrawny arms and legs, leap onto the deck and come skidding to a halt just before the door. She straightened, standing tall, pushed her tangled hair back from her face, smoothed her hands down her T-shirt and then stepped gracefully, almost regally through the open door. The transformation reminded him a little of Chastity's. "How was that?" she asked expectantly.

"Beautiful," Chastity said. "Very elegant."

The child beamed and pirouetted. As she spun, she saw Gabe; her Bambi eyes widened and she froze. He half expected her to bolt from the room.

"Sophie, this is Gabe Masters," Chastity spoke quietly. "Gabe, this is Sophie, a friend of mine."

"Hello, Sophie." He wasn't entirely sure of child protocol, but he held out his hand. Sophie, who he guessed to be somewhere around ten or eleven years old, studied his hand. Her gaze darted to Chastity, who gave a small encouraging smile and nodded. Slowly, Sophie extended her hand and shook his. Her fingers were adorned with rings made of shells polished to smoothness by the ocean. A pink shell necklace that rattled faintly as she moved hung around her neck. He felt like he was shaking hands with a sea sprite. "It's a pleasure to meet you, Sophie," he said, smiling.

The girl smiled shyly back.

"I see you have the same beautiful earrings as Chastity."

Sophie touched a hand to her ear and then spun to look at Chastity. "You're wearing them?"

Too late Gabe realized that Chastity would have changed her earrings when she changed her outfit. "She was earlier," he said quickly.

"Of course I'm wearing them." Chastity pushed her hair back behind her ears to reveal her earrings.

"We match," Sophie said, almost breathless. She looked at Gabe as though seeking a witness.

"You do indeed. I feel like the thorn between two roses." He hadn't quite gotten the expression right, but it didn't seem to matter to Sophie who stood taller, her smile widening. Then suddenly recalling herself, she turned back to Chastity.

"Mum wants me to ask if we can borrow a couple of eggs. We've run out."

"Of course."

Chastity crossed to her kitchen and opened the refrigerator.

"She says we'll replace them next Tuesday." The girl looked at the floor. "After Dad's payment comes through. If it's not late again."

"Tell her not to worry. These are from my friend with the farm. She's given me far too many again." Chastity spoke a little too quickly, a little too brightly.

From where Gabe stood, he saw her behind the screen of the open fridge door, transferring eggs from what looked a lot like a store-bought carton into a plastic container.

"Sophie," he said to distract the girl who was craning

her neck to watch Chastity, "I have a friend who used to make her own jewelry from bits and bobs she collected, buttons and glitter and things like that. She now works as a jeweler in London, England. She's designed pieces for movie stars and even royalty."

"Really?"

Gabe nodded. "And it all started with her making things for herself and her friends."

"Really?" she asked again, all breathy excitement.

"Yes, really."

Chastity shut the fridge door and passed the container to Sophie.

"Thanks, Chass." The girl held the eggs to her chest and looked up adoringly at Chastity. "You want to walk on the beach later? I'll show you my cartwheels. I've been practicing."

"Sure." Chastity returned the girl's smile, looking for a moment not that much older than Sophie.

"Great." Sophie headed for the door. "Bye." And then she was gone, running with the eggs clutched under one arm.

He watched Chastity. "'My friends call me Chass?'" That was what she'd said to his mother. And at the time he'd been unable to imagine anyone shortening Ms. Elegant and Sophisticated's name so informally. Not quite so hard to imagine now.

Her smile changed, hinting at a vein of mischief he'd not seen before, and then vanished. "Thank you for distracting her."

Gabe shrugged, still searching her face, her eyes. "She's cute."

"And?"

"And nothing."

"Then why are you looking at me so strangely?"

"Because you keep surprising me. That doesn't happen very often."

"Maybe you shouldn't mix with such boring people." He knew she meant her comment as an insult, a means of distancing them. But Gabe thought of the endless rounds of meetings with architects, accountants and financial controllers that comprised his life lately.

"Maybe you're right." It was her turn to look surprised. About time.

Finally she turned away, busied herself minutely adjusting the position of a fruit bowl on her counter. "Do you really have a friend who's a jeweler who got her start as you said?"

"Yes. I'm not sure about the designing pieces for royalty, but I think she mentioned something like that, and it's entirely possible given what's happening with her career."

"It's so good for Sophie when people recognize her interests and encourage them. To not focus only on how she looks."

That sounded personal. Gabe watched her, curious, but he knew he'd get nothing from her if he probed.

She looked up and he could read nothing in her expression. She was cool and remote. And beautiful. He wanted to strip that practiced neutrality away. He wanted her to smile at him like she'd just smiled at Sophie. He wanted to strip away more than just that, perhaps starting with her sundress. The unbidden thought stilled him. He reminded himself that that wasn't at all what he wanted. He'd written her off the second he'd learned she'd gotten engaged to his brother. "I'll get going, too." Leave, straighten his thoughts out. Maybe that was how she'd snared Tom, by bewitching and confounding him.

She nodded. No argument there.

They walked out onto the deck, and her gaze went to the freshly planted shrub in the corner of the garden.

"Think about the lodge," he said quietly, doing his best to be nonthreatening. "I leave tomorrow and we'll be there for a week. It'd be good if you came. In the meantime, happy birthday again." He picked up the slim parcel from where he had placed it on the outdoor table and handed it to her.

"Thank you." She eyed it dubiously. "You shouldn't have."

He'd never heard a more sincere *you shouldn't have.* "Believe me, it's nothing." And suddenly he didn't want to see her open it. He'd taken too long over the decision of what to get her. He usually delegated gift buying to his PA. In fact, he'd probably even delegated that chore to Chastity in the time she'd worked for him. He hadn't for this gift, despite the fact that Julia was already buying something for his father from him, because he'd been unable to frame the parameters to someone else. *Get something for my dead brother's wife. The woman who's carrying my child. The woman I need to sweeten up.* So, he'd undertaken the job himself. He'd looked in high-end jewelry stores for something tasteful and expensive, but not too personal, nothing that smacked of bribery, although undoubtedly that's what it was. But ultimately he'd ended up buying something that caught his eye on the bargain tables of a bookstore as he'd been striding past. Cheap was touching when it came from a ten-year-old. Not so touching from a millionaire. He should have left it to Julia after all. He mentally shook his head. Way to go, Gabe.

"I'll see myself out."

She nodded, still holding the unopened parcel slightly away from her body, like something distasteful.

Gabe headed slowly, thoughtfully, for his car. Had he played that right? He'd opened his door when she came hurrying around the side of the house, her hair catching the gold of the sinking sun. She drew up, slightly breathless. The book—a journal for recording her thoughts during the weeks and months of her pregnancy—was still clutched in her hand, but now held close to her. He saw its cover, the soft-focus silhouette of a mother cradling her baby that had initially caught his eye.

"Thank you," she said. "This was really thoughtful. I'd thought you might try to do something tacky."

"Tacky?"

"You know what I mean. Try to soften me up with something expensive your PA bought on your behalf, jewelry or whatever. I misjudged you. I'm sorry."

Actually, she'd pegged him just right but she didn't need to know that. He lowered himself into the seat.

"I'll come. To the resort. If that's still all right?"

Victory. He hid the rush that came with it and turned the key in the ignition. "I'll pick you up tomorrow morning."

# Five

As the gusts from the helicopter died away and the dark spot in the sky receded, Chastity realized the quick, heavy thumping that continued was her heartbeat and not the rotor blades.

What had she done?

She was on Gabe's territory now and that shifted the balance of power between them.

"What do you think?"

She shot a glance at him, but could read nothing of his expression or intent from behind his dark sunglasses. She knew only that he was watching her, as he had been, subtly, since the moment he picked her up. "That coming here was a mistake."

Her almost overpowering urge was to flee. But she couldn't. Not only because her best means of escape from the island—Gabe's helicopter—had just disappeared from view, but because she needed him to trust her. Trust her enough that he wouldn't make any attempt to fight her for her daughter. If she kept that end in sight, she would get through this.

Besides, she wasn't completely stranded. Here. With him. He'd told her about the arrangements he'd made for the mail ferry that stopped at neighboring islands to also call regularly at Sanctuary Island. But it still felt like being stranded.

One corner of Gabe's mouth stretched into a grin. He, too, was aware of the shift of power. "I meant, of the island? The resort?"

Oh. She turned to look about her. The lodge's buildings were a short stroll away. The largest timber building, with its steep roof and massive windows and a welcoming semicircular entranceway, stood in the open, but other smaller structures—the chalets, she guessed—were nestled in the edge of the forest where it came down to meet gently sloping grass that in turn gave way to white sand. From the beach, a wooden jetty, where the ferry would dock, stretched into the sheltered bay. Water lapped at the shore, and behind her birdsong rang out in the forest. "It's beautiful."

"It is, isn't it?" There was a quiet, awed pride in his voice.

"And not at all what I expected."

"Because it's not like my other resorts?"

"I guess. It doesn't look as much like a playground for the wealthy as the others."

"It's not. This one's a retreat. It's…more personal. I wanted to buy the island from the moment it first came on the market nearly two years ago."

Was Gabe sharing something of himself with her? "Why didn't you?"

"George Tucker wanted it, too. He pushed the price well above what it was worth, and I backed out."

"And?"

"And now Tucker's bankrupt, though not just because of this decision, and I own the lodge he started building."

Or was he subtly warning her? Gabe got what he wanted.

Trouble was she didn't know precisely what he wanted from her, what his agenda in bringing her here was. She knew only that he would have an agenda. And she didn't for a moment believe his claim that he only wanted to get to know her. She still had the message on her answer phone, the one where he suggested he adopt her child. She wasn't about to let herself forget that.

She was trapped in this situation. It wasn't her fault that Tom had tricked them both. If she hadn't been pregnant, Tom's tragic death would have been the end of any contact between them. But—she pressed a hand to her abdomen—she was most definitely pregnant. With Tom's/Gabe's baby.

He wouldn't want the baby for its own sake. She couldn't imagine anyone less likely than workaholic Gabe to want a child in his life. But he wouldn't want Chastity raising his child, either, not when he thought she was nothing more than a gold digger. And not when he blamed her for Tom's estrangement from his family.

"You know with Tom's—your—shares in the company, you're ultimately a part owner of this." His gaze swept the bay and the resort.

She looked again at its quiet beauty. "I hadn't thought of it like that. I don't often—"

"What?"

"Nothing." She didn't think of the shares as hers. She'd use them for her child if she needed, but nothing else.

She reached for the handle of her case, but Gabe beat her to it and hefted it up with a sideways glance at her. He said nothing, but she imagined disapproval in those brown eyes. Disapproval that her case was twice the size and immeasurably heavier than his. She shrugged and walked ahead. "Which way?" she called back over her shoulder.

"Take your pick. Any one of the chalets. They're all mostly finished."

Chastity headed for the one farthest away. Not because she wanted to make Gabe carry her case all that way— that was just an added bonus—but because she wanted her privacy. She'd seen the signs of workmen, scaffolding and ladders against the side of the main building. She wanted to be on her own as much as possible.

"There are no land lines on the island yet," he said as they walked, "but there is cell phone coverage." Chastity nodded.

At the last chalet, Gabe pushed open the door. "And the locks haven't been fitted yet, but it's safe on the island." He looked around the room. "Like I said, it's not completely finished, but it has a bed in it at least."

He waited for her to pass him and enter. She lowered her gaze from the hint of challenge in his dark eyes, but her eyes caught instead on his chest and the dark, button-down shirt that stretched across it, and as she passed him she caught a trace of the cologne that had teased her senses throughout the helicopter flight. She didn't want to be aware of him this way.

But she was.

She fixed her gaze straight ahead. Sunlight shone on a wicker armchair in the far corner of the room. A dresser and a bed with a cream linen coverlet were the only other furnishings. The walls and polished wooden floors were bare.

"I like it," she said. "It's restful."

"Do you mean Spartan?" She heard humor in his voice.

"I mean sparse. But I like sparse. Too many things and I start feeling weighed down."

He hesitated. "But?"

He didn't expand on his question and she knew he was thinking about the apartment she'd shared with Tom. An apartment that overflowed with rugs and furnishings and objets d'art. An apartment she'd been both relieved and pained to leave.

She caught a faint lingering trace of fresh paint—the walls had recently been given a pale mushroom color. "Do all the chalets have beds already?" she asked, changing the subject.

"No."

"Then why does this one?"

"Lucky guess. I called ahead yesterday, told them to make it up. But I wanted you to have the choice. If I'd been wrong it would have been no trouble to change things around."

"Am I that predictable?" She didn't want him to think he knew her. Because he didn't.

"No. This one made sense. It's farthest away from

any construction noise." He lowered her case to the floor. "I'll leave you to get settled in."

But he didn't leave. She waited for him to speak, certain there was something on his mind—probably a warning, or a criticism or an admonishment. But no words came. Finally—finally—when her nerves had stretched to snapping point, his phone rang and he turned and sauntered out to take the call. His crisp, deep voice gradually faded from her hearing.

Chastity ran, her legs pushing through the water. And when the water got too high for her to run, she dove. The ocean closed around her, streaming her hair behind her, cocooning her in cool, muted silence as she swam beneath the surface till the need for air sent her to the top. One breath and she dove under again. Oh, to be a dolphin or a mermaid. Carefree. Being immersed in the water was as close as she could get.

When next she surfaced she swam with strong, easy strokes deeper and farther into the bay. A hundred meters from shore she stopped and looked around the curving shoreline of the small cup-shaped bay. Gabe's bay, despite what he'd said about it being partially hers. What had she done? It was the question that wouldn't leave her alone. A week effectively trapped here with Gabe. A Gabe who could be—and would be, if the day so far was anything to go by—relaxed and charming. Seven days in which she had to be on her guard. Of all the ludicrous ideas. She flipped onto her back and floated.

A dark-haired head broke through the water beside her and she gasped and sank, spluttering, then turned upright and trod water. "Don't do that to me." She pushed wet hair from out of her eyes.

"Me? Don't do this to *you?*" Anger flashed in his dark eyes.

"You startled me."

"What about what you did to me, coming out here alone and then disappearing beneath the water for five minutes?" He was close. Too close.

"It wasn't five minutes and I didn't realize anyone was watching."

"Someone had to watch. You shouldn't swim alone. Fundamental principle of water safety." Droplets of water clung to his dark, spiky eyelashes. She caught sight of broad, slick shoulders, the muscles glistening and shifting as he, too, trod water. She wanted to touch them. She should *not* want to touch them. Beneath the water she made out the indistinct shape of muscular legs working.

"It's a safe beach. I'm a good swimmer." Her foot brushed against his calf and she backed away.

"It doesn't matter how good you are. You shouldn't swim alone." He moved closer again.

Time to set some boundaries. "I may have come to the island with you, but that doesn't give you the right to tell me what I can and can't do." She tried to keep her tone reasonable.

He glared at her. "It's not just you anymore."

The baby. It all came back to that microscopic joining of a part of him with a part of her.

She couldn't bring herself to admit that he might be right this time so she turned from their confrontation and swam toward the pontoon anchored at the northern end of the bay.

Gabe swam beside her.

Chastity strengthened her stroke. She was, as she'd said, a good swimmer. Good enough to get into a U.S. university on a swimming scholarship. Good enough to leave many men in her wake.

But apparently not Gabe.

She swam faster. He kept pace. They were racing hard out as they neared the pontoon. Their hands touched the wooden planks in unison. Her only consolation for not beating him was that he was breathing at least as heavily as her. A couple of seconds later, Gabe surged out of the water and twisted in one lithe movement to sit on the edge of the pontoon, his feet dangling in the water, his shoulders glistening in the sun. That was when Chastity realized her mistake. She would have to sit—bare thighed—next to Gabe and hope he didn't notice.

"Come on. I'll help you out." Gabe held his hand toward her. She had no choice. She reached up and grasped it.

"Ready?" She nodded, and in one swift, effortless movement he had her up and sitting beside him, practically touching. She repositioned herself, edging away from his slick, muscled contours, carefully, casually, positioning her hand on the side of her thigh.

"You were right about the good swimmer part," he conceded.

"I know," she said between breaths.

"You competed?"

"For a few years." Swimming had been her way out of the life she'd had, the path to her transformation. The new, improved Chastity.

"Seems like most of the women I've known never swim in anything other than a pool, and even then they never got their hair wet."

Chastity smiled. "I don't know that pushing off from the submerged seat to drift to the far side and order another cocktail really counts as swimming."

"You knew Amber?"

She laughed at his feigned surprise.

Gabe lay back on the damp planking, lacing his fingers behind his head. Her glance caught the curve of his biceps, the pale, softer skin of his inner arms, the contours of defined pecs and toned abs. There was that urge again—the urge to touch. He wore boxers, not swimming trunks. Had he really been that concerned that he'd stripped off his clothes and come in after her? She searched the shoreline and saw a small dark heap that had to be his discarded clothes.

"Thank you," she said quietly, "for your misplaced concern."

She lay down beside him, let the sun warm her skin, and reminded herself who he was. Tom's brother. The man who didn't trust her with her own child. She laid her hands protectively over her abdomen.

White clouds drifted overhead and she heard the faint sound of Gabe's breath next to her ear.

She turned her head to look at him. His face was angled toward hers. She looked into his deep espresso-brown eyes—that's where the danger of sudden drowning lay, and yet she couldn't turn away, couldn't break free of their pull.

She blamed the water, the bay, the sunlight on bare

skin; she blamed pregnancy hormones. She blamed everything she could for the fact that she still wanted, more than ever, to touch him—her fingertips to his jaw, his hair; her lips to his. It was almost a compulsion. The logical part of her brain screamed denials. The blood rushing through her body screamed something else altogether. And she saw his response, a provocation in return.

When and how had this started happening? And what could she do to stop it? The only thoughts she should be having about Gabe were how to get him to trust her. If he guessed what she was thinking, he'd probably try to have her committed. If she didn't beat him to it and check herself in first.

Gabe sat up and his gaze tracked to her thigh. His eyes narrowed.

She glanced at the outside of her leg, saw the pale mismatched patch of skin and sat up, too, positioning her hand over the scar.

"That's what the insurance claim was for?"

As Tom's wife, she'd been covered by the company's medical insurance. And clearly Gabe had seen at least something of her claim from the surgery. "It wasn't for breast implants, if that's what you thought."

Gabe said nothing. His silence and the look on his face told her clearly that was precisely what he'd assumed.

She was tired of fighting him, tired of always putting up a front. "I had a skin cancer removed." She didn't have to tell him, but she wanted to put him in his place. He made far too many assumptions—wrong ones—about her.

His startled expression was at least some compensation. "I'm sorry. Tom never said."

"Why should he? It was none of your business."

"You're right. It wasn't. Isn't. I just figured that you were so...perfect, that it couldn't all be natural."

"Perfect?" It was her turn to frown in disbelief. Gabe thought she was perfect?

"Perfect hair, beautiful face, stunning body," he said dismissively.

"How is it you manage to make what should be a compliment sound like an insult?"

"It's not meant to be either. Just an observation. A statement of fact. You must know it and work at it."

Her looks had been both a curse and a blessing in her life. Chastity looked at their feet dangling in the water.

"You're all right now?" he asked quietly. "The skin cancer?"

She could feel his gaze on her, but didn't look at him. "I'm fine. It wasn't an aggressive type. But they always take out a decent chunk. To be on the safe side."

"I'm glad you're okay." He sounded almost sincere. She wasn't going to be swayed by it. "So am I."

He reached for her hand, slid it away. She stiffened. She hated people seeing the scar, its ugliness. With a blunt finger he traced the edge of the patch. She tensed even further and grasped his wrist. No one else had ever touched it.

He met her gaze as he drew his hand away. "Does it hurt?"

She released his wrist. "Not exactly. More an uncomfortable sensation."

"I'm sorry. I'd kiss it better if I could."

She gave him her most disbelieving expression before she covered the scar again with her hand. Even Tom had preferred that she keep it hidden.

In a lightning-fast motion he captured her wrist, swept her hand aside, then leaned down and placed his lips over the scar in a quick, searing kiss.

# Six

Gabe straightened and Chastity stared dumbfounded at his profile, his relaxed face and posture as he looked out over the water, showing no sign of the shock assailing her. If anything, there was the faintest hint of a smile playing about his lips.

"I like it," he said, aware of her confusion. "Not what it meant for you, but it's so real, so not perfect. So… human."

"You didn't think I was human before?"

"It's difficult to get past the perfection, the reserve."

"Maybe I'm actually shy and that's how it comes across." He wouldn't believe her, but it was the fundamental truth. She usually took a long time to become comfortable with someone, not through want of trying. It's just how she was.

She wasn't surprised when Gabe laughed, though he

cut his mirth short and shot a probing look at her. She didn't want to be the subject of his consideration, didn't want him spending time thinking of her. "So what's the difference?" she asked, needing to distract him.

"Between?"

"Between implants and real? Seeing as how you're such a connoisseur."

"I wouldn't say connoisseur," he said, shaking his head in denial.

"If only I could do the skeptical eyebrow raise."

A smile tugged at his lips. "One or two of the women I've dated…"

"Hmmph."

They lapsed into silence.

"So, what is the difference?"

"I'm not sure that a gentleman would remember."

"No, but you might."

"Seeing as I'm no gentleman." He lifted his hand and a devilish challenge lit his eyes. "Perhaps if I could just…?"

He was teasing and it changed his persona entirely. He didn't seem at all like the Gabe she knew. Hard, uncompromising, unforgiving.

"Not in this lifetime." She, too, kept her tone light. Trouble was, she could almost want his touch. Almost imagine it. That large competent hand… She banished the thought.

The silence returned. His hand lay flat on the wood between them, almost touching her own, with its pink, carefully manicured nails.

"Your fingernails?"

"Mine," she sighed, flicking his thigh in irritation.

He trapped her hand beneath his. "And...your hair? You're a real blonde?"

It was time to put a stop to this before he beguiled her, made her laugh, made her forget completely who she was and, more importantly, who she was with. She slid her hand from under his, turned to him, went for her haughtiest expression. "You'll never know."

The look was one that years ago she'd worked on in front of the mirror as she was sloughing off the old Chastity, the Chastity who was frightened and uncertain and far too easily intimidated. It was a deliberately frosty expression that saw most men back off. It didn't work on Gabe. Clearly, he wasn't most men. The barest hint of a smile registered on his full lips and his stare lingered and heated. "Is that a challenge?" And Chastity was certain her own body temperature rose with it.

"Just a statement of fact." She tried to be as coolly dismissive as he had earlier, but given the masculine appraisal in his dark eyes, he wasn't going to be that easy to dismiss. She'd forgotten how competitive Gabe was, how he took on any challenge he thought he could win—and won. She wasn't going to get into any kind of power play with him.

Pushing off with her hands, she slipped into the water, let it close around her again, let it shield her and cool her. She began a lazy breaststroke, keeping her head above the water so she could get her bearings and enjoy the view.

She had only gone a few strokes when Gabe drew level and began to swim beside her. "There's a chef here at the lodge." He spoke briskly, the detached Gabe she felt safe with.

She breathed a sigh of relief at his change of subject.

"He's overseeing the installation of the kitchen and providing meals for the tradesmen and the few staff who are here. You can eat in the dining room with everyone else or get him to prepare something to take back to your chalet."

"A chef? That must thrill him, feeding a bunch of hungry manual laborers. Macaroni and cheese all round."

"Adam's a friend of mine. He wanted to do this. He gets a break on the resort, some time away from a few…issues that he's having. And the guys appreciate it, too. Just because someone swings a hammer doesn't mean they don't like good food."

"No. I know." Chastity swam a little faster. How about that? She'd just been told off by Gabe for being judgmental. The very worst part about it was that he was right. All the same, she could allow herself to resent him for it. Because if she was busy resenting him, she could put out of her mind those feelings, urgings, she'd had on the pontoon.

They walked from the water. As Gabe picked up his clothes, she veered across the sun-warmed sand toward her chalet.

"Can you do me one favor?" he asked, catching up to her, heedless of his bare chest, of the way his damp boxers clung to his hips.

She kept her eyes fixed straight ahead. "Depends on what it is."

"Tell me before you go swimming?"

She wanted to say no, but the earnestness in his voice stopped the word. Instead, she lifted a shoulder. "Okay."

"Promise?"

"Yes," she agreed on a reluctant sigh.

* * *

"Books?"

Gabe watched Chastity as she looked up, startled, from the page she was reading and seemed to take a moment to focus. Though she was sitting beside a large window, the early evening light was fading and she probably should have turned a lamp on.

He leaned a shoulder against her door frame. Her door had been open, so naturally he'd looked in. And seen her, legs curled beneath her in the armchair, engrossed in a book. "That's what was in your suitcase?" he said when she didn't respond.

She glanced at the nightstand beside her bed and the half dozen books haphazardly stacked on it. "Among other things."

She shrugged—a simple lift of a pale, bare shoulder beneath the white strap of her sundress. Nothing that should captivate him. But something had changed from the moment he'd seen her kneeling in her garden. Despite his best intentions he saw her differently, as something more than just a gold-digging Ice Maiden. He'd had to admit that even gold diggers had feelings and that Chastity just might be a woman with hidden strengths and vulnerabilities. That didn't mean he wasn't still going to get what he wanted, needed—a father's rights. Because he was determined that he be a part of his daughter's life and that she be a part of his. He wasn't going to lose any more of his family to this woman. But there were ways and means of achieving his ends; they didn't all have to be unpleasant or confrontational.

"I don't like to be caught without a book." Defiance and apology mixed in her voice.

"We're only here for a week."

"You think I should have brought more? In case it rains?" Her voice was deadpan and he couldn't figure out whether she was serious or teasing. Her full lips didn't so much as twitch, but an intriguing light danced in her eyes.

He watched her as he strolled into the room, noting how quickly that light disappeared as she uncurled her legs and placed her bare feet on the floor. The flight response? He needed to cure her of that.

She flicked out the skirt of her sundress, smoothing it over her thighs. He touched the top book in the stack and looked to her for permission. Another lift of that shoulder. Not captivating, he told himself firmly. Again. But he could see a slight, inviting hollow above her collarbone.

He picked up the first book, a thriller that had been recommended to him. He'd been meaning to read it, but never had time these days. Beneath it lay a couple of romances, beneath those a book of essays by a political columnist. And last the pregnancy journal he'd given her.

"Eclectic." And far more stimulating than the financial reports that constituted the bulk of his reading these days.

"I don't always know what I'll feel like," she explained.

"Well, do you feel like dinner?"

She glanced at her bare wrist, which showed a faint strip of paler skin, then scanned the walls of the chalet, looking for a clock, as if the time made a difference whether she was hungry or not.

"There are no clocks here," he supplied.

"And I'm guessing it's not just because the decorating isn't finished?"

"You're right. Because the point of the lodge will be for people to forget about time while they're here."

She stood. "It's working then. And yes, I do feel like dinner."

While she slipped her feet, with their berry-red toenails, into her sandals, Gabe crossed back to the door to wait for her. She ducked her head as she passed him. What was it going to take for her to relax in his presence? In the gentle warmth of the evening, they walked side by side along the forest edge. The sun hung low in the sky, burnishing the clouds with orange.

His cell rang. "Marco?" He spoke to his right-hand man as he walked beside Chastity, his attention only partially on the call. He finally pocketed the phone just as a plump wood pigeon flew past with its characteristic slow wing beats, heading into the trees. He and Chastity stopped in unison.

"Did you see where it went?" she asked.

"There." He pointed over her shoulder. "In the puriri tree. It's going for the berries."

She narrowed her eyes but kept scanning.

Gabe moved to stand behind her so he could put his arm over her shoulder and give her a line of sight. And though he was careful not to touch her, he sensed her tense up. "Out on the second branch from the bottom."

She wasn't the only one who'd tensed with their proximity. He'd caught the scent of her freshly shampooed hair and had a sudden urge to lower his face to the top of her blond head.

"I see it," she gasped. "Oh, look, there's another one."

He was the one who was supposed to be charming her, not vice versa. How much of this was an act? The Chastity who'd lived with his brother had been a glamorous socialite. Photos of her and Tom used to appear regularly in the social pages of magazines and newspapers. They'd epitomized city sophistication, had vacationed in the Greek Islands, attended gallery openings in Paris and operas in Rome. And yet here she stood beside him, delighting in the sight of a native bird feeding.

She glanced over her shoulder, caught him staring at her and her excitement leached away, to be replaced by a small frown. She started walking again, and Gabe matched his stride to hers.

"Both adults brood the egg. The female during the night and morning, then the male takes over for the afternoon and through the evening."

"You're not exactly subtle, are you?" She looked over her shoulder at him.

"Meaning?"

"Oh, please. Don't play innocent. The whole two-parents-sharing deal. Not to mention the 'Gee, with my font of knowledge won't I be a great Dad' angle."

"Can't be ignored."

"Yes, it can be." She looked away.

If she thought it was going to be that easy, she was sadly mistaken. He touched a deliberate hand to the small of her back as they entered the dining room. Nothing intrusive, perhaps a little possessive. Another not-so-subtle message. He was not about to let her shut him out. He needed her to get used to him, used to the sizzle that existed between them, because regardless of what she wanted, her future now included him. And he needed her to not feel threatened by him so that she'd stop looking for ulterior motives in everything he said and did. Even if they were there. And for a moment, when she neither stepped away nor tensed, he thought he was making progress.

But then he saw the apprehension in her face as she looked at the six men already seated at one of the dining tables. Apparently, he was only the lesser of two evils. He could live with that, and use whatever advantage it gave him.

He shifted his hand, laid it on her shoulder then, the one nearest to him so that his arm wasn't even around her back. He meant only to give it a reassuring squeeze, but he hadn't expected the silken feel of her skin to heat his palm.

She wasn't the only one who had to get used to the sizzle. He dropped his hand and touched it once more to the small of her back. Here at least was the protective barrier of fabric. He urged her forward. "They're good guys," he said quietly in her ear. She gave her head a quick shake that feathered her hair over her shoulders, and as she lifted her chin a transformation came over her. Uncertainty vanished and before his eyes, she became the Chastity of those social pages photos—bright, sophisticated, untouchable.

And yet he still wanted to touch her.

The men had looked up and were watching them. Her. He knew it was her, because men didn't generally forget to chew just because they were looking at him.

Dave, the foreman, lifted his chin by way of a greeting, then stood and pulled out the chair at the table next to him. Gabe was betting that also wasn't for his benefit. Chastity seemed to glide across the room. She stopped at their table.

"You guys are doing an amazing job on this place."

And six men started talking at once to try to tell her what they'd been doing. He watched in fascination and, he had to admit, admiration. The woman could work a room, or table, as it were.

After a few minutes he maneuvered her to the next table, before the men could shuffle up and make room for one more, monopolizing her.

Adam brought out their meals. Gabe was expecting the warm lamb salad that the others were eating. It took him a single horrified moment to recognize the meal the Paris-trained chef had set in front of Chastity was macaroni and cheese. He looked at Adam's impassive face. Although he'd shared Chastity's comment with him earlier, Gabe hadn't expected him to make anything of it. Adam was normally a customer service genius, allowing nothing and no one to get under his skin.

A small frown pleated Chastity's brow and then she laughed. Full on, stomach-holding laughter. She looked up at Adam who was now grinning from ear to ear.

The last thing Gabe expected was for Chastity to push her seat back so she could stand and embrace his chef. Nor for his chef to enfold her in a bear hug in return—a hug that in Gabe's opinion lasted far too long. It was his turn to frown.

Finally, Chastity stepped back, smiling widely and slowly shaking her head as she looked at Adam. "Wow. Look at you." She most definitely was, so Gabe did, too, trying to see what put that awed smile on her face. All he saw was Adam, part Maori, a little rough around the edges, his too-long dark hair tied back, a gold stud in one ear, a tattoo just visible beneath the sleeve of his T-shirt, encircling his biceps. He supposed some women would find him attractive in that living-on-the-edge kind of way. But he really wouldn't have thought Adam was the type Chastity would go for. He didn't smack of wealth, though that was deceptive. His restaurants had been phenomenal successes both in New Zealand and in London. Part of that success was due to the image Adam had created and perpetuated for himself as being a hell-raiser from the wrong side of the tracks.

"Wow, right back at you," Adam said tugging on a lock of Chastity's hair. "If Gabe hadn't told me your name, I don't think I would have recognized you for the skinny kid with hair almost green from too much chlorine. Of course the macaroni and cheese comment helped."

"Grab a chair, Adam," Gabe said. "You two clearly have some catching up to do." He pushed aside the relief that had swept through him at the realization that they knew each other from a long time ago. And, more importantly, hadn't seen each other since. Now might just be a good time to learn more about Chastity.

"Sorry, can't." Adam jerked his head in the direction of the kitchen. "Got stuff to do." He reached for Chastity's plate. "I'll bring out your proper dinner."

Chastity grabbed hold of her plate with two hands. "What, and miss out on the dish that started it all? No way."

Adam smiled and tugged her hair one more time. "Catch up with you tomorrow?"

"Of course."

Chastity watched Adam leave, and Gabe watched Chastity, studying the sweet reminiscent expression on her face. She turned slowly back to him and the expression vanished. With a small shake of her head she became Social Pages Chastity once more.

He wanted to know the other.

She ate a forkful of her pasta, heedless of the calorie-laden carbs, and the smile returned. She looked up and caught him watching her. "Adam grew up in the same place I did."

"I said my mother had another side. She's got nothing on you."

Chastity ignored the comment. "He had a hard time of it. People always expected the worst of him and his family." There was a subtle challenge in both her words and her eyes. She broke the gaze, blinking, and then looked over Gabe's shoulder at the bay behind him. She gave a small, sad laugh. "Often as not, he delivered. He's a couple of years younger than me, but he always made out that he was older and tougher. I found him one time down at the beach. Not so tough. He'd been beaten up. I was…going through a rough patch, too. We got to talking about how we were going to get away from that…town. Make something of our lives."

"Looks like you both did."

"I guess." She returned her attention to her food, eating with a deliberate and concentrated precision.

"Good macaroni?"

She smiled. "The best."

They talked a little more throughout the meal. Gabe kept the topics neutral, wanting her to relax. She was easy to talk with, but there was a measured quality to her conversation as though she weighed her words before she spoke, careful not to reveal anything she didn't want to. But each time she smiled or laughed at something he said, it felt like a victory to be savored.

Once they'd finished they chatted a while with the

workmen who were leaning back nursing beers, and then they left. Outside, they walked in unspoken agreement to the water's edge. A full moon hung in the sky, bright enough to cast shadows and shimmering on the still bay.

"Look at it." Chastity sighed over its beauty, but Gabe was far more captivated by the way the light caught softly on her hair and pale shoulders. She slipped off her sandals, letting them dangle from one hand as she walked ankle deep in the water in the direction of her chalet. With her other hand, she pulled up the skirt of her dress.

Gabe kept to the sand, keeping pace with her. Watching her. Wanting to know her, needing to pin down who it was that he was dealing with. "Where was this town you and Adam grew up in?"

"Nowhere you would have heard of," she said, not looking at him.

"Try me."

"No point. It's on the east coast, but not on the way to anywhere. No one who hasn't actually lived there has ever heard of it. Small town, small minds. At least back then."

"It's changed?"

"I wouldn't know. I left when I was seventeen."

"You've never been back?"

"No."

"What about your family?"

"Nothing to tell."

"A town I wouldn't have heard of. A family you have nothing at all to say about. Could you be any more evasive?"

She stopped in the water and turned to face him,

hands planted on her hips. "Fine. One mother, dead for six years. Two half sisters. No genetic diseases or deformities you need to worry about. All our vices are of choice. And, like I said, I didn't know my father. He left when I was a few months old, so I can't vouch for him. Is that enough for you?"

Not nearly. "Are you close to your half sisters?"

"If by close you mean have I spoken to them since our mother's funeral, then the answer's no."

"So you have no one?"

"I can take care of myself."

"That's not what I meant." What was she hiding behind that bristling defiance?

Her expression clouded. "I had my grandmother until a little under a year ago. She was an amazing woman." And then, as though regretting letting him see she'd cared about someone, as though it was a weakness, she lifted her chin and glared at him, and that sorrow he'd glimpsed in her eyes vanished. "Is there anything else you'd like to know?"

"Yes. How heavy is that chip you're carrying around on your shoulder?"

She paused. "Mostly I forget about the chip. Except when some privileged rich guy starts looking down his nose and asking questions, ready to judge me because of where I come from."

"By that, you mean me?" Gabe didn't react because he sensed old hurts beneath the insinuation.

"If the shoe fits."

"I don't judge a person on their upbringing or their past," he said quietly. "I'd like to think I don't judge at all."

Her silence was telling.

She turned away and started walking quickly through the foam of the lapping surf.

"Wait up." He wasn't surprised when she didn't. He kicked off his shoes, jogged along the beach then rolled up the legs of his pants and waded into the water, catching hold of her hand. "What did I say or not say that made you think I was judging you?"

She didn't look at him, just kept walking. Her hand lay utterly passive in his. "Nothing. It's just what people do. Particularly successful people from wealthy backgrounds. I moved away from there because I didn't want to be defined by my family." She made to pull her hand away and he tightened his grasp.

"No one wants to be defined by their family. I knew Adam's background had been tough. He's told me snippets, and I've met some of his family. I never thought it defined him."

"Maybe not. But a lot of people do and some definitions definitely look a lot better than others."

Was she aware that her fingers had curled around his?

"So, you think a judgmental snob from a wealthy background, as you're happily labeling me, is better than a woman who grew up poor but made something of herself?" He wondered what she'd had to overcome to become the woman she was today.

"You really have no idea." She faced him, standing close. "And you do make judgments. Everyone does."

There was nothing passive about her now. Energy leaped from her. And God help him he wanted to kiss her, to cover her mouth with his, to drink in the taste of her, fill his hands with her. To pull her hard against him. Why her? Why did this woman have this effect on him?

It was sorcery; he was under some kind of spell. He broke free of it, furious at his weakness. Furious at her. At himself. He opened his fingers, let go of her hand. Perhaps without the contact of skin, he'd get his head back on straight.

"Maybe. But if I were to judge someone it would be based on solid evidence—my own interactions with them and on their actions. On facts. Like marrying a man for his money, like coming between him and his family." The words were finally out in the open. He waited for her denial, watched carefully for her reaction.

The moon was full and bright, but not *that* bright and he couldn't read her expression. She drew herself up taller. "I'm not having this conversation. It can't achieve anything."

Gabe stared. That was it? Disappointment washed through him. If she'd said she married Tom for love he wouldn't have believed her, but he'd wanted her to at least have convinced herself that she did. He wanted the pretense rather than the mercenary silence of admission.

They walked toward her chalet, not together, but as two strangers who happened to be following the same path.

At the door to her chalet she paused and looked in his direction, not quite meeting his gaze. "Good night." Cool, haughty. Unrepentant. She slipped inside, vanishing from the night.

# Seven

Chastity heard Gabe's voice before she saw him. So much for slipping into the back of the kitchen for lunch and a visit with Adam. She looked up in the direction of the surprisingly close sound and did a double take. If it had been up to her eyes alone, she probably wouldn't have seen him at all, or at least not recognized that it was him. He and Dave stood high above the ground on a scaffolding plank inspecting something on the roof.

She turned away from the sight of Gabe in worn, fitted jeans with a leather tool belt slung low across his hips, and kept walking. She'd planned on avoiding him today, had spent the morning reading and if she could leave her book alone this afternoon, would go for a walk or even try fishing. The weather wasn't as nice as it had been yesterday so she convinced herself she didn't have to swim—because swimming meant time, or at least communication, with Gabe.

Last night, needing to quash the strange stirrings of feeling she had for him, she had taken his accusations about her marriage without argument, but she wasn't ready or strong enough for more.

"Yo, Chastity!" Dave called out. "Lunchtime already? Wait up, we'll come with you."

Great. Looked like she didn't have a choice about being ready or strong enough. She watched the two men climb down from the scaffold.

Gabe would never have believed the truth, that she had married Tom because she had lost the last family member she felt any real connection to, that she was alone and lonely, because she didn't honestly believe in love—for her—not the soul-deep, lifelong connection touted in the movies. Tom had been kind and friendly and up-front about his reason for wanting marriage. Another reason Gabe would never believe.

Gabe jumped lightly to the ground.

"You two go ahead. I'll go round up the guys." With a smile in her direction, Dave disappeared.

Right. Good. Gabe drew level with her and they started walking. Forget about last night. Forget about the animosity. Forget about the strange other heat that had preceded it. Today was a new day, could hopefully be a neutral day. "When you said you'd be working, I didn't think you meant *working*, working."

He looked at her, relaxed and seemingly blessedly neutral. "As in manual labor?"

"Precisely."

"Judging me, Chass?" Okay, so he wasn't going to

forget about last night. But he said it with a half grin that softened his face. And so maybe at least he, like her, was moving forward, putting the past, both recent and more distant, behind him.

"Apparently."

"Actually," he continued, the grin stretching into a smile that spoke to something deep within her, "I didn't think I'd be doing this kind of work, either. But the lawyer who was coming out for a meeting had to reschedule for the afternoon and Dave was down a man this morning, so…" He shrugged, broad shoulders lifting casually beneath the soft cotton of a white T-shirt.

"You know what you're doing? With a hammer?"

"I know enough. I used to volunteer with a charity at building sites during summer vacations."

And suddenly it wasn't hard to imagine at all. Gabe was the sort who could do whatever he decided he'd turn his hand to. Another difference between the brothers. "Tom didn't."

"It wasn't Tom's thing."

She laughed at the thought. "It wouldn't have been. If there was anything that needed doing at the apartment, his first, his only, reaction was to call a tradesman. Several times I stopped him because it was something I could do myself."

"You?"

"Who's judging now?"

"We really do need to start again, don't we?"

"Maybe we just need to be a little more open-minded," she said.

"Maybe." They walked on a few steps. "I guess working on the building sites was my way of spending less time around home."

Was that an admission that the family life Tom found so stifling and repressive had also impacted Gabe? "From what I learned, Tom's way was partying." She could just imagine fun-loving Tom breezing through his summer vacations in a whirl of socializing.

"Something like that." The shadow of his grin still lurked as he opened the door to the restaurant and waited for her to enter.

She smiled up at him, remembering. "He was so easy to love." She regretted her words as the grin disappeared and his eyes narrowed on her. Her step faltered. Not like Gabe, who wouldn't be at all easy to know or to love. But wasn't there some saying about the things worth having not being easily attained?

He stood waiting, arm outstretched, still watching her. She sucked in a deep, supposedly fortifying, breath as she passed close to his masculine warmth, to the contours of his chest.

They ate in silence, her words apparently having killed the conversation. She put down her fork. "What if it wasn't me?"

"What if what wasn't you?"

"What if it wasn't me who drove a wedge in your family? You practically just admitted that you used work to avoid your family, too."

Gabe stared at her, intent. "You're saying it wasn't?"

She should never have spoken, but she had and so now had to continue. "I'm saying laying all the blame at my door is a cop-out." Tom had worked at avoiding his family. Yes, he'd used her as an excuse, at first without her knowledge, but even once she realized what he was doing she hadn't especially minded. And from what she saw, the family wasn't overly concerned. At least they hadn't been until Tom went and died on them all.

"You were all adults, capable of making your own decisions. It's just easier to blame someone else. You can't blame Tom because he's dead, you don't want to blame yourselves because that would mean accepting guilt, so you blame me."

"What were we supposed to assume when Tom said the two of you couldn't come to a family dinner because you'd made other arrangements, or you weren't feeling well, over and over till it was undeniably obvious that it was nothing more than a phony excuse?"

"How hard did you really try? So often the invitations were for Tom alone that it could be interpreted as nothing more than insulting. Do you blame him for sticking up for his wife? What effort did you personally make to see Tom outside of work, to try to understand where he was at?"

"What needed to be understood? He had a great job, a great life. And he had you."

Silence fell as he challenged her with his gaze. There was so much about Tom that Gabe had needed to understand. And now it was too late. But mainly she fixated on his last sentence. "And he had you." As though Tom's having her was…something Gabe envied?

The builders turned up then, arguing and joking, and soon Adam joined them, insisting that he have the seat next to Chastity. She felt finally like she had a friend at her shoulder, someone to shield her from Gabe. She turned to Adam, let him regale her with stories of his times in London and around the world.

When the helicopter touched down outside, Gabe excused himself from the table.

As conversation flowed around her, Chastity watched through the massive windows as he greeted the suited lawyer who stepped from the chopper, and she tried to figure out how it was that Gabe, in jeans and a T-shirt, was subtly, yet clearly, the man with the power.

She also tried to figure out why Gabe held an undeniable fascination for her, how he affected her on so many levels. She couldn't help but wonder, if things had been different... He'd invaded her thoughts, claimed her senses. She wanted to look at him, to touch him. She'd even, as she'd passed by him earlier, had the craziest urge to press her face to his chest and breathe in his scent.

But things weren't different, and the crazy compulsions were just, she told herself, repercussions from the knowledge that she carried his child. Maybe she was a vehicle for the unseen and unseeing person getting to know her father. Just as her appetite for food was a way to nourish the child, her appetite for Gabe was also stirred by the child.

Appetite for Gabe? She wanted to bang her head on the table.

"You look like you've got it bad."

Startled, Chastity turned to Adam. She'd forgotten he was even there. "I've got something bad, that's for sure. I just don't know what it is, or what I should do about it."

"I know the feeling."

"Woman trouble?" she smiled.

He nodded. "Man trouble?" he asked in return.

"Always is," they said in unison.

"This time," Adam said, "it's not something I can run away from."

Chastity looked back out at Gabe. He and the lawyer were striding across the lawn. He glanced in her direction, his gaze a direct contact despite the distance and the glass between them. This man was the father of her child. There was no running away from that fact. "Me neither."

Gabe watched Chastity across the table. The setting sun behind her burnished her hair as she finished her salmon and salad, and aligned her knife and fork neatly together on her plate. He hadn't seen her all afternoon. She'd reluctantly joined him for dinner, but had scarcely spoken to him, let alone looked at him. And yet when she talked to Dave or Adam, he caught glimpses of someone else, someone relaxed with a ready laugh and a dazzling smile.

She wore a white tank top with jewel-like stones studded around the neckline. A neckline that dipped low but clung faithfully. He knew because it had nagged at his attention all through their meal.

Chastity glanced around the dining room, her gaze sliding past him. "I think I'll head back to my chalet."

"Adam's made dessert."

"I'll pass." She stood, so Gabe did, too.

Surprise—or was it that latent fear he'd seen before?—crossed her face. Either way he made her edgy. "You stay."

He shook his head. "I'll walk with you."

He saw a protest form on her lips, but then she looked at him and whatever she'd been about to say died away.

She went for a nonchalant shrug instead, lifted her chin. A nonverbal *whatever*.

His phone rang and while he took the call, she made her escape.

But it was a quick call and he followed her outside. In the balmy evening she hesitated at choosing between the direct path to her chalet and the walk along the fore-shore. She headed for the water. Sandals dangling from her fingers, she walked along the wet sand, heedless of the waves that periodically swept up and around her ankles.

He caught up easily, but she didn't acknowledge his presence. "I've been thinking about what you said at lunch, about the blame for Tom's estrangement not being yours."

"I've been thinking about it, too, and I'm sorry. I shouldn't have said what I did. I'm also sorry that you missed out on so much of Tom's life in the last two years."

"Who *are* you?" He unintentionally voiced his thoughts. She was such a puzzle, sometimes confirming his opinion of her, sometimes confounding it.

She paused and looked at him.

The more time he spent with her the less he felt he knew her. Two steps forward and two steps back, or sideways, ending up somewhere different but no more enlightening. Was it possible to confuse reserved and perhaps uncertain with haughty and cold? Just a few weeks ago he'd been so sure he knew her, or knew her type. An ever-climbing socialite, all gloss and no substance. But he was starting to wonder whether that wasn't precisely what she wanted him to think. Whether her refusal to defend herself last night was just that and no more? Too many things about her didn't quite add up. How did her friendship with

Sophie, her love of reading and swimming and walking barefoot in the water fit with the socialite persona?

"Who am I? What do you mean?" She was immediately defensive and he didn't want her defensive.

"Nothing." He had to be more subtle. Watch and wait for her to reveal herself.

"I've got a question then. Who are *you?* Does work really consume as much of your life as it looks like it does, as Tom always said it did?"

He thought about that for a moment. "Yes." It was the only honest answer. "But that's my choice. I could just as easily choose to do other things, as well. But work is what gets me fired up—the making of deals, seeing projects come to fruition." Although lately, if he was honest, he hadn't found the same satisfaction that he used to. "When I'm a father, that will change."

Chastity made a dismissive noise, almost a snort. Then when she looked at him, her derision turned to horror. "You really think you want to play Daddy?"

"It won't be playing."

She turned and kept walking. "I just have a hard time picturing you in the role."

Gabe narrowed the distance between them so that they walked almost shoulder to shoulder. "I don't find it so hard. I've been thinking about it a lot lately."

"And?"

"And I've realized I do want children. I just hadn't thought about it before because I haven't met the right woman. But I can imagine building sand castles at this very beach, walking along the sand with a woman, a child between us, each holding a hand, swinging my little girl over the waves." He allowed himself to picture the scene.

She was silent a moment as they walked slowly on. "There are so many things wrong with that picture."

"Like what?"

"Like you're picturing some idyllic time, forgetting things like sleepless nights and childhood illnesses and dirty diapers."

"I'm a realist if nothing else. I know about those things. Doesn't mean that has to be what I choose to dwell on. It's not what you think about, is it? You think about cuddles and gurgling laughter and butterfly kisses."

"I guess," she admitted. "But what about the woman part? You're already picturing a woman on the scene helping you. There might not be one. You'll likely be doing it all alone."

"I'm more than happy to, and capable of, doing it alone. But chances are there'll be a woman. A wife. At some stage."

A small frown pleated her brow as her gaze found his across the foot of evening that separated them, but he couldn't read what was in her eyes. "Is there someone?" she asked as though considering the possibility for the first time. "Does she know? About this?" Chastity gestured to her stomach.

"There's no one at the moment. But there will be one day. It's on my list."

"It's on your *list*?" A gurgle of laughter, like sunlight on water, escaped her. "What, somewhere between 'buy next resort' and 'pick up dry cleaning'? Like when you get to number six on your list, you'll look around and the perfect woman will be waiting?"

"That didn't come out quite how I meant it."

"No, but it was probably how you were thinking it. And I've seen the women you date. They might not be so keen on Bachelor of the Year if he has a little girl taking up too much of his time and attention."

"That's not the kind of woman I'll marry."

"Just the kind you like to sleep with."

He ran his hand through his hair in frustration. "You are so twisting this."

"You're doing a pretty good job of that on your own."

"You know nothing about the women I've dated."

"Aside from all the cosmetic surgery," she cupped and lifted her breasts, momentarily riveting his attention there, "and Amber who never got her hair wet when she swam."

He dragged his gaze upward. "Amber who was a pediatric oncologist."

"Was she really?" Surprise sprang to her face and he felt momentarily bad for tricking her.

"No. Sadly, she was actually a lingerie model."

"Really?" And this time she sounded intrigued.

"No. Sorry again. I was joking."

She looked away.

He slung his arm around her stiff shoulders and leaned in. Brotherly, he tried to tell himself. He wasn't going to let her dismiss him on any level. "Are you always this gullible?"

"Pretty much. It's a failing." The shoulders softened beneath his touch. And for the life of him, he couldn't force himself to drop his arm. He barely managed to stop his fingers from caressing the warmth of her skin.

"It's a very endearing failing."

She looked back at him, a very endearing earnestness in her gaze. "Anyway, back at your apartment that first night, you said you never joked."

"I don't. Usually." What was it about being with her that changed him? And why? He thought again about dropping his arm, and just as quickly dismissed the thought. There was no harm in it. Friends.

"This woman on your list, what does she do, what does she look like?"

"She's a kindergarten teacher."

Chastity laughed, the sound dancing over the waves.

"Actually I wasn't joking that time."

She laughed harder, her slender frame shaking beneath his touch.

In one movement Gabe snaked a leg out in front of her ankles and pivoted her so that she fell backward till the only thing keeping her from the water were his arms, one behind her shoulders, one around her waist. Her hands flew to his shoulders, clutched at him.

"Not so funny now, is it?" He met her deep blue eyes, mere inches away from his, the laughter still dancing there. His gaze flicked to her softly parted lips. And he wanted nothing more in all the world than to haul her against him and kiss her. To lose himself in her. To lose both of them. Forget everything except this moment. Not brotherly. Not friendly. Something else altogether, something hot and insistent.

He righted her again, released her and walked slowly on as though nothing at all had happened. As though his world hadn't tripped and tilted in much the same way he'd done to her. He wanted Chastity Stevens. Wanted himself deep inside her.

And that wanting could only lead to disaster.

She caught up to him. "But a kindergarten teacher? Really?"

Gabe fought for composure. Ruthlessly quashed the erratic, erotic thoughts. "Doesn't have to be. That was just an example."

"Someone wholesome and innocent." A shadow passed over her face.

"No, someone kind and gentle and trustworthy."

The shadow deepened.

"Though I don't have a problem with wholesome and innocent."

"And why would Miss Kind-Gentle-Trustworthy-Wholesome-and-Innocent want to have anything to do with Mr. Ruthlessly-Successful-Workaholic? Aside from money? Which naturally she won't care about. When are you even going to find time to locate this perfect woman?"

"I'll make time."

"You're what, thirty-four? And you haven't made time yet."

"I've been busy. I haven't felt the need."

"You've been busy your whole life. It's not that easy to stop."

"I can stop whenever I want."

"The world will keep turning if you take a step back from it."

"A fact I'm well aware of, thank you." His phone rang, and he clenched his fists to stop himself from reaching for it.

"Then give me your phone."

"No." He let the call go to voice mail.

"Why not?"

"People need to be able to contact me. I need to be able to call them, arrange things."

Chastity's eyes danced with merriment and superiority as she…smirked.

"It's not that I can't."

She nodded, ostensibly agreeing. "When did you last take a vacation?"

"That's none of your business."

An I-told-you-so look of satisfaction spread across her face. "When were you last separated from your phone for more than an hour?"

"This conversation is ridiculous. You think you know me. You have no idea."

"Ditto," she said quietly. Then a little louder, "Here you are building this exclusive lodge so people can take some real time out, no clocks, no newspapers, the beautiful ocean at their doorstep, the simple pleasures of life and you can't even do it yourself."

"It's not a good time at the moment." He was well aware of both the irony and the flimsiness of his excuse. Chastity's eye roll proved she was aware of it, too.

"Children don't wait till it's convenient to need you. Prove that you can do it. Give me your phone."

His hand tightened around it in his pocket.

"Spend an entire day without it. Show me that you can."

He wasn't sure how she was somehow making this about him, as though he was the one who needed to prove himself worthy to be a parent. He didn't have to prove anything to her. Except that he deserved rights when it came to his child. But it could work both ways.

He pulled the phone from his pocket, and after checking who the last call had been from, switched it off and held it out to her. The surprise in her eyes was some consolation. She really hadn't thought he'd do it. Slowly, she reached out and took his phone, held it carefully yet gingerly.

Gabe slid his hands into his pockets. "If I'm going without my phone or work for the day, what do you have to do?"

"Keep you honest."

"Not good enough. You can go without your disguise."

"Disguise?" she sounded genuinely confused.

"The glamour, whatever. The makeup, the hairstyle, the designer clothes." Her eyes widened, making her look both startled and vulnerable. "It's all about simplicity, right?" She took a step away from him and he saw the *no* form on her soft pink lips. "Don't tell me you can't," he challenged, suddenly wanting this, and not just because it would even the balance of the challenge, but because there was someone different beneath the glamour, someone she only let him get glimpses of. But the glimpses intrigued him and he was curious, more than curious, to explore them.

"Of course I can, but—"

"Good. It's a deal." He knew better than to give her time to dwell on it or back out. "So, how are we spending this day?" It was his turn to push. "You and me. Together." He held her gaze, expecting that subtle fear he sometimes caught, but instead her eyes reflected her acceptance of the challenge and he saw a switch from defensive to offensive. He tamped down the flare of admiration and anticipation.

"You start by sleeping in. Then when you wake up you have coffee and breakfast brought to your chalet."

"No staff for that." He took pleasure in pointing out the first flaw in her plan.

"I'll do it." She smiled sweetly, countering him. "Then you sit in your pajamas—"

"I don't wear them."

"Or a bathrobe, or a pair of boxers," she said, after only the briefest hesitation. "Anything that's not proper clothes. You wear that while you sit on the veranda of the chalet eating your breakfast slowly and drinking— sipping—your coffee. Doing nothing other than enjoying the food, each and every bite you put in your mouth," she said, apparently unaware of the sensual images she conjured. "And appreciating the sight of the blue ocean in front of you, and the sound of the birdsong behind you."

"And you'll be with me?"

"Absolutely. Someone has to make sure you don't cheat, don't borrow a phone or a laptop. And obviously I'll have to have your laptop, too."

"Obviously," he said, not meaning it. "Then what?"

"Then nothing."

"What do you mean nothing?"

"I wouldn't have thought there were too many inter- pretations."

"But—"

"Oh, we'll do something. Probably. But the point is not to have it all planned out, not to schedule your time. We're not watching a clock." She gave a lazy shrug of her pale shoulder. "We might swim or read a book or go for a walk. Or we might do nothing. No thing. And you don't need to look so horrified. If you're going to have days where you have *my* child, then there will most definitely be days when you get absolutely nothing done—when if you manage to have a shave in the morning, you'll count that as an achievement."

"I hardly think so."

"Ever spent time around a baby?"

"No."

"Then let's just start with tomorrow, okay?"

"Sure."

She spun around, her skirt spinning and lifting with the movement, showing long, slender legs. "I'll see you with breakfast, then."

"What time?"

She laughed. "This is so going to kill you."

# Eight

Chastity was far from laughing the next morning when she set the breakfast tray down on the outdoor table and tapped on the door of Gabe's chalet. Suddenly her brilliant idea seemed positively dimwitted. She'd backed herself into spending the day with Gabe. A Gabe who wouldn't have work to distract him. And somehow he'd known that without her careful facade of elegance she would feel vulnerable.

"It's open."

Like she'd step willingly into the lion's den? "I'll wait out here." She thought she heard his quiet chuckle. He was going to make her pay. A few seconds later his door swung open. The sunlight streaming onto the veranda caught on his bare chest, on the definition of his abs. Black silk boxers rode low on his lean hips. She dragged her gaze upward to his tousled hair, his beard-shadowed jaw, to his slumberous eyes. Chastity swallowed past the sudden dryness of her throat. "Have you really been in bed till now? Or is this a careful ruse and you've actually been up for hours secretly working?"

He stepped back so that she could see the unmade bed. "It's still warm if you want to test it."

"No. Thank you."

His gaze returned her assessment, traveled over her freshly scrubbed face, over the loose tank top, over her shorts, bare legs and the flip-flops on her feet. "Like the outfit."

"Thank you," she said, studying the wooden decking beneath her feet.

He tapped a gentle knuckle to the underside of her jaw urging her to look at him. "So what's for breakfast? I'm starving."

For a moment their eyes locked and her body heated. Chastity forced her legs to move and stepped back so that he could see the tray on the table. Gabe strolled past her.

She carried his child. The thought ricocheted around inside her. And there was a part of her—the part that could ignore the untold complications that fact caused—that was glad of it. It was only, she told herself, that on a purely primal level he was…her ideal of physical perfection.

Gabe sat, leaning back in his chair. "Everything okay?"

She shook her head to clear it. "Fine."

A knowing smile tugged at the corners of his lips. "Coffee?" He lifted the French press from the tray.

"No, thanks. There's a chamomile tea there for me." Though she was well beyond the point where the supposedly relaxing chamomile could give her any help.

"So, are you joining me?" He looked at her where she still stood by his door, one hand gripping the frame. She released her fingers, gritted her teeth and made her way to the second chair. Gabe passed the plate of melon slices to her. "Is something wrong?"

She could hardly tell him to put a shirt on without breaking her own rules of the day being about informality or worse, without revealing quite how distracting that bare chest, with its light covering of hair, was. "No." She picked up a slice of honeydew melon and bit into it.

When she looked up again he was staring at her. "What is it?"

"You have beautiful skin," he said with a note of surprise.

"Thank you. I think."

"You don't need all the makeup you wear. You don't need anything."

"My choice."

"What is it you're hiding?"

"Don't try to make it into something it's not." What she really meant was, *don't delve, don't try to figure out anything about me.* She wanted to keep her barriers against him, wanted even now to run back to her chalet, fix her face and her hair, change her clothes, because there was safety in the facade she presented to the world.

He shrugged. "I like it."

They lay on sun loungers in the shade of the veranda. Gabe was seemingly immersed in his—her book, the thriller, the one she'd planned on starting today. But when she'd brought out a selection for him to choose from, he'd gone straight for that one. She'd heard it was good. Sadly, the one she'd chosen for herself just wasn't grabbing her. For that the blame lay in part with the man a few feet away. The man turning the pages with great rapidity, the man who chuckled occasionally. The man with those long legs that were more enticing than the words on the page in front of her. Fortunately, he'd put on cargo shorts and a dark polo shirt after breakfast. The shirt at least saved her from his chest though it still managed to hint at the contours it shielded.

She tried her book for a couple more minutes before looking over at him again. "Shall we go snorkeling?"

It was a few seconds before he looked up. His gaze came to rest on her. "Sorry? Did you say something?"

"I thought you might like to go snorkeling. Adam says the next bay around is great for it. And I want to collect some shells for Sophie—those ring-shaped ones that fit over her fingers."

"No, I'm…" He checked out the book open in her hands, where she was clearly only a scant way into it, "Sure. Sounds good."

This wasn't how it was supposed to be working. He was the one who was supposed to be getting antsy at the enforced relaxation, not her. Still, she jumped up, discarding her book on her lounger. Gabe closed his book, set it on the floor and stood. He lifted his arms above his head, stretching. That chest was too close. Too inviting.

Gabe watched Chastity rest her dessert spoon on the side of her plate. He loved watching her eat, the sensory pleasure she took in food. He'd noticed it these past days. No picking at her meals, just her own brand of careful savoring. Often on her first mouthful she would even close her eyes, devoting all her attention to the flavors in her mouth.

She looked up, caught him watching her. "So, how'd you find it? A whole day without your cell phone?"

"Remarkably pleasant." And it had been, if he ignored the constant thrum of physical awareness. Reading, snorkeling, swimming, even a siesta. He couldn't remember the last time he'd spent such an indolent day. He couldn't remember the last time he'd spent such an easy day with a woman. It had been Chastity who needed time to relax into it, but finally she had when they'd gone fishing. Her wariness around him had receded and they'd talked, or not, as they sat on the end of the jetty, helped each other with the fish they finally caught. He liked that she wasn't squeamish. He liked that his fish had been bigger than hers and that that had subtly annoyed her. Funny how he could like having her both relaxed and unaware of him and like getting under her skin.

In the fading light they walked along the beach. Chastity *in* the water as usual. Gabe fingered the shell rings in his pocket.

When they were even with her chalet, she stopped and kicked up a small splash of water with her toes. "It's still so warm."

He heard the wistfulness in her voice. "You want to swim again, don't you?"

"Yes." She looked at him. "Do you mind? I know you don't want me swimming without you watching. But it'll be safe. There's light left and the moon is already up. I love swimming at night. It's so…otherworldly."

Just as she was, standing there like a mythical goddess in human form with the water lapping around her calves. A siren sent to tempt and bewitch him.

"Swim. I don't have anywhere else I have to be. Unless you're letting me off the hook now and giving me back my phone?"

"Nope. One whole day. That was the deal. I'll just change." She skipped from the water and jogged toward her chalet. Gabe breathed a sigh of pure relief.

He was waiting for her when—bikini clad—she came back out. He caught her scanning the shoreline and looking back toward the chalets. "Gabe?" she called. Her soft voice carried across the water.

"Here."

She spun to face the bay where he trod water, waiting for her.

"Oh."

"I wanted to be close. So I didn't lose sight of you."

"I didn't mean to make you swim, too."

"It's no hardship." The hardship lay in watching her standing there hesitant in the moonlight, her pale limbs long and slender. She walked slowly into the water. He swallowed and turned away. Good thing the water and darkness hid his reaction to her. If she was anyone else, if he didn't know the things he did about her, if they didn't both have agendas, if she hadn't been his brother's wife… He swam a few lazy strokes deeper. *Stay in control here,* he warned himself.

He heard the quiet splash of her stroke as she caught up to him. They breaststroked in unison toward the jetty and stopped a few meters shy of it and trod water. Over the lap of the waves on the shore, they heard the occasional burst of laughter from the men still in the dining room. Gabe looked toward the sound—away from her pale face and shoulders, away from the swell of her breasts just visible beneath the waterline.

The dining room was the brightest spot of light on the shoreline, and he could make out the men sitting inside. Through a second window he could see Adam with a phone pressed to his ear. Adam—who knew Chastity. The more time Gabe spent with her, the less he felt like he knew her. He looked back at her. And wanted her.

"Why Tom?" That easily he shattered their fragile truce.

She backed away a little, putting physical distance, as well as emotional distance, between them. "I thought you'd already decided the answer to that. For his money. Maybe what you really mean is why did he marry me?"

He said nothing.

"Oh, right. You've decided the answer to that, as well."

He wouldn't be swayed by the hurt in her expression and looked away, toward her chalet, just one solar-powered outdoor light indicating its location. When he turned back she was no longer beside him. He waited, then turned a frantic full circle, and when he still didn't locate her, panic flared. "Chastity?"

Nothing.

"Chass!" he shouted.

Still nothing. He was about to shout again before diving down to search when he heard the faintest splash. He spun toward the sound to see her surfacing halfway to the shore and swimming in her graceful freestyle for the beach.

Gabe surged after her.

She had a big enough head start that she'd reached water shallow enough to walk in by the time he caught up with her, and she was pushing through the waist-deep ocean.

He caught hold of her wrist. "Don't do that to me."

She turned, pulling her wrist from his grasp. "Do what?"

"Disappear in the water."

She looked up at him, her eyes sparkling with anger in the moonlight. "I'll do what I please. I'm not a child and I'm not your responsibility. And I'm not going to wait passively around while you insult me."

When she would have turned away he grabbed her shoulders. "You're here with me, you are my responsibility. And you're carrying my child."

"Don't pretend you care."

"I do care. You frightened me." He could barely keep the anger from his voice. He'd never known panic like those infinite few seconds when he couldn't see her.

Some of the fight went out of her, he could feel it in the softening of her shoulders beneath his hands. "I'm not going to do anything that could harm your child, because first and foremost she's my child."

"It's not just the baby."

"Oh, please. If it wasn't for the baby, you and I would never have seen each other again. You can't stand me. That much is obvious despite your halfhearted efforts at hiding it. I know what you're trying to do. But give it up because—"

He cut her words off with his kiss. Dammit. He couldn't help himself. Without thought he'd lowered his mouth to hers. Her lips were cool and salty from the water, but her mouth was hot and open beneath his because he'd caught her midsentence. And he couldn't stop. With his hands still on her shoulders, he pulled her closer till their bodies pressed together in the water. He tasted her sweetness, reveled in the soft contours of her body—breasts, hips, thighs—and he felt her response coursing through her. Her body communicating directly with his. Her hands clasped his head, her fingers threaded through his hair and her tongue moved against his. He was in heaven, a deep, drugging ecstasy that obliterated all thought, left only sensation and desire. He could feel the press of her breasts against his chest and he groaned his helplessness into her mouth, eased his thigh between her legs and she bore down against him.

Her hands shifted to his shoulders and for a second she clung fiercely to him, and then she flattened her palms and pushed. She stepped away, turned and surged through the water. Gabe watched her go. Watched her run for her chalet as soon as she hit the sand. Watched her open her door, heard her slam it behind her.

What had he done?

Kissing Chastity hadn't been part of his plan. He wasn't even supposed to like her. She'd trapped his brother. She was a mercenary, conniving, manipulative, beautiful…fragile, sweet woman who had let his family vilify her to protect Tom, and who was carrying his baby. And who kissed like she was on fire. For him.

And he wanted her.

His dead brother's wife. Gabe knew right from wrong and this was wrong on so many levels. He wanted to blame her. She shouldn't have kissed him back. But he couldn't. He'd started the kiss, caught her by surprise and she had ended it. He tried to tell himself that he wished she'd ended it sooner, but he was only grateful that she hadn't.

\* \* \*

Chastity couldn't identify the sound that woke her at first. When she finally recognized it for a helicopter, she leaped from her bed. The helicopter meant escape. A way off this island without having to wait for the mail ferry—the option she'd settled on as she'd tossed, sleepless, through the night.

She raced to her window in time to see the chopper lift into the air—leaving, not arriving.

At breakfast she made the discovery that Gabe had gone with it. He'd left no message. He obviously wanted to get away from her. He must have felt her response last night. Her hunger for him.

Stupid. That's what she'd been. Seven kinds of stupid.

If and when he came back she'd be ready for the helicopter. She had to get away from here. Away from him.

Adam found her reading on a sun lounger after lunch. "There's a path that leads up through the forest. Takes about half an hour."

Chastity dropped her book, jumping at the chance to do something different. Something that might distract her. The book, the thriller she'd snagged back from Gabe, had scarcely held her attention. It had scant power in comparison to the memory of last night, of Gabe's kiss, and of the desire that had flamed through her.

She pulled her sundress on over her swimsuit. Adam would be good company. He would ask no questions.

Instead, she found, it was her who had questions. "How do you know Gabe?"

"We've been friends for years. Ever since I catered a function for him in London."

"What's he asked you about me?"

"Gabe?"

She nodded.

Adam looked blank. "Nothing."

"Nothing about where we grew up?" She didn't need to spell it out for Adam—about her childhood full of taunts, about the town that had shunned her because of whose daughter, and whose sister, she was. "My family?"

"No. And even if he had, I wouldn't have said anything."

"I know that. I just thought he'd try to probe."

"If Gabe had questions, he'd ask you. That's how he is."

She acknowledged his point. Gabe had no trouble asking direct questions.

They were standing at the lookout on the island's highest peak and admiring the 360 degree view when she first heard and then saw the returning chopper.

"Oh, no." She turned for the track.

"What?" Adam called after her, alarmed.

"I need to catch that helicopter." Her case was packed in preparation, ready and waiting at the door of her chalet. She ran—sprinted—back down the forested trail and burst into the open just as the helicopter disappeared out over the ocean again. She wanted to scream her frustration.

Standing in front of her was Gabe.

Adam came out of the forest and stood at her shoulder. "Everything all right?"

Gabe walked toward them. "Fine," she panted. "I've just got to go." She hurried toward her chalet. Hopefully he'd talk to Adam. Hopefully he wanted to avoid her as desperately as she needed to avoid him.

But she'd scarcely shut her door behind her when

Gabe knocked and pushed it open. He stood in the doorway, a white business shirt on, the top few buttons undone, lines etched into his face. Concern showed in his dark eyes.

"We need to talk." His gaze swept the bare room, paused at her case. "Planning on going somewhere?"

She, too, looked at the case. "Home. It's not working, me being here with you."

"You don't have to go."

"Yes, I do."

"I brought you here to rest, relax. And so we could get to know each other. I never meant… It was wrong. *I* was wrong. It won't happen again. I promise."

"You can't make that promise."

"I'm not that weak. I can and I will promise."

She looked at him then, held his gaze. "It wasn't just you, though, was it? There were two of us in that kiss."

His eyes narrowed warily. "I started it. I won't do it again." She could hear anger and blame, directed at himself, in his words.

She closed the distance between them. "I know you're not weak. But what if I am?" She caught his masculine scent. "What if I kissed you? Are you strong enough for both of us?"

"What?" His surprise was almost comical.

She turned away, walked to the vase of orange tiger lilies on the dresser. She touched a finger to the soft petals. "There's something you should know."

Gabe didn't say anything. As far as she could tell, he hadn't even moved. But he was listening. She knew it. "It's about Tom and me. About our relationship."

"I don't need to know anything about it. I didn't

before. I don't now." He couldn't disguise the tension and anger in his voice.

"Yes, you do. I need you to trust me because I'm going to be raising your—our—child. You already think badly enough of me. I'm not going to add this to the list. And you don't have to think as badly about yourself as I think you might be." She took a deep breath and looked at the flowers in front of her. "Tom and I, we didn't…we weren't…" she began, then took another even deeper breath. "We never slept together." The words rushed out.

She heard him move then. Quick footsteps. She turned in time to see him drop heavily onto her bed. "What? Why? No?" He looked at her in patent disbelief.

"Yes." She sat next to him, kept a careful distance and stared at her feet. "I'm not going to give you our reasons. They're private." Of all the things Tom had hidden from his family, that was the biggest. "But I just wanted you to know so you didn't think I was some kind of…"

"Never?" The question was laced with incredulous disbelief.

"Never," she said quietly. "And don't think that means I cheated on him. I didn't. I wouldn't."

"But what did you do for… Never mind."

"Sex?"

"It doesn't matter. Forget I asked."

"That's the easy part to answer. I never found sex to be all that it was cracked up to be. I'm quite happy without it."

His jaw dropped open and she smiled.

"I think it's maybe a lack of the normal hormones or something. Because usually I never even think about it.

The trouble is that's kind of changed since I've been pregnant. And lately I do think about it. A lot. And the real trouble is I think about it…with you. Even now, this very moment. You're sitting on my bed and I'm thinking about it, about you. So, you see, I need to leave."

"Damn."

"Exactly."

He stood, as though not wanting to be so close to her, as though worried, given her admission, that she'd try to jump him. Sensible man.

"Can you get the helicopter to return?" She spoke to his broad back as he stared out her window. Noted against her will his lean hips. His very nice, clutchable butt.

"Not till tomorrow. The pilot's on another job."

"The ferry?"

"Doesn't come Sundays."

"Oh."

He turned. "We can manage this."

"You'll have to do the managing because you're at least not being driven nuts by hormones."

"You at least have an excuse."

She didn't get his meaning. "Maybe if I slept with someone…other than you, the cravings would pass."

He said nothing. A muscle worked in his jaw.

"Adam might help me."

"Over my dead body."

"You're right. We spent too much time together growing up. He's too much like a brother."

"That's got nothing to do with it. If you're going to sleep with someone, it's going to be me."

In the echoing silence that followed his fierce pronouncement, she stared at him.

"You're having my baby anyway," he added.

"I'm not going to be your pity—"

"It wouldn't be pity, Chass. It'd be desire. The same thing you're fighting."

"Yes, but you're fighting it because you don't like who I am. I don't want to sleep with a man who doesn't like me. And I won't. I just won't. I'm not like—"

"Like who?"

"No one." She pushed past him. "I'm going for a swim. That will cool me off. And you are not swimming with me. And tomorrow I'm going to leave." She strode outside and across the sand. At the water's edge she peeled her dress off from over her swimsuit, dropped it on the sand and ran into the water. When she was chest deep, she turned to see that he'd followed her. "Don't come in. I'm not going any deeper than this." She swam for a hundred strokes parallel with the shore, turned and swam back again. All the while Gabe kept pace with her on the land.

When she stood again she was cold, deliciously cold, some of the awful, restless heat had gone. She walked from the water. "Actually, I think I'm better now. My little…problem has passed. But it will still be best if I leave tomorrow."

Chastity woke from a fevered dream in a tangle of sheets, the need within her almost unbearable. There was only one thing that seemed to help. Actually, there would be two things that would help, but she wasn't going near the second one.

Her one-piece swimsuit was still a little damp so she pulled on her bikini, threw a T-shirt over the top of it and in the half-light that preceded sunrise, she walked the short distance to Gabe's chalet. Promises. Why did she make them?

"Gabe," she whispered loudly. She tapped on his door. It swung open just as she was about to try the handle. He wore only boxers. The soft light of dawn washed over him, all contours and shadows. His gaze traveled over her, eyebrows rising as he took in her loose T-shirt, her bare legs. "I need to swim again," she whispered, embarrassed. She saw him swallow. "I'll be okay on my own though if you want to go back to bed."

"I'll change and come with you," he said, his voice raspy with sleep.

She turned, headed for the moonlit water. "I won't go in far this time, either. You don't need to come in," she called back over her shoulder.

"Don't look, but I could use a cold swim, too."

She looked and tried not to be awed and a little flattered. "Me?" she whispered.

Gabe was not amused. "Only you."

Really? Best not to dwell on that. These feelings—yearning, craving, hunger—were a temporary insanity. Chastity turned away again and dropped her T-shirt and her towel to the sand. She ran for the water and dived under as soon as it was deep enough. She swam. And when she finally stopped and looked for Gabe he was a distance—a safe distance—away. She swam for the pontoon, figuring that because Gabe was in the water, too, he wouldn't mind her being out so far. She touched it, then headed back for the shore, pushing herself hard. By the time she could touch her feet to the sandy bottom, she was tired and had cooled and most importantly had exorcised with exercise the fevered longing.

Gabe already stood on the shore, drying himself off. As she approached he picked up her towel and held it out to her. He was so beautiful.

"Better?" he asked.

"Yes. You?" She reached for the towel.

"Completely." He didn't let it go.

They stood facing each other, his gaze held hers. And the heat returned. She remembered the last time they'd been in the water together.

"I don't know what it is about your collarbone," he said.

"My collarbone?"

Gabe ran a finger along the bone, from her shoulder, over the strap of her bikini top, to the hollow at the base of her throat. The finger began its slow exploratory journey back and again encountered the strap. This time it slid beneath the thin strip of Lycra, eased it to the edge of her shoulder.

He gently thumbed where the strap had lain. Chastity stood, rendered immobile as he lowered his mouth to that very spot and pressed heated lips to her cold skin.

"Two choices. Water or bed?"

"Water," she croaked, grasping for the tattered shreds of her sanity, hoping it would douse the desire.

He eased her strap back into place then took her hand, led her back to the water. Chest deep, they stopped.

"Is this working for you?"

Mute, she shook her head.

"Me neither."

"Swimming might help?"

"It might."

He didn't release her hand though. Instead he turned toward her and tugged her closer till her breasts grazed against his chest, till her hips pressed against his and she could feel just how much it wasn't working for him. He slid his hands along her jaw, threaded his fingers into her hair. For a second he held her gaze and she could see the echo of her own hunger in his darkened eyes. And then he lowered his head.

# Nine

Gabe's mouth was hot on hers, his kiss kindling the flames within her into an inferno. Chastity clutched at his shoulders and then, as his tongue danced with hers, slid her arms around him, needing to get closer. Needing to feel every part of him against every part of her. She wanted him. Desperately. He was strength and power and heat. He was solidity in a world that was spiraling. He was the only thing that made sense in the midst of her insanity.

For so long she had denied the way she wanted him, and then when she'd had no choice but to acknowledge her desire, she'd thought she would be strong enough to fight the clamoring need. Only now, she realized her utter weakness for him. All the willpower she had was focused not on running from him, but on getting closer, on sating her desire by claiming him in the most elemental of ways.

His seeking hands explored the length of her back, trailing sparks along her spine and over her skin. Those deft, pleasuring hands lowered till they cradled her hips, fingertips digging in to her buttocks, massaging, as he lifted and pulled her harder against him.

Buoyed by the water, Chastity lifted her legs, wrapped them around his hips and felt the delicious pressure of him against her. Closer. Better. And yet still not enough.

She tipped her head back as he trailed kisses down her throat, devoting himself for a time to her collarbone before his mouth moved hungrily lower. She hadn't realized he'd undone the strap of her bikini till the triangles of fabric covering her breasts fell away with the slightest tug of his teeth, revealing her tautly peaked nipples.

She should have felt vulnerable, and yet she felt like a goddess. He covered one nipple with his hot mouth, working dark magic with his lips and tongue and teeth, and she arched into him, a whimper escaping her. It was as though there was a direct line between her nipple and the swollen, aching flesh between her legs. And all the attention he lavished on her breasts only intensified her cravings. She pressed herself harder against him. She hadn't known need the like of it. Hadn't even known a need this powerful, this all-consuming, existed. She had to do something to ease it. And the only release to be had was with Gabe. Gabe, who should have been all wrong, but who was so very right.

She slid her hand between them, slid it inside the waistband of his swimming trunks, closed her fingers around the length of him and freed him. She nudged aside the narrow fabric of her bikini and positioned him at her entrance.

"Chass, wait." The raw weakness of his voice thrilled her. His grip was fierce on her hips.

"No. I won't. I can't. This is just sex. We both know that." She knew what she wanted. And what she wanted was Gabe. Only Gabe.

She touched a finger to his lips, silencing any further protests. He sucked the finger in, tugging hard on it, and she sighed with pure pleasure as, giving in to the demands of her body, she lowered herself onto him. She slid him in deep, stretching over the glorious length of him, till she was filled with him. *This* was what she needed. *He* was what she needed.

He pulled her on harder still. For a second they paused in wonder and pleasure, her gaze locked on his, and then at last he was moving, thrusting into her, guiding her hips to meet his. As she slid her arms around his shoulders, he again lowered his lips to cover her damp breast with his hot mouth as he rocked with her.

And she was so primed with need that that was all it took. Just that.

She cried out as her climax took her, surging outwards from her very center.

As the shock waves spilled convulsively through her, Gabe kissed her again, and she felt his release pulsing into her.

Afterward he wrapped his arms around her and held her to him in the water. She dropped her head to his shoulder, sated. And waited to come back fully into the world.

Slowly, sanity returned, and along with it came humiliation. What had she done? Who had she been for that brief, exquisite time? She eased off him. When he lifted his hands and retied her bikini top, she looked steadfastly over his shoulder, fixing her gaze on her chalet. The first rays of sun were touching the forest canopy. A light came on in a chalet at the other end of the bay where the workmen were staying. Wordlessly she started to move away. Gabe grabbed her hand, turned her back to him. And when she didn't look at him, he placed gentle fingertips beneath her chin and tilted her head up.

"I think we need to talk."

"I think we don't."

Ignoring her assertion, he kept hold of her hand, led her from the water toward her chalet. Inside, she moved to stand at the window overlooking the bay. He stood right behind her. Waiting. She could sense him. "I told you I should have left."

Silence settled over them. Neither of them moved.

"I'm sorry," she finally said.

His hand came to rest on her shoulder, warm, comforting—almost. And then he turned her, and again when she would have avoided his gaze, he tipped her head up so that short of closing her eyes, she had no choice but to look at him. "Don't be sorry. It wasn't your fault."

She allowed herself a small smile. "So, when I…took hold of you, slid onto you, while you were saying wait, that wasn't my fault?"

He smiled back. His hand cupped her jaw. "I started it. I kissed you. And I could have stopped you if I'd really wanted." His dark, unreadable eyes were intent on her. "But I didn't stop you because I didn't want to. Not even a little bit. So don't blame yourself."

"It was just sex. I remember saying that."

His hand slid into her hair, curving around the back of her neck. "If I agree with that, will you stop beating yourself up about it?" His voice was so kind.

Against her will, her gaze dipped, slid over him, his broad shoulders, sculpted chest, narrow hips. She looked back at his face. "Maybe."

"Then I agree. It was just sex." He nodded, encouraging her to agree, too.

She nodded along with him. "Good sex." She swallowed, her mouth suddenly dry. Damn. It was starting again. The wanting. "But just sex."

"Great sex, in fact. But still just sex."

The heat was building again and she started to turn away.

"Chass, wait, my—"

But she couldn't wait. She couldn't let him see the reawakened hunger in her eyes. As she pivoted, she felt a tug behind her neck and the black triangles of fabric fell away from her breasts.

"Fingers are caught," he finished, before the power of speech deserted him. They both stilled. Gabe sucked in a breath, suddenly needing the oxygen. "Perfect," he said quietly, awed by the sight of her.

Slowly, he disentangled his fingers from the thin straps. He watched her face as he slid his hand forward, his fingers traveling slowly downward till he cupped one soft, rounded breast in his palm. He lifted his other hand to do the same and brushed his thumbs over her nipples.

Hunger burned in her eyes. Her lips parted, but it was several seconds before she spoke. "Don't," she said, but the word came out breathy, and she leaned into his touch.

Gabe swallowed. "Do you really mean 'don't'?

Because if you do, I need to know now." She didn't say anything, gave just the smallest sideways movement of her head. Slowly, he lowered his head, took one peaked nipple in his mouth, and teased it with his tongue.

"That's not fair," she whispered, arching into him.

Reluctantly he gave up the exquisite pleasure of her nipple, but he didn't seem able to keep his lips, or his hands, off her. This time he kissed her mouth as he slid his arms around her, bare skin against still-damp bare skin. She was so slender, she should have felt vulnerable within the circle of his arms, and yet the power of her need radiated from her.

She pressed against him and he was lost. He drank in the sweet taste of her, tried to keep control of the kiss, tried to keep at least a portion of his brain functioning. He gripped her hips, fingertips pressing into the softness of her behind. Did she have any idea what she did to him? He broke the kiss and tucked a strand of damp hair behind her ear.

"You're not fair. I have no strength, no defense against your beauty, your perfection. You are my every fantasy."

Chastity opened her mouth to say something, but no words came out. She licked her lips, about to try again, but Gabe bent and scooped her into his arms. He held her gaze, let her see his hunger.

In three steps he'd laid her down on the bed and sat beside her. She reached for him, but he encircled her wrists with his fingers and raised her arms up above her head. With his other hand he drew her top away, tossed it to the floor. Her bikini bottoms followed. "Beautiful," he said on a rough sigh. She was laid bare for him, and he was honored. This woman was so many things he was just beginning to guess at.

He looked into her eyes as, starting at her hairline, he trailed his fingers down the side of her face, her jaw, along her throat and through the dip between her collarbones that, against all reason, he considered his. Heat bloomed in her cheeks as he moved his hand lower, over the swell of her breast and the straining nipple. Her eyes darkened as he traced the outline of her ribs, the curve of her waist, the flare of her hips.

He slid his palm across to rest on the gentle swell of her abdomen.

His child grew within her.

The rush of protectiveness and possessiveness that knowledge caused stunned him with its ferocity.

"Gabe." She whispered her need through parted lips, a whisper that spoke directly to the answering need in him.

He brought his hand to rest at the apex of her thighs, covering the blond curls. With his fingers he parted her folds, found her slick and hot. She rose up and opened to him.

"Please." She sounded as desperate as he felt. "I need you inside me."

He slid fingers inside her tightness.

"But you?" she said, puzzled.

"This one is just for you." With his thumb, he explored till he found the spot that made her gasp. And then he pleasured her, felt the fierceness of her desire building ever higher, till she was writhing and gasping. He covered her mouth with his, tasting her ecstasy as she climaxed, her hips rising up, her muscles convulsing around his fingers.

They were both breathing hard as she sank back into the bed. He let go of her hands and she clung to him. The early morning peace settled over them, and despite his own need for release, Gabe felt a contentment he hadn't expected, a pleasure in just knowing he had given her pleasure. Somehow it meant more than anything he could remember.

And then she was moving again. She insinuated herself more completely beneath him. Her hands tugged at the waistband of his trunks and he took the hint, shucking them before settling himself between her thighs.

Her hand found him more than ready. She stroked his length as she guided him home. He paused at her entrance. She raised her hips to him, wrapped her long legs around him. He slid in, slowly, exquisitely slowly, sheathing himself in her.

Chastity smiled. "This one's for you."

Just as slowly he pulled out—almost completely—before sliding in again. He repeated the movement again, watching her.

Her smile disappeared and she frowned. "Don't expect me to… I won't be able to… Not so soon."

It was Gabe's turn to smile. "I don't expect anything of you," he said as he kept moving within her, his rhythm building.

Chastity's frown turned to confusion and then surprise.

He plunged deeper, faster, into her heat, watched her eyes darken. He slid a hand between them, found the same spot he had earlier, saw its immediate effect, heard it in her ragged breathing.

They were moving together, a powerful physical joining.

And something more than just physical.

The blood roared in his ears as he watched the need and passion overtake her. He thought for a moment that she resisted it before giving in. And as her climax took her, he exploded into her.

Gabe could hear Chastity in the bathroom—quietly crying. That wasn't the effect he usually had on women. He hesitated outside the bathroom door. If he called to her, asked if he could come in, she'd only tell him to go away. So he opened the door, thankful that the locks hadn't yet been fitted and walked in.

Chastity sat in a corner, wearing a bathrobe, hugging the knees pulled up to her chest. The sight cut a hole in his chest.

"Go away. It's nothing. Sometimes I just need to cry." She turned her head so that her still damp hair curtained her face.

He sat down beside her.

She wiped at her eyes with the sleeve of her bathrobe. "What part of 'go away' don't you understand?"

He slid his arm behind her back. "Don't cry, Chass. What's wrong? Did I hurt you?"

She leaned in to him, pressed her forehead to his shoulder. "Don't worry, it's not you." She sniffed. "Well, not what you think."

"What do you mean?"

"Nothing. Just go away."

"I'm not going away and leaving you like this."

"I'm fine. Really. It just looks bad."

"You're right about that. It looks bad. Really. I'd have to say you're not fine."

"But I am. That's why I'm crying."

"This is woman's logic, isn't it?"

She gave a hiccuping laugh that did little to ease the bands tightening his chest.

"Why did it have to be you? No one's ever…done that to me before."

He stiffened, thought back over their morning. "Oh, God. You weren't a—"

This time she laughed properly. "No. I wasn't a virgin."

"Then what did you mean? No one's ever…"

She buried her face in her knees. "Made it good for me. Like that. Like you did. Took time for…me."

Something burned within him. Why hadn't she been treasured? "Who've you been sleeping with?"

"No one, actually. Not for a long time. Like I said, I thought it was overrated."

Did she still think that? He wasn't going to ask the question. His masculine pride was not important right now.

She turned her head, resting her cheek on her knees so she could look at him. The sweetest smile played about her lips, her blue eyes sparkled. "I don't think it's overrated anymore. I can kind of see what the fuss is about. Although I'm not sure if that's you or just pregnancy hormones."

Again he said nothing, though the effort cost him.

"I only ever slept with one other guy."

"One?"

"My swim coach in college."

"Wasn't that unethical? Of him," he added quickly.

"Yes. It was. He was good-looking, he'd been an Olympic swimmer himself. It was all so cliché. I thought he cared. Turns out so did two other girls on the team. That I knew of."

"Did you do anything about it? Did anything happen to him or did he get away with it?"

"One of the other girls, Monica, was much stronger, and more bitter, than me. I was just…humiliated. She took it higher."

"And what happened?"

"I don't know."

"What do you mean?"

"I left school and came back to New Zealand."

He pulled her closer to him. Wished he could undo the last few hours, have them over again. One guy? She'd only ever slept with one other guy and he'd been a self-centered louse. She deserved the magic, not the insatiable hunger that had driven him. She deserved dinners and flowers and romance. He could give her that, at least.

A uniformed crew member handed Chastity up onto the yacht, nodded as Gabe spoke quietly to him, and then disappeared into the night. Chastity looked around in awe. How did something this big, with not a sail in sight, come to be called a yacht? Her survey took in the darkening water, the stars that were starting to appear in the sky, then the gleaming handrails and fittings of the yacht. She smoothed her hands over her white linen pants, adjusted her turquoise halter-neck top. She looked anywhere but at the man beside her. His subtle scent, almost like that of the ocean itself, and his very nearness invaded her senses.

She'd spent another day in his company. He'd left his phone behind. Voluntarily. Another day of nothing and yet everything. They'd forgotten about the past and the future and had a day of moments, of nows. Created memories Chastity knew she'd treasure once this was over.

Apart from the lap of water against the hull of the yacht, all about them was still and quiet. Finally she looked at Gabe, who she'd known was watching her. He stood casually, hands loose at his sides, a single step away. His dark eyes held hers.

She saw the dark hair, the strong jaw, the eminently kissable lips and the broad shoulders. And she'd seen so very much more. The perfect whole. Yet she hadn't the faintest idea what was going on beneath his enigmatic appraisal. So much had changed between them, for her at least.

A second crew member materialized, wearing the same white shirt and long white pants as the first. With a friendly smile to her and a respectful nod at Gabe, he led them to the dining area. Candles flickered on a table laid with a linen cloth and set with gleaming silver cutlery for two. The scent of roses from an enormous white bouquet perfumed the air. Soft, smoky jazz played from unseen speakers. As a low rumble vibrated through the boat, the man who'd led them here pulled out a chair for Chastity. After he'd seated both her and Gabe, he, too, disappeared.

"So, this seems awfully like a—"

"Date. Yes." Gabe smiled.

"Why?" He wasn't known for his spontaneity. He was a calculator, a planner. She couldn't help but be anxious that his calculations and plans were suddenly including her. Now seemed like a very good time to start worrying. "I'm not going to sleep with you again," she jumped in before he could even answer. "You're wasting your efforts and both of our time if that's where you think this is going." He studied her. Waiting. "Because that was a monumental mistake. I'm not saying it wasn't... Well, I'm not saying anything aside from the fact that it was a mistake. Which you have to know, too. So now I'll shut up because clearly I'm babbling, which I do when I'm nervous. But you can talk and you can tell me why you think we're here."

Chastity clamped her lips together and silence fell. Gabe waited a couple of beats, all the while watching her with that unwavering, unnerving gaze. "It's not because I want to sleep with you again. Which I'll concede wasn't the wisest thing we could have done. And if that—" he continued—"but at his emphasis on the word *that* and the subtle darkening of his gaze, Chastity felt her traitorous body respond "—was what I wanted, or thought you wanted, this isn't where we'd be right now." And that was all it took for her mind to flash back to tangled sheets and tangled limbs and Gabe over her and inside her.

She recalled, though she'd forbidden herself from recalling it, how very, very good it—he—had been. How physically he'd intuited so much about her, almost more than she herself knew, and then used it—with her consent, if you called pleading consent—to overwhelm her, carry her to places of fantasy.

She swallowed, looked down and realigned her cutlery.

He touched the back of her hands with his fingertips. A fleeting…caress. "And I don't mean to make you nervous."

She regretted that particular admission of weakness. Gabe was of the "knowledge is power" school and she'd just given him power. It was time to claim some back for herself. Folding her arms, she lifted her chin. "Then why are we here?" She was prepared to confront him. She wasn't prepared for the melting gentleness in his brown eyes.

A waiter appeared and set bowls of aromatic soup in front of them and a basket of assorted breads between them. When he'd withdrawn from the room Gabe spoke. "Because everything has happened backward. Pregnant first, sex second." He held her gaze and it was all she could do not to look away in embarrassment. How was it that he could be so seemingly blasé about…that? He had rocked her world. "A date seemed like the next logical step."

The next logical step. So he did have a plan, or was at least formulating one. It was time to be worried. Time to shore up her own defenses. Because there was a warning voice in her head shouting at her to watch her step, and even to watch her heart, that if Gabe decided to be charming, she was history. She'd already shown him far too much about herself. She reached for a chunk of bread. "Maybe we don't need to get to know each other. Maybe we just need to figure out—when it becomes necessary—how we're going to manage your contact with my daughter."

"Our daughter." He spoke calmly, quietly.

"My. Daughter."

"You're going to try to deny that she's mine?" Still calm, almost quizzical.

"Not biologically. And not in private."

"But legally?"

"It's not about me denying it. It's about you being clear on precisely what the letter of the law is."

"But we're not talking about the letter of the law, are we? It's never that clear-cut when people and emotions are involved."

"No," she said on a sigh. "I know." And that was where the problems lay. Her emotions where this man was concerned. The fact that he might be a good father. In fact, there was no *might* about it. If it was what he wanted, as he said he did, he would be a very good father. If he accepted, as he seemed to, that it was worth spending less time immersed in his all-consuming work to spend time with a child, her daughter, then her little girl would be one very lucky child. Because he was so good at everything he did. And beneath the Granite Man exterior, beneath the strategist, lay someone gentle and loving and strong.

Chastity turned her attention to her soup. It was the only thing that wasn't confusing her. After a couple of delicious mouthfuls she looked back up at him, so calm, so patient, so sure of himself. And she wanted to be angry at him, or to at least find something that would level the playing field, give her a sense of power. "Is there anything you're not good at? Do you have any failures in life?"

"Yes."

"What?"

He took a deep breath. "My relationship with Tom."

She set her spoon down. Of course. Tom who'd gotten them into this mess. Tom whose relationship with his family had broken down almost completely, as he'd wanted it to, from the moment Chastity moved into his apartment.

"Was he gay?"

She broke a chunk of bread in two, keeping her focus fixed on it. "You can't ask me that."

"I just did."

"He was *your* brother."

"And now he's dead, so I can't ask him."

She sometimes forgot that Gabe had suffered the same loss as her, the loss of Tom. From what she knew, they hadn't had a great relationship, especially in later years, but a brother was a brother and death was forever. "Then don't worry about it because it doesn't make any difference, does it? It can't bring him back."

"But it would explain so much." She saw the puzzlement in his eyes. Gabe with all the answers didn't know what he needed to figure this one out. "We were close once. And then it all changed. It started well before you came on the scene. Probably in his late teens. A distance came between us. He became more and more secretive about his private life. I asked him once, outright."

"And?" Tom had never told her this. He'd said his family didn't have a clue, but that it was willful ignorance because knowing would destroy them.

"He bloodied my nose for it."

"Really?" She almost smiled. Tom would have been secretly both shocked and proud of himself.

"Only because he caught me by surprise."

"Naturally."

Gabe grinned. Then the lift of his lips disappeared. "I never asked again. I figured if he was, he'd tell me if and when he was ready. Then later he took up with you and I thought, okay, definitely not gay. Now the envy of every red-blooded male he knows. But through eighteen months of engagement and six months of marriage you never slept together. And it's the only explanation I can think of."

"It is possible for people to wait."

"It wouldn't be possible for me if I was going to marry you. Not unless I could arrange a same-day marriage."

"Is that a backhanded compliment or an insult? No, don't answer that, this conversation's not about me. I don't care."

"How could it possibly be an insult?"

"As in clearly that would be the only real reason for marrying someone like me, nothing worth waiting for, nothing worth celebrating. Step up to some hole-in-the-wall place, that'll be fine."

"How can you think so little of yourself?"

"I don't. But I'm more than used to it in others."

"If I loved someone enough to marry them, I wouldn't want to wait for any of it. I would want the world to know she was the woman I'd chosen and that she'd chosen me back. I'd want her to take my name. I'd want to share it all, with her as my life's partner. Sunrises, sunsets and everything in between. The walking, the talking, the moments of stillness and, yes, the making love."

She saw the passion and intensity in his eyes, heard it in his words. And it made her feel almost sorry for herself. She didn't know that she'd ever find the sort of love Gabe would one day offer. "She'll be a lucky woman. The woman who marries you."

"And he'll be a lucky man. The man who captures your heart."

"Let's hope he thinks so." She looked out the window to a night that revealed nothing.

Firm fingers touched her jaw, turned her face back to him. "He couldn't possibly think otherwise." His eyes. Did he know he had the kindest eyes? The sexiest, kindest eyes.

Those warm, sure fingers stayed on her skin for several beats before he lowered his hand to the table, clenched it around his knife and turned his attention to spreading pesto on a chunk of bread. "So, Tom was gay?"

"It's not for me to tell you one way or another."

"He was gay." Gabe chewed a piece of perfectly cooked fillet steak. "I just can't believe I ever doubted it. And I can't believe he didn't trust me enough to tell me."

"The perfect Gabe? He was going to reveal what he considered, and what he knew your family considered, such a flaw, to you, the Golden Boy?"

Gabe looked at her. And she realized she'd as good as told him what she'd vowed to herself she wouldn't.

Gabe sat back and for a minute looked into the distance. He was somewhere else altogether. Then, abruptly he leaned forward in his seat. "I get why Tom did it. It was an elaborate sham. You were his smoke screen. But why were you with him? Why even agree in the first place to the pretense of an engagement?" His gaze had changed, was now assessing, intent. There was no lingering sadness or softness, just a determination to get answers. "You must have had reasons. More than I initially thought."

Chastity put her hands flat on the table. "Why the inquisition when this is supposed to be a date?"

Gabe was about to respond, to counter, she was guessing, when the waiter appeared. When he'd gone Gabe spoke quietly. "Sorry. You're right." But the assessment was still there in his eyes. She didn't know what he was thinking, but whatever it was unnerved her. "At one time I thought you might have had feelings for me."

So he had known. "I did," she admitted because there was no point denying it.

He frowned. "Then, why Tom?"

"You transferred me. I thought you'd figured out that I was attracted to you and that you didn't want… that. Me."

Gabe leaned forward, his stare intense. "You didn't think that maybe I transferred you precisely because I did want you? But because I was such a staunch and vocal advocate against relationships between people who worked closely together within the company, that I wanted to put some distance between us first?"

"No." She'd never in her wildest dreams thought that. Gabe's rejection, which is what she'd viewed it as, had seemed perfectly reasonable for someone like him.

"Beneath it all, I was jealous of Tom. That's why I allowed the distance between us to grow."

"I never thought."

"No. Perhaps neither of us thought things through properly."

As much as she wanted to believe that things might have been different, a relationship with Gabe couldn't have lasted. Tom understood about secrets and imperfections. He let her keep her secrets just as she let him keep his. Neither of them pried into the other's life. Gabe would never accept something that superficial.

"I still don't understand why you two suddenly decided to get married and have a child though."

Chastity was quiet a moment. "It was after my grandmother died that we got to talking about it. Tom wanted the appearance of a real family and he said he wanted an heir. And I wanted…someone to love. I wanted a real family, too, I guess. And I didn't want to have a baby outside of marriage."

A tear leaked from her eye and she wiped it away. "This wasn't a good idea. Can we go back to shore? I'm tired." She was tired of trying to figure out where she was with him. There were too many layers. There was Gabe the man she'd made love with, Gabe the father of her child, Gabe the brother of the man she'd married. And they were all layered together in the man sitting opposite her, watching her. It was too much to keep straight in her head.

"Let's finish eating. Adam prepared the menu specifically for you."

"He's here?"

"No. The yacht has its own chef, but Adam planned the menu."

"Oh." She had no friend here to shield her from Gabe. Though thinking Adam could help, when it was her own feelings that were the problem, was futile. She squared her shoulders. This was for her and her alone to deal with. "Okay. But no more questions?"

"No more questions. And then afterward, there's one thing I'd like to show you."

"I don't know." She should get away. She was spending far too much time with him and it was confusing her in so many ways.

"I think you'll like it. And there's nothing devious, no ulterior motive in it." He held his hands out, palms toward her.

"It won't take long? Because I really am tired." Tired of trying not to be beguiled by him.

"No."

"Okay then."

He smiled, a gentle approving smile that coaxed one in return from her. Far too beguiling. She had to turn away from the warmth in his eyes before it kindled back to flame the embers of desire that had taken up permanent residence within her.

# Ten

They stood together at the railing, a careful distance between them, as the boat motored through the water. "What is it I'm supposed to be looking at?" she asked. Dusk had bled into night. But the moon again hung unobscured and bright in the sky.

"Just wait. You can't see it yet."

"How long? Because soon I'll scarcely be able to see anything at all."

"I can't say. Maybe a few more minutes, maybe longer. Just wait."

"But—"

He quieted her with a hand on her shoulder. "Soon. I promise. Or we'll go back to shore."

"Can't you at least tell me what I'm looking for?"

"No. Watch the water."

His hand tightened, but before he could say anything,

she saw it. A flash of glistening silver-gray curved in the water where there should have been nothing. And then another. "Gabe. Was that—"

"Just watch."

Suddenly several dolphins broke the water, leaping and diving in graceful arcs through the yacht's wake. Then up ahead first one and then another leaped into the air, seeming to stand for an instant on their tails before dropping back down. A mother and young dolphin played together at the edge of the pod. For ten minutes Chastity watched in awed silence as the pod performed— because it felt like a performance—for them. And then just as suddenly as they'd appeared, they were gone. And she was leaning back in Gabe's arms stunned by the beauty and privilege of what they'd just seen.

For long minutes more they just stood there. She didn't want to move. Didn't want to break the magic of what they'd experienced or the subtler magic of leaning into Gabe's strength, of having his arms around her.

Later as they stood on the jetty, the big yacht's tender heading back out, she turned to Gabe, whose hand she still held from when he'd helped her off the boat, whose hand she couldn't quite bring herself to let go of. Yet. "Thank you."

"You liked it?"

"It was amazing. I've never seen anything so beautiful." She'd moved closer to him so they were separated by only a whisper of air.

He threaded his fingers through her hair, a thumb pressed gently against her jaw. His eyes searched her face. "I have."

Slowly, he lowered his head. She could have stopped the kiss if she'd wanted to. But the very last thing in the world she wanted was to stop his kiss. As his mouth covered hers with an aching tenderness, she melted against him. She forgot every one of the multitude of reasons why she shouldn't be doing this and clung to him instead—the one real, solid thing in her universe. He tasted of the coffee they'd finished dinner with. His hint of stubble abraded her palms as she touched his face, slid her hands into his hair. She tried to let this be enough. This one consuming kiss that fired her senses. But it held the promise of so much more.

She pulled away from him. "We shouldn't."

"No. We shouldn't."

He lowered his head again, tasted her, savored her once more.

He held her to him and she felt the passion vibrating through him, an echo of her own pulsing need.

He lifted his head. "So, I'll just walk you back to your chalet."

Chastity nodded, mute.

Neither of them moved, till finally, her hand, of its own volition, lifted and her fingertips grazed over his chest. Still ignoring the protest of what remained of her sanity, they shifted and flicked the fabric from around the first button, and then the second and third so that she could slide her palm inside his shirt and rest it on the warm skin there, feel the beat of his heart beneath her touch.

She looked up from what she was doing and into his eyes. If onlys—her mind teemed with them. If only she'd met someone like Gabe earlier in her life. If only she'd met…Gabe. There was no someone else like him, there was only him. And she was in deep, deep trouble.

She could never have him. He didn't want a woman like her. Warm fingertips traced the shape of her collarbone. Well, he might want her now. But not permanently. Not in the way she was realizing she wanted him.

His lips found hers.

He deserved someone from his own background. Someone he could make a life with. Someone who wasn't faking that she could belong in the strata he lived in.

She had to leave before she was hopelessly lost. His kiss deepened. And she knew she was too late to stop losing herself. Live in the moment. Wasn't that what she'd told him to do?

She would take tonight. What was one more night of passion between them? She took hold of his hands. "Your chalet. It's closer." His hands cupped her jaw as he searched her face. She could only hope that in her eyes the desire overrode the love.

Chastity was dreaming of drums when something woke her. Lying on her back, she stretched out alongside Gabe and allowed herself a moment to savor the sensation, the bliss and contentment of his warmth and nearness, his subtle male scent. There was surely no better place in the world to wake. She opened her eyes to find Gabe lifted up on one elbow, a lock of his hair falling forward, brown eyes studying her, and the softest of smiles playing about his lips. Morning sunlight streamed in through the window behind her, bathing him in gold.

He touched his fingers to her stomach. "It's a good

thing you were already pregnant, because if you weren't, you surely would have been by now." His smile widened. His gaze full of tenderness.

An ache bloomed in her heart. Was there a way they could make this work? Could she make him love her? Could they have a future?

Two quick raps sounded on the door before it swung open. Gabe's body blocked her line of sight. "Gabe," the high, cultured voice cut through the air and Chastity tensed. She didn't need a line of sight to recognize his mother.

Not drums—a helicopter.

She tried to shrink down beneath the sheet, but Gabe's touch, his fingers in her hair, stilled her, his calm gaze locked on hers, held her where she was, promised that everything would be okay. For long seconds he stayed just like that, then with a caress of her cheek he slowly turned, still shielding her with his body. "I really have to do something about getting locks fitted."

"Gabe, your father and I were worried. No one's been able to reach you for two days. And after Tom…" Chastity heard the tension in Cynthia's voice and then the slow, ominous tap of her footsteps as she came farther into the room. One more step and Chastity could see her, see the worry in her eyes. Guilt bloomed. She hadn't been thinking of his family when she'd taken his phone. She'd forgotten how an inability to reach Tom had been the first sign that anything was amiss.

"And," Cynthia continued, "Marco's going crazy. The Turner deal is floundering. He's had to bring the Tokyo delegation—" Her gaze finally lighted on Chastity, and worry turned to horror. "What is that…slut doing here?"

Chastity shrank back at the venom of her words as Gabe swung himself to sitting, still shielding her with his body and keeping the sheet both over her and his hips. "Do not *ever* call her that again."

For a moment, Cynthia looked taken aback at Gabe's vehemence, but she rallied instantly. "I speak as I find. As I know."

"You're wrong."

"You're telling me that you didn't just sleep with her? Let me guess, you didn't finish *talking* the other night she stayed with you? And you needed to be naked and in your bed to have the rest of the conversation?"

Gabe folded his arms across his chest. "I'm not telling you anything that's none of your business."

"By my definition, sleeping with another of my sons only months after burying the first, the one she was married to, qualifies as a—"

"It's not how it looks."

"You mean walking in here and finding that—"

"Cynthia," he cut her off again before she could call Chastity anything else. "Go to the restaurant. I'll come talk to you there."

Cynthia's face was tight-lipped and livid with fury as she sucked in a breath through her nose. She pointed a manicured finger at Chastity. "Leave my son alone. You've cost me one already. You're not getting your conniving, money-grubbing hands on another."

"Cynthia—"

But Cynthia had turned and gone.

He turned to Chastity. "I'm sorry about that."

"It's okay."

"It's not okay." He reached for a strand of her hair,

ran it through his fingers. "And I really am sorry. She shouldn't have said that. When she understands what's really going on—"

"There's no need to apologize. It doesn't matter to me what your mother thinks."

His gaze held hers. "I'd be happier if I believed that." He ran a gentle knuckle along her jaw.

"Then believe it." She slithered past him and out of the bed, pulled on her underwear, picked up her bra from the floor. As she struggled with its catch, Gabe, who'd managed to get at least half-dressed too, came to stand behind her, shifted her fumbling hands away and did it up.

With his hands on her shoulders, he turned her. "I can't believe it when it's clearly not the truth."

Chastity stared at the smooth muscle of his shoulder and tried to find the right words to convince him.

"Come with me to talk to her."

She swung out of his grip and lunged for her linen pants and stepped into them. "Not if my life depended on it."

"Why not? If you don't care what she thinks, it shouldn't make any difference."

She pulled her top over her head. "Because she's right. I was married to Tom." She crossed her arms, holding on to her shoulders.

Gently, Gabe uncrossed them, his hands holding her wrists. "It wasn't a real marriage though, was it?"

She shook her head.

"You've slept with a grand total of two men. The first, a guy in a position of authority over you who you thought you loved, and the second whose child you're already carrying and who took advantage of a moment of weakness. Well, several moments of weakness. But who's counting?"

Chastity smiled. "That's very chivalrous of you, but we both know that if anyone was taking advantage, it wasn't you."

"Stop trying to take the blame or I'll take advantage of you again, right here and right now just to prove my point."

Chastity tried to take a step back, but he still had her wrists and instead of releasing them, stepped up to her. She caught, and recognized, the look in his eyes as he lowered his head. She turned her face so that his kiss landed on the corner of her lips. So gentle. He shifted so that his next kiss connected properly and he coaxed her lips apart. Chastity leaned into the kiss, into Gabe, as his arms slipped around her, holding her to him. His kiss held the sweetest tenderness and longing. She softened against him, wanted to meld herself to him, wanted to stay like this forever, loving Gabe.

Chastity pushed herself away. Loving Gabe? Please, no.

Gabe blinked and studied her. "See what I mean? That, Chastity, was me taking advantage of you. Not the other way around. Now, I'm going to talk to my mother before she has a coronary. Are you coming?"

Chastity shook her head. She couldn't love Gabe. She wouldn't let herself. Loving Gabe would only mean pain and heartbreak.

"Don't look so terrified. She can be a drama queen, but she doesn't know you. She's never had the chance. If she did…"

And if only he knew why she was really looking terrified. She tried to focus on the conversation Gabe thought they were having. "She'd what? See a gold digger trying to trap another of her sons."

"She'd see an incredibly strong woman who's true to herself and who's made something of herself against the odds. A woman with a kind, loving heart."

If only he knew just how loving. If only he knew that her loving heart had given itself to him. He'd be in the water and swimming for the mainland. Or worse, laughing pityingly at her.

"Go and see her. She needs you."

"What about you? Do you need me here? I'll stay if you do."

She couldn't stop the leap of her heart at his question even though she knew he was talking about the present moment only. "No. Go. You're her only son now. She's hurting."

"Wait for me. I'll be back soon."

Chastity watched him leave and felt the tears well and then trickle down her face. It was over. All good things must come to an end. Wasn't that how the saying went? She'd had her days—and nights—of perfection. But Gabe would come to his senses. Pick up the mantle of responsibility again. Which is exactly what he should do. And the fact that he would was part of why she loved him.

He was going back to the world he belonged in. A world she couldn't be a part of. She'd been able to make a life with Tom because Tom, rightly or wrongly, had believed he needed to be apart from his family. But Gabe and his mother and father were all each other had now and she knew what it was like to lose the last of your family. She couldn't come between them. Even if Gabe wanted her.

She stared out the window, watched him stride toward the restaurant. The words needed to escape her and make themselves heard. Just once. "I love you." He paused and looked back, though he couldn't possibly have heard her. Then he kept right on walking.

Chastity rested her forehead against the glass. Of all the stupid things she could have done.

Gabe set a cup of coffee down in front of Cynthia. "So, what's the problem with the Turner deal? What's Marco doing with the Tokyo delegation?"

His mother's hands clenched into fists on the table. "You think I can talk about the Turner deal after what I just saw, knowing that woman's here? With you?"

She had a point there. Gabe, too, didn't want to talk or even think about the Turner deal, knowing that Chastity was here and probably now in her chalet fretting, blaming herself. "Her name's Chastity and we're not going to have any kind of conversation unless you can remember that."

"I can remember that. Can you remember that she ensnared your brother, cost him his family?"

Gabe looked at his mother. She excelled at laying blame at other people's doors. And far too often she got away with it. "Maybe we cost him his family. Maybe Chastity was a convenient excuse for cutting himself off and not the real reason."

His mother stared in horror. "She's poisoned you, too, hasn't she?" Sniffing, she reached for her handbag and started rummaging for a tissue. It was an act though. She wouldn't cry; it would ruin her makeup.

"No. But I've learned some things about myself and about Tom from Chastity. Things I should have seen a long time ago."

Cynthia pulled out a tissue and dabbed at her eyes. "What sort of things?"

His mother wasn't going to take this well, but it was time his family stopped hiding from their secrets before what little remained of it self-destructed. "Where's Dad?" If he had to break this news to his mother then he may as well tell both parents at once, and Cynthia would need his father here, too.

"Playing golf. Where else would he be? These days it's all he ever—never mind." The tissue disappeared within her fist. "Why, Gabe? Tell me why that woman's here. What sort of hold has she got over you?"

Maybe his mother was partially right. Chastity did have some kind of hold over him. But it was the very best kind of hold. And he was suddenly hoping that their days here had been enough to give him the same kind of hold over her. The very best kind. He quelled the smile that threatened before his mother could see it.

If Chastity was here with him now, he could admit that to her and they could tell Cynthia about the baby—their baby. Once his mother accepted that news it would do her good, give her something positive in her life to look forward to. But Chastity wasn't here. And he wasn't telling his mother without her permission.

"I can see why you might be attracted to her. She's a beautiful woman. But there's no shortage of beautiful women."

"Not like her."

Cynthia's mouth dropped open at his defense of

Chastity. Her eyes blazed with a bitterness he hated to see there. "She's nothing more than a gold digger. You've said it yourself in the past. Have you forgotten that? Is she really that good in—"

Gabe held up a hand to stop her words, and he frowned.

She was no gold digger. She didn't seem to care at all about money. She loved the beach and wore shell jewelry made by a child. She cared about others. She protected those she cared about, took the blame for things like seduction when it didn't belong to her. And she was everything he wanted in a woman and more. She was more than he deserved.

He thought about the hours he'd spent making love with Chastity. Chastity, who was kind and loving and passionate and vulnerable. And he remembered, too, that time two years ago that she had first touched his heart as they'd sat in the sunlight on a river bank. He thought of their walks along the beach, of her delight in the simplest things in life, of the wonder in her eyes as she'd watched the dolphins. It was, he realized, just last night, as they'd stood on the deck of the yacht and he'd been watching her rather than the dolphins, that everything had come together for him, the physical and the emotional becoming something more. It was then that everything had changed irrevocably.

He loved her.

Completely and utterly. He wanted to share his life with her; he wanted to share hers. She was the woman he wanted to walk along the sand with, swinging their child between them. Her and no one else.

"We had her investigated, you know," Cynthia finally said when he didn't respond.

"You did what?" he asked, still processing his re-alization. He loved Chastity Stevens. He wanted her to be Chastity Masters, to take his name and be his wife in all the ways she'd never been Tom's.

"When she moved in with Tom, your father and I had her investigated."

Gabe stood up. "How dare you?"

"She's completely unsuitable." Cynthia clearly failed to comprehend his outrage. "We tried to tell Tom, but he wouldn't listen. Her family, if you can call it a family, is trash, perfectly revolting. Her mother was an alco-holic and died of cirrhosis of the liver, but was known as the town slut. Her half sisters, from different fathers, I might add, are no better."

Gabe turned on his heel.

"Where are you going?" Cynthia's voice climbed several notches.

"To Chastity."

"Don't you dare walk away from me for her."

Gabe stepped out of the restaurant in time to see the mail ferry tied up at the jetty and Marco leading a party of dark-haired and dark-suited businessmen toward him. His heart sank. He had a few scant seconds to look in the direction of the chalets, seeing nothing and no one, before the men were upon him.

"I couldn't get in touch with you. We had to rearrange the schedule, and they wanted to meet with you person-ally," Marco said quietly as they approached. "As far as they're concerned, *you* are Masters' Developments." Gabe accepted the explanation with a nod. He knew the importance of perceived status and personal relation-ships. "And," Marco continued, "they want to see what's going on here first." The Turner deal, a joint venture in conjunction with the men now in front of him, would be their biggest yet. Three linked resorts on three Pacific islands.

And then the formalities began. The greetings of those he already knew, the introductions to those he didn't, the presentation of business cards. Gabe tried to focus.

"We'll need to arrange some kind of entertainment for this afternoon," Marco suggested just a short while later as they were touring the resort's facilities. "They've also been seeing Jacobs. He's trying to woo them."

"I'll call Julia, get her to organize a big-game fishing expedition." He looked up and saw his mother walking toward the restaurant—from the direction of Chastity's chalet. His gaze lighted on a solitary figure making her way down the jetty, hauling a too-heavy suitcase.

# Eleven

He turned back to Marco. "You handle this. I have to go."

Marco followed his gaze. "You can't seriously be thinking about leaving this for her?"

"Apparently I can."

"Are you crazy? They're already jittery. If you leave now, the deal will fall through. You know how touchy they can be. And there's nothing more important to us right now than this."

The low rumble of the ferry's engines carried to him. "Maybe I am crazy, but there is something, *someone,* more important than this. And I'm not going to lose her for the sake of a few million. You handle it. It's what you do." He turned to the delegation. "Excuse me, gentlemen. Please accept my sincere apologies."

And then he was sprinting for the jetty.

He made it onto the ferry with a leap that barely cleared

the rapidly widening gap of water. On deck, he pulled out his cell phone and called his PA. "Julia, forget about whatever else you have planned for today. I have something you need to organize. Bring in any and all help you need. Pull out all the stops." He talked to her for a few minutes longer then made his way to the bow of the boat, eased alongside the woman facing forward, her tousled hair blowing in the breeze. Their shoulders touched and she stiffened.

"The helicopter's faster," he said. "The ferry has to stop at several more islands farther out before heading back for the mainland. It'll be a few hours still."

"The ferry was leaving sooner." Her hands were clenched around the railing.

"Ahh."

"Shouldn't you be back on the island?"

She still hadn't looked at him and he studied her profile, her pale, perfect profile. "Perhaps that's where I *should* be. But I'm precisely where I want to be."

She slid the briefest, concerned glance at him and he saw the redness of her eyes, and the pinkened end of her nose.

"Am I right in thinking you've had the pleasure of a chat with my mother?"

"Pleasure's probably not the word I'd use."

"No. I don't suppose it would be. So, what did she say?"

Chastity said nothing.

"Let me guess. She ranted for a while and when that didn't achieve what she wanted, when she figured out that you had…feelings." He watched her stiffen. "Real feelings for me, she changed her tack. Said that a relationship with you would harm my standing in the business community, make me a laughingstock. She said that you would cost me my family. That if you really loved me, you'd walk away."

"You've pretty much nailed it."

"And do you? Love me?"

"No." She kept her focus firmly fixed on the wide ocean, but he heard the catch in her voice and his heart swelled.

"You really are a terrible liar."

She pressed her lips together.

"I think you do love me."

"It doesn't have to mean anything."

"It means everything. To me." The ferry pushed through a wave and Gabe put his arm around Chastity, pulled her closer to him. "So, back to my mother."

"She's lost so much."

"She's not the only one."

"I told her that I would leave you…alone. I mean, it's not like we even had a real relationship."

"No."

Chastity smiled sadly. "She can be very gracious when she's getting her own way."

"And I can be very pigheaded until I get mine."

She slid a glance at him, a frown marring her brow.

He turned her toward him and pushed a strand of hair behind her ear, then left his palm resting against her cheek. For a moment she leaned into his touch. "Did I mention that I loved you, too?"

Tears welled in her eyes. "Don't, Gabe." She tried to turn away.

His lifted his other hand so that he cradled her face

between his palms. "Don't what?" He held her gaze. "Tell you that I love you?"

She closed her eyes. "Yes. That."

"But I do," he said quietly. "Nothing about you is how I'd convinced myself you were. But I had to do that. Because if I'd let myself see who you really were, I would have wanted you too badly for myself."

"That's just it. You don't know who I really am."

"I do."

"No. About my family. My mother. My sisters."

"I don't care."

"Only because you don't know."

"No. I do not care. The only thing, the only *one* I care about is you."

"Your mother cares. She knows about my family. And your parents have already lost one son. They're hurting. I won't cost them another."

"And what about you? What about me? My hurt. Do I have to lose Tom and now you, too?"

"When you're ready, you'll find someone. The right kind of woman for you."

"Right for me or right for my mother?"

"I believe you'll be on the lookout for a kindergarten teacher."

He half laughed. "I forgot I said that."

"I didn't."

"Ever thought about taking up early childhood education?"

A sad smile quivered about her lips. God, he loved that smile. Still holding her face, he leaned forward and tasted her lips. "Do you have any idea how much I need you?"

"Yes. I think I do."

"Because?" When she didn't answer he filled the silence, "You need me, too?" She nodded and his heart soared. "There's nothing we can't overcome together. Did you tell her about the baby?" he asked.

"No. I think that might be best for you to do. Alone."

"Coward," he teased.

"Craven."

"I had hoped we'd tell her together. But given what's happened today and what's still to happen, it's probably best if I tell her now." Gabe pulled his phone from his pocket, hit a programmed speed-dial number. "Dad, how soon can you get out to the island?" He overrode his father's objections. "Yes, it's important. More important than your game. I'm about to tell Mum that Chastity and I are having a baby." He smiled. "Call Julia, she'll get the helicopter." He frowned as his father spoke some more. "It's okay. I'm way ahead of you. You'll see when you get out there. But do me one favor. Give it ten minutes and then phone Mum." He eased the phone back into his pocket.

"Why did you tell him to go to the island?"

"To be with Mum."

"But—"

"Just trust me."

She nodded her acceptance. "What did he say about the baby?"

"He said I should marry you."

"No."

"Yes. I knew he would. He's old-fashioned like that. Besides, he was looking for the path of least resistance. He's on the seventeenth hole and wants to finish his game." He took both her hands between his. He couldn't seem to stop touching this woman. His woman. "Dad will like you. And you'll like him, too." He saw the doubt in her eyes. "You both play the piano and like Beethoven."

"That means nothing."

"It's a start. Besides, Dad's easy. Smile at him, tell him you're having his granddaughter and he'll be putty in your hands.

"Now for the big one." He looked at Chastity and winked then hit another button on his phone.

"Cynthia."

Chastity could hear his mother's voice as she launched straight into a tirade. "Mum!" He cut her off. "Chastity and I are having a baby." A shriek—and not of joy—came from Gabe's phone, then a rapid, shrill string of language. Chastity caught words like "dead to me," and "destroying our family." She turned away from him, walked a couple of slow, numb circuits of the ferry, then paused at the stern to stare at the foamy wake trailing behind the boat.

By the time she made her way back, Gabe was chatting with a group of smiling, nodding passengers. He saw her waiting at the bow and came to join her. He leaned back against the rail, looking perfectly calm as he watched her.

"The phone call didn't sound like it was going well."

"She's coming round. You have to trust me on this. She has both snobby and drama queen down to an art, but beneath it all she has a heart. And she'll love having a grandchild. Particularly a granddaughter. She's complained often enough about being surrounded by males in the family." He looked at her, his brown eyes serious. "It *will* be okay."

"I know it will be okay because it'll be your problem, not mine." He'd said he loved her, but it was a bitter-sweet admission because their love wasn't going to be enough. Not if it meant hurting others.

In the distance a helicopter headed for what looked like Sanctuary Island.

He took her hand and led her to sit in the white plastic chairs affixed to the deck. "Let's enjoy the trip." Two seagulls took up sentry positions on the rail at the front of the ferry.

How could she possibly enjoy it when her heart was breaking? Being with him like this was torture. She wanted the simple togetherness to go on forever to delay the moment of their parting, but she also wanted to get the pain over and done with.

By the time the ferry pulled away from the last wharf of its rounds, there were only a few passengers dotted about the boat. Some indoors, one or two out. Gabe left her side and went to the bridge to speak to the captain. He then made the rounds of the remaining passengers, pausing by each of them for a few words. Chastity shook her head. It was like he was campaigning for some-thing. And by the look of their smiles and nods, he was winning them over. She looked away. Not her problem.

Gabe came back.

"I'll put you on the birth certificate." She needed to assure him of that before she began to distance herself from him. Perhaps she should go away somewhere. Somewhere with no phones, no Internet, almost like Sanctuary Island. She could have laughed. She needed to go somewhere she couldn't give in to the temptation to call him, to talk to him, or even to follow what he was doing in the business world. "I know that's all you really wanted."

He clasped her hands. "It was all I wanted at the start. It's not now. Now I want so very much more."

"And all I wanted was to convince you that I'm not a bad person. I'll be a good mother."

"I know you will. Which doesn't mean we won't sometimes have differing opinions about how to raise our children, but we'll work it out."

"Children?"

"I thought four, but if you only want one I guess that's fine, too."

"Gabe, have you lost your mind?"

"I'm not sure about my mind. I don't think I've lost it. My heart, on the other hand, I'm positive about. I've lost it completely."

She took a half step back from him. "I'm going to get off this boat and then it'll be best if we don't see each other for a while."

He closed the gap and she didn't have the strength to widen it again. Not yet. "What kind of marriage would it be if we didn't see a whole lot of each other? Certainly not the kind I'm hoping for."

One word had her mentally stumbling as confusion, hope and then reality coalesced. "Marriage? You have lost your mind. We're not getting married."

"That could complicate things."

"Ladies and gentlemen," a deep voice sounded over the speaker system, "this is your captain speaking. We'll be making a brief unscheduled stop at Sanctuary Island and then getting underway on the trip back to the mainland. I understand some of you will be disembarking here. For those continuing on the journey, our arrival will be fifteen minutes later than scheduled."

"What's going on?"

A smile twitched at Gabe's lips. As they began rounding the point into the bay, the helicopter again came in low overhead. Gabe's phone rang. "All set?" he asked. Apparently receiving a satisfactory answer, he pocketed the phone.

He dropped down onto one knee and grasped her left hand as he pulled something from his other pocket, keeping it hidden, clenched in his fist. "Will you marry me?"

Chastity tried to pull her hand free. "Get up."

"Not till you answer."

"Then, no."

"Why not?"

"I answered, now get up."

"You didn't say why."

"I just can't."

"Can't? Not don't want to?"

"It amounts to the same thing."

Finally he stood. "Not at all. Do you love me? And this time I want the truth."

"Yes. I love you." The smile that lit his face only hurt her more. "But sometimes that's not enough."

"It's enough. I want to spend my life with you."

"I don't fit in your world."

"You fit perfectly because you are my world."

Her breath caught in her throat. She wanted what

he was offering so desperately that it scared her. "Gabe, we can't."

"Will you wear my ring while you think about it?"

He was sliding one of the shells they'd collected for Sophie over her ring finger before she could even answer. He silenced her protests with his kiss. "So, this *can't,* is it really because of my mother?"

"No. Maybe."

"What if we get her blessing? Scratch that, what if we get her grudging consent? Will you at least consider it?"

"Yes." He didn't have a hope in hell. He hadn't been in the room with Cynthia. Hadn't seen the fear of losing a son, and the determination to prevent it, in her eyes. "I'd consider it."

Gabe smiled. Confident and triumphant. "She'll want to put the blame on you. Trapping me into this marriage. But if you won't do it without her consent, then the blame falls on her. So she's going to agree. And then she can blame you for making me miserable, for being a terrible mother, a bad example to our children. Although what she'd like best of all is to give her consent and for you to refuse me. It just depends on who you care about making happy. Cynthia or me. And yourself. Because we will be happy together."

"What about your father?"

"Dad's wholly on the side of an easy life. Which, incidentally, he's not going to get either way."

He kissed her again. "I do have a proper engagement ring for you, one that's been in the family for generations. Julia's bringing it out."

"That's not necessary."

"I thought it was. Out of curiosity, once we get my

mother's consent, how long do you think your *considering* will take?"

"I don't know," she said hesitantly, when all she wanted was for him to take her in his arms again. Because when she was in his arms, she could believe that it really all would work out for them. Because it didn't seem possible that it wouldn't.

"All right then. We'll just have a party today. A thinking-about-marrying-me celebration. Though really now I'd rather be alone with you. I think I'd have a pretty good chance at speeding up your consideration if it was just the two of us."

She frowned her confusion and with gentle hands on her shoulders he turned her. Beyond the sparkling blue of the bay, bathed in sunlight, a white marquee stood on the shore, pennants blowing in the breeze. A crowd of people, most of them holding champagne flutes, stood near the jetty, waiting.

Chastity looked from the marquee to Gabe and back again, suddenly picking out people she knew. "You didn't?"

He lifted a shoulder. "I always knew when I found the woman I loved I wouldn't want to wait, that I'd want to marry her that very day. But I'm not going to pressure you."

"This is what you call no pressure?"

"Chastity, we host functions all the time. It's not pressure. These people are going to enjoy themselves and have a party whether it's a marriage or a thinking-about-marriage celebration. It's not like they've been looking forward to it for months."

"You helicoptered them out?"

"Some. Chartered boats for others."

"All these people are here for you?"

"And you."

"How could there be anyone here for me?"

"The upside of Cynthia having you investigated, in case you never thought there could be one, is that the investigator could give Julia a list of your friends."

To one side, along the shoreline a young girl twirled, her white skirts spinning out around her before she stooped to pick up shells. "Is that Sophie?"

Gabe smiled. "Yes. I thought she'd make a beautiful flower girl. When the time comes."

The ferry moored and all of the passengers got off, calling their congratulations to Gabe and Chastity. "I invited them to stay. They all accepted," Gabe said by way of explanation. As the last passenger cleared the gangplank, Cynthia picked her way up, her heels entirely wrong for the grated surface. She made her way straight to them, heels now clicking purposefully on the decking.

"I don't want to interrupt," she said, "but I need to talk to Chastity for a minute. Alone."

Chastity's heart pounded against her ribs.

"You okay with that?" Gabe's eyes searched her face.

"Yes." She'd avoided Cynthia for long enough. Their discussion in the chalet, while far from amicable, had made her stop viewing Cynthia as someone to be frightened of and rather someone who was herself frightened. And grieving. Whatever happened she had to have some kind of relationship with this woman who would be a grandmother to her child. Gabe nodded. "Call out if you need reinforcements. Or rescuing." He looked pointedly at his mother. "Remember that I love this woman." He walked to the other side of the boat.

Cynthia fixed her with a gaze very much like her son's. "Gabe never rebelled like Tom did. Growing up, he was always such a good boy. He always did the right thing. And by the right thing, I guess I mean he did what we asked of him. But just occasionally he would get something in his head, something he really wanted, or wanted to do or didn't want to do. And then…then there was no way on earth I or anyone else could convince him otherwise."

Chastity waited.

"It appears he feels that way about you. About marrying you."

"I won't marry him without your consent."

"He told me that you wouldn't. I'm not sure whether that's very honorable or very cunning."

Chastity remained silent.

"Gabe would have me believe—honorable. And Gabe is a good judge of character. Usually. Look, Chastity, I don't really know you, but Gabe has…clarified some things. And I might have misjudged you. If you do decide to marry him today, or even if you don't, I want you to have this." From around her wrist she unclasped a diamond bracelet. "It was my grandmother's before me. It can be your something old. And if you want, someday you can pass it on to your daughter. My granddaughter." She held the bracelet out to her.

"I don't know what to say." Chastity hesitated. "Thank you."

Cynthia smiled. "Now pass me your wrist." She encircled the glinting bracelet around Chastity's wrist.

"I'm not easy to know. Or to like. I understand that." Cynthia took a long time fastening the clasp. Finally she lifted her eyes to Chastity's. "But please don't take Gabe or my granddaughter away from me."

Chastity did something she'd never imagined doing and put her arms around Cynthia. "I won't. I would never."

Cynthia hugged her back, a single fierce squeeze. "I'd withdraw my consent if you did."

"So you do consent?" Chastity pulled back to study the other woman's face.

"Yes." Cynthia lifted her chin and smiled. "And graciously, I hope. Not, as my son might have suggested, grudgingly. And now it's up to you."

Gabe's hand came to rest on her shoulder as she watched Cynthia walk away. "And now it's up to you," his deep voice sounded in her ear. "Will you marry me?"

She slid her arms around his waist, tilted her head up to look at his face, the face she loved, the man she loved. "Yes."

"I want you to take my name."

"I wouldn't have it any other way."

\* \* \* \* \*

## MASTER OF FORTUNE by Katherine Garbera

Astrid Taylor was the only woman Henry Devonshire wanted. But mixing business with pleasure could cost Henry a fortune.

## MARRYING THE LONE STAR MAVERICK by Sara Orwig

He needed a wife and fast. And his lovely new assistant would do just fine.

## BACHELOR'S BOUGHT BRIDE by Jennifer Lewis

When his new wife slammed the bedroom door in Gavin's face, he realised his feelings for her were very real. But was it too late?

## CEO'S EXPECTANT SECRETARY by Leanne Banks

Betrayed by his lover, CEO Brock Maddox discovered she'd been keeping an even bigger secret.

*Series – Kings of the Boardroom*

## THE BLACKMAILED BRIDE'S SECRET CHILD by Rachel Bailey

Nico Jordan's world shattered when his lover Beth married his brother. Seven years later, Nico wants answers. But that's not all he wants!

## FOR BUSINESS...OR MARRIAGE? by Jules Bennett

She had one month to plan Cade's wedding. And one month to change his mind.

### On sale from 18th February 2011
### Don't miss out!

*Available at WHSmith, Tesco, ASDA, Eason and all good bookshops*

www.millsandboon.co.uk

0211

# 2 FREE BOOKS
## AND A SURPRISE GIFT

We would like to take this opportunity to thank you for reading this Mills & Boon® book by offering you the chance to take TWO more specially selected books from the Desire™ 2-in-1 series absolutely FREE! We're also making this offer to introduce you to the benefits of the Mills & Boon® Book Club™—

- **FREE home delivery**
- **FREE gifts and competitions**
- **FREE monthly Newsletter**
- **Exclusive Mills & Boon Book Club offers**
- **Books available before they're in the shops**

Accepting these FREE books and gift places you under no obligation to buy, you may cancel at any time, even after receiving your free books. Simply complete your details below and return the entire page to the address below. You don't even need a stamp!

**YES** Please send me 2 free Desire stories in a 2-in-1 volume and a surprise gift. I understand that unless you hear from me, I will receive 2 superb new 2-in-1 books every month for just £5.30 each, postage and packing free. I am under no obligation to purchase any books and may cancel my subscription at any time. The free books and gift will be mine to keep in any case.

Ms/Mrs/Miss/Mr _____ Initials _____

_____

Surname _____

Address _____

_____

_____ Postcode _____

E-mail_____

Send this whole page to: Mills & Boon Book Club, Free Book Offer, FREEPOST NAT 10298, Richmond, TW9 1BR.